CW00506866

Memory of Water

Memory of Water

A Rosemary and Thyme Mystery

BRIAN EASTMAN
with
REBECCA TOPE

This edition first published in Great Britain in 2006 by
Allison & Busby Limited
13 Charlotte Mews
London W1T 4EJ
www.allisonandbusby.com

A catalogue record for this book is available from
the British Library.

10 9 8 7 6 5 4 3 2 1

ISBN 0 7490 8132 5
978-0-7490-8132-4

Printed and bound in Great Britain by
Bookmarque Ltd, Croydon, Surrey

BRIAN EASTMAN heads one of the UK's leading independent production companies, Carnival Films, and has produced a wide variety of TV programmes and feature films including Agatha Christie's *Poirot*, *Jeeves and Wooster*, *Shadowlands* and *Traffik*. He created, and produces, *Rosemary and Thyme* for ITV.

**Also available from Allison and Busby
in the Rosemary and Thyme series:**

And No Birds Sing
The Tree of Death

Prologue

The two boys crouched in the long grass, heads close together, the shiny colourful biscuit box on the ground between them. 'Will it go rusty?' asked Martin wistfully, as he carefully placed one of his Dinky cars on top of a copy of the *Beano*. The car was a Mini – not one of his favourites, but he valued it nonetheless.

'Not if the box is watertight,' said Jim. 'And airtight,' he added. 'However long it stays closed, everything will look exactly as it does today when it's opened again.'

'How do you know that?' Martin was frequently impressed by his cousin's knowledge of science and his powers of observation. Jim's contribution to the box included a slightly dented metal robot and a completed Airfix model of a Second World War Lancaster, delicately painted. To Martin's mind, Jim had a dazzling array of skills. All Martin could do was read prodigiously and attract the notice of fond relatives with his long eyelashes and thick wavy hair. It seemed deeply unfair, then, that Martin's father, a mere two years older than Jim's, would inherit Abbotslea when Grandpa died. Jim and his parents would have no claim on the great house. Already the brothers and their wives were struggling to maintain polite relations, knowing how divisive things would soon become. Their sons, born only weeks apart with Jim, ironically, the elder, had grown up in a harmony that they believed could never be fractured. Their first ten years had been spent in a carefree union, with frequent visits to their grandfather's mansion.

But now Grandpa was old and very ill and the adult talk had filtered through to them, making them anxious. 'Let's make a pact,' said Jim. 'To be friends for ever. We can sign it in blood and bury it in the walled garden.'

The idea had blossomed into a larger exercise. The pact was solemnly composed and written, and placed in the time capsule that was the biscuit tin. But the blood signature had proved too daunting, so they dipped the pen in Vimto, hoping it would leave an equally indelible mark. Then they dug a deep hole close to the disused chapel that Great-Great-Grand-daddy had built in the old walled garden, and carefully placed the tin inside.

'Nobody will find it for a thousand years,' said Jim. 'And when they do, they can read about how we were friends for our whole lives.'

Outside the garden wall, a small girl waited. She could not hear what the cousins were saying, because the nearby river was running in full spate, drowning other sounds. The October leaves were rustling, too.

But her wait was soon ended. Her beloved Martin emerged through the garden door, with Jim close behind. 'Hi, Gwynne,' said Martin. 'Want to play Pooh sticks at the bridge?'

She nodded eagerly, taking care not to notice the way Jim's face lit up at the sight of her. For an eight-year-old, the complexities of a love triangle were just a little bit too much.

Chapter One

'Quick!' called Laura, 'it's stopped raining. You can finish trimming the creeper now, while I get the rest of the mulch under the rosebushes.'

Rosemary threw down her magazine and jumped to her feet. 'At last,' she rejoiced. 'I thought we were going to lose another whole day.'

'So did I,' Laura agreed.

They left the gloomy claustrophobic lounge of the Bellwether Hotel at a trot, desperate to finish the job which had already taken ten days longer than anticipated. Although not frightened of a spot of rain, the relentless downpours of recent weeks had made their work impossible. Their chief task was to deal with a vicious attack of blight on a historic creeper clinging to the façade of an even more historic court house. Much of the work involved climbing ladders, made unthinkably perilous by strong winds accompanying the rain. They had also been asked to dig out several rosebeds around the sides of the building, replacing the plants and giving them a good start. The claggy soil turned to a powerful adhesive during a downpour.

The Gloverton Court House was Georgian in origin, but had a number of more recent features. At some point about a century ago, a handsome *parthenocissus quinquefolia* had been trained all over the façade and then left to its own devices. The result was a romantic and impenetrable tangle, obscuring half the windows and invading the stonework. While terrible crimes were heard and tried inside, the exterior of the building presented a gothic image that many found almost comforting.

Rosemary set the ladder against the top of the high window of the main courtroom, and swarmed up it clutching her secateurs. This was the last area needing attention. She had tried twice before, only to be ordered to leave it while the court was in session. Twice she had missed gaps in the rain because of this. Now, she was dismayed to find that the room beyond the window was once again in use.

'They're sitting,' she hissed down at Laura. 'I thought you said there wasn't anything happening today.'

'Must have run over from yesterday,' said Laura. 'It's Jardine, again, isn't it? You know how long-winded he always is.'

'Well, I don't care,' Rosemary decided. 'I've had enough of Gloverton. Finished or not, we're away from here tomorrow.'

She snipped ruthlessly at the straggling tendrils, causing a shower of wet leaves and stalks to cascade around the foot of the ladder. The proceedings in the courtroom had evidently reached a high pitch of tension, since nobody took any notice of her at the window. Warwick Jardine QC was on his feet, chest puffed out, wig slightly crooked, like a Roman orator. He clearly had the entire room in thrall to his brilliance.

The window had decorative stone mullions between the panes of glass. There were protruding carved leaves and flourishes which Rosemary found convenient to hold on to as she reached further and further sideways in her attack on the creeper. Suddenly, with only the toes of one foot still on the ladder, a piece of stone broke off. With her balance utterly lost, she flailed with hands and feet, grabbing at the creeper, the windows, anything to save herself from falling.

Laura habitually kept close by when Rosemary was doing anything that involved leaving solid ground. With considerable presence of mind, she rushed over, straightened the ladder and tried to aim a steadying rung directly beneath her friend's feet. 'Here,' she called. 'It's all right. Stop thrashing about.'

Rosemary dangled from a slender stem of Virginia creeper, still scrabbling frantically with her feet. A particularly frenzied kick went through a pane of glass, with much more noise than might have been expected.

Everything froze for a few seconds. Rosemary could see a hundred faces inside the courtroom all staring up at her in horror. She felt a nudge beneath the sole of her boot and suddenly she knew she was safe again. Safe from falling, at least. The look on the face of Jardine QC was anything but reassuring. *If he had a gun in his hand, he would definitely shoot me,* she thought, only dimly realising what she had done.

The unfortunate part was that Jardine already had reason to abhor Rosemary Boxer. Two days previously, she had accidentally permitted a fine spray of toxic blight remedy to land on his Daimler. The paintwork had instantly turned dull and discoloured. Ten minutes later, flakes were starting to peel off. Anybody could see that a full respray of the car would be required. Hoping he might not notice until they'd gone, Laura and Rosemary remained silent on the matter for a full day.

But Warwick Jardine had the eyes of an eagle, and in the face of his direct accusation, nothing else was possible but a full confession. Issues of insurance and liability and compensation continued to rage.

Shakily she backed down the ladder. Through the broken window, she heard the judge announce that they would adjourn for lunch at this point in the proceedings.

Her instinct was to run and hide, but there could be no escape. Within seconds, it seemed, the black gown-clad figure of Jardine was approaching, his face contorted with fury. 'Miss Boxer!' he bellowed as if she was half a mile away instead of right in front of him. 'How dare you! You utterly ruined my closing speech. Can you not understand that a man's whole future rests on those few minutes? Have you no notion of what you did just then?' He drew a deep breath that did nothing to calm him. 'You have perverted the course of justice – no less than that. I could have hoped that you were satisfied with vandalising my car, but no—' He spluttered for a moment, uncharacteristically lost for further words. Then he revived, with a parting shot: 'If I were in your shoes I would suffer many a sleepless night after today's shameful performance.'

Rosemary swallowed and stood her ground. 'Don't be ridiculous,' she said, her voice sounding much too squeaky in her own ears. 'If the man's innocent, the evidence will show it. Justice can't possibly rest on a single speech from you.' She wanted to add more, but her courage had deserted her. Jardine's face turned puce at her impertinence. She suspected that nobody had spoken to him like this for a very long time – if ever.

'You have no comprehension of what's at stake,' he barked. 'You are a silly, empty-headed woman who ought never to be allowed near a court of law.'

'Steady on,' said Laura, taking a step to be shoulder-to-shoulder with Rosemary. 'That's going a bit too far.'

But Jardine had had his say, and was flapping back into the court house, where his assisting barrister, Martin Frazer, hovered apprehensively.

Ruefully, Rosemary shook her head. 'He didn't like me before,' she groaned to Laura. 'Now he absolutely loathes me.'

'Who cares?' demanded Laura. 'We'll never have to see him again.'

Behind them, a procession was emerging from the court house in search of lunch. There were only two or three places close enough to get a meal within the allotted time, and the Bellwether Hotel was one. Another was a cheerful Italian restaurant, which had taken the fancy of Laura and Rosemary when they had first arrived in town. The long drawn-out trial was a novelty for Gloverton, happening at the same time as Rosemary and Laura's commission to improve the appearance of the court house purely by coincidence. The court normally heard minor cases involving burglary and car theft. Many people thought it unfortunate that the complicated process by which a certain James Stanley Beaver was tried for the crime of defrauding Messrs Higgins and Forrester, proprietors of the local cattle market, should take place in their town. Mr Beaver insisted on his innocence and had hired a top QC to make his case. Most of the personnel had been staying at the Bellwether Hotel for the past three weeks. When Laura and Rosemary arrived they had initially been told there was no room for them, before some early departures and strange shufflings had liberated a small room at the back on the third floor.

Rosemary took a while to recover from her second

confrontation with Warwick Jardine, her jaw set rigid with indignation for a full hour afterwards.

'We'll go to Giovanni's,' Laura said firmly. 'Maybe Martin will be there and you can tell him what you think of his boss.'

They had quickly made the acquaintance of Martin Frazer. He occupied the room next to theirs and seemed to be in urgent need of cheering up at the end of each long wet day.

'It isn't fair,' he had grumbled, some time towards the end of the first week. 'I do all the work and he gets all the glory. Not to mention the money,' he added. Laura and Rosemary had not needed to ask who he meant. They had quickly grasped the nature of the relationship between Martin and his superior. Mr Jardine was a self-important, overpaid, arrogant beast – accord-ing to Martin. He was also a brilliant performer who seldom lost a case. His mind was razor sharp and his breadth of knowledge astounding. 'He knows *everything*,' Martin had said. 'He'll make a marvellous judge one of these days.'

'And you'll make a splendid QC,' Rosemary had assured him warmly. 'It's only a matter of time.'

Martin had been mildly encouraged by these words and from then on he had sought out the two whenever things depressed him.

Now, with the trial in its final stages, all three found themselves heading for Giovanni's for a last lunch together. At the sight of Rosemary's face, Martin made a show of quailing in fear. 'Still angry, then,' he ventured.

'How you manage to work with him, week after week, beats me,' said Rosemary. 'The man's not human.'

'He *was* provoked,' Martin said mildly. 'He'd put a lot of work into that speech.'

Rosemary's gaze slid away, and she stared for a moment at the floor. 'I suppose it must have been annoying,' she conceded. 'But he didn't have to be so rude.'

'It's his trade mark,' sighed Martin. 'He thinks it makes people respect him.'

'Never mind him now,' said Laura. 'What's done is done. Have you got another thrilling trial lined up?' she asked Martin.

He laughed. 'I actually have a couple of days free, thanks to the Bank Holiday next week. It's a restless life I lead, flying from one trial to another, all over the country. I have to be in Leeds first thing Wednesday morning, which means I've got to go up there on Tuesday. Poor Suzanne hates it that I have to be away from home so much, but there doesn't seem to be much alternative. She has to manage everything on her own and it's quite a job. Not that she ever complains.'

'Do you have children?' Laura asked.

Martin nodded. 'Timmy and Toby. They're eleven and twelve. We had them very close together, not entirely by design. They remind me of myself at that age.' He looked wistful. 'Seems a long time ago now.'

They all devoted some moments to their pasta, before Martin asked, 'What about you? Where do you go from here?'

'Good question,' nodded Rosemary, with her mouth full. 'With the weather like this, nobody's keen to hire gardeners. But we'll find something – we always do.'

'We'll have to,' said Laura. 'Or we'll starve. As it is, this Gloverton commission has been a financial disaster. They paid us for the whole job, a flat rate, and all the delay has meant we've barely covered the cost of staying at the Bellwether. Next time, we'll have to sleep in a tent.'

Martin's head tilted sideways in a parody of deep thought. 'What?' laughed Laura. 'You look as if you've had an idea.'

'I have,' he smiled. 'I think you might be just what I've been looking for. I'm surprised I didn't think of it before.'

'Explain,' invited Rosemary.

Martin launched into a description of his home, a large Elizabethan house named Abbotslea. 'It was actually a small monastery originally,' he said. 'At least, it's on the same site. It stands beside the river Mallam and has its own fifty-acre wood. The village is just beyond the gates. You'd like it – it has a wonderful quality of timelessness.'

'You want us to do something with a fifty-acre wood?' Rosemary frowned worriedly.

Martin chuckled. 'No, no. I'm just setting the scene for you. It also has a walled Elizabethan garden, which has been neglected since before I was born. For as long as I can remember there's been talk of restoring it, with herbs and knot gardens and all the rest of it. I did make a start last year, doing a bit of clearance work and scouting round for some new plants. It's been slowly climbing up the list of Things To Do until it's just about at the top now.'

'Sounds interesting,' said Rosemary carefully. 'What exactly did you have in mind?'

Martin scratched his cheek. 'That's open to discussion. I'd like it to have a period look. It's been messed about with over the generations, but the basic structure's still visible. Last month I demolished a dreadful Victorian ruin that was there, which has been a big step forward.'

Laura gave him a look. 'A Victorian ruin? Do you mean some sort of folly?'

He frowned, and attended diligently to his meal for a few moments. 'A chapel, actually,' he mumbled, as she waited for a reply. 'I had some help available for a week or so, and decided to make good use of it.'

Rosemary caught Laura's eye, managing to convey excitement and some kind of warning. To Martin, she said, 'The Elizabethan style is very distinctive, you know.'

Martin nodded eagerly. 'Oh yes. It needs experts to do it properly. I've never been able to afford anybody I could trust to do as I want.'

'Until now,' said Laura, hoping she wasn't saying anything that Rosemary might object to. It was generally left to Rosemary to negotiate new commissions and discuss the technical details.

'Well, it sounds awful, I know – but I did think your rates might be slightly more...um, *affordable* than some people's.'

'We've never done a real Elizabethan garden,' said Rosemary with a gleam in her eye. 'How big is it?'

Martin shrugged. 'Pretty big,' he said. 'I've never actually measured it.'

'And you'd want us to do the whole job, from start to finish?'

'I could find you some manual labour for the heavy stuff,' he said, with a mysterious smile. 'In fact, a phone call this very afternoon might set that in trail.'

'When would you want us to start?' Laura asked.

'Right away, I suppose,' he shrugged. 'If you've got nowhere else to go. You could come down on Sunday. I'll give Suzanne a call and tell her. She'll be delighted that I'm finally getting the garden seen to.'

'Are you leaving here today?'

Martin sighed. 'I doubt it. Jardine's going to want to do

a comprehensive debrief after this shambles of a case. And it's still not concluded, remember. If I know him, we'll be at it till midnight. I'll try and make a really early start tomorrow and be with Suzanne by mid-morning. At least I'll miss the Friday evening traffic. It'll be chaos tonight, with half-term starting. My boys are arriving back from school this evening.'

'Half-term,' Laura echoed wistfully. 'I've almost forgotten about all that. I wonder if the weather's going to pull itself together.'

'It is,' said Rosemary emphatically. 'Definitely.'

'I hope you're right,' said Laura. 'Because I actually wasn't joking when I mentioned a tent.'

Rosemary stared at her in alarm. 'What?'

Laura patted her arm. 'Don't panic,' she soothed. 'It'll be fine, you see.' She looked at Martin. 'We'll need to have a little think before we finally agree to come.'

'Oh?' He seemed disappointed. 'I thought it was settled. I was going to make that call about finding some labour, as well as telling Suzanne.'

Rosemary poked Laura. 'Stop pretending there's anything to discuss,' she said. Smiling at Martin, she told him, 'It's fine. We'll come. Give us the directions, and we'll be there on Sunday.'

'Excellent,' he said, finishing his after-lunch coffee. 'Now I suppose I'll have to go and watch His Majesty at work, one last time.'

'Will your client get off, do you think?' Rosemary asked him.

'Oh yes,' said Martin with little enthusiasm. 'Mr Jardine never loses a case.'

'Even though I interrupted him when I broke the window?'

'He'll turn it to his advantage, somehow. But if I were you, I'd wait until everybody's gone before you go up that ladder again.'

'Don't worry,' Rosemary shuddered. 'I've learnt my lesson.'

The afternoon continued dry. At four o'clock there was even a suggestion of watery sunshine. 'Would it be reckless to say that summer might have come at last?' Rosemary ventured.

'Slightly,' said Laura. 'After all, it's not the end of May yet. But I have to admit I'm optimistic.'

Rosemary jabbed her fork into the mulch beneath a rosebush. 'So we'll do Martin's knot garden, then?'

Laura laughed. 'Need you ask? It sounds perfect, and if Martin's wife and sons are as pleasant as he is, we'll really enjoy the company.'

Rosemary nodded, and then gave Laura a probing look. 'So what was that stuff about a tent?'

'Oh yes,' Laura breezed. 'We'll go and buy it first thing tomorrow. Won't that be exciting!'

Most of the legal people packed up the moment the trial was over – Jardine having managed to salvage his speech and win as predicted – and sped back to their homes and families. The Bellwether became eerily quiet. Nervous of meeting Jardine again, Rosemary kept to their room while Laura went down to see if the QC and his barrister had finished their dinner. Only then would Rosemary risk the dining room.

Arrangements having been made with Martin, Laura insisted that they go on a shopping expedition first thing the following morning. 'What for?' asked Rosemary, having forgotten Laura's words of the afternoon. Or rather, not so much forgotten as deliberately buried.

'Essential supplies,' was all Laura would tell her. 'But if you want a clue, I can say that the weather forecast is promising a fine warm spell.'

Chapter Two

Most of the legal people packed up the moment the trial was over – Jardine having managed to salvage his speech and win as predicted – and sped back to their homes and families. The Bellwether became eerily quiet. Nervous of meeting Jardine again, Rosemary kept to their room while Laura went down to see if the QC and his barrister had finished their dinner. Only then would Rosemary risk the dining room.

Arrangements having been made with Martin, Laura insisted that they go on a shopping expedition first thing the following morning. 'What for?' asked Rosemary, having forgotten Laura's words of the afternoon. Or rather, not so much forgotten as deliberately buried.

'Essential supplies,' was all Laura would tell her. 'But if you want a clue, I can say that the weather forecast is promising a fine warm spell.'

Rosemary was forced to accept that Laura had been all too horribly serious when she bullied her into getting up at eight, and driving off to the shops right after breakfast. She led the way to a large camping shop, with a display of dozens of ready-erected tents, from tiny child-sized ones, to a monster that would make some houses look pokey.

'We need a tent with space for two,' Laura told the assistant. 'It must be easy to erect.'

Following at a reluctant distance, Rosemary watched as Laura inspected five or six possibles. 'This one's great!' she enthused. 'See – there are two little rooms that zip together, with another area for general purposes. Isn't it clever!'

Rosemary had been speechless with horror until then. 'No!' she pleaded. 'No, Laura. I don't want to sleep in a tent. I've managed to avoid it all my life till now. It's too late to change. Think of the bugs, and the damp. And the *cold.*'

'Don't be pathetic,' Laura chided her. 'You'll love it.'

'I won't,' Rosemary insisted. 'Listen, I've got a bit of money tucked away. We can afford a hotel. Please. Please let's stay in a hotel.'

But Laura was implacable. 'Trust me,' was all she would say.

'Have you been camping before, madam?' asked the youth who was patiently following Laura from tent to tent.

'Oh, yes,' she assured him. 'I was in the Brownies.'

Rosemary gave a loud guffaw at the expression on the boy's face. Laura's Brownie days must have been long before he was born.

'We'll take it,' Laura decided. To Rosemary, she said, 'Just imagine how much money we'll save. There's some packet food over there as well, look. All you do is add hot water to make all kinds of things.'

'Lovely,' muttered Rosemary miserably. 'I still wish we were going to stay in a hotel.'

Laura pretended not to hear her.

* * *

The following morning, having finally tamed the court house creeper and found a glazier to repair the broken window, Laura and Rosemary were on their way to Lyvedon and Abbotslea, home of Martin Frazer. The roads became narrower and more winding, sometimes diving steeply down country lanes that felt more like tunnels with great trees meeting overhead. 'This is exciting,' said Laura. 'Are you sure we're on the right road?'

'You've got the map,' said Rosemary, slowing for another corkscrew bend. 'It's like another world, isn't it.'

'The land that time forgot,' said Laura. 'Isn't that a quote by somebody or other about this part of the country?'

'I have no idea, but it does seem to fit. Look at that road sign.' She ducked her chin at a fingerpost that looked as if it had come straight out of an Ealing comedy. 'I bet that's been there since Queen Victoria's time.'

'I doubt it,' said Laura. 'I'd say it isn't a day older than George V. That's when they started to think they might need signs, when people first began to use cars on any serious scale.'

'Thanks for the lesson,' said Rosemary, still chafing at the prospect of sleeping in a tent.

'Must be nearly there,' said Laura, twenty minutes later. 'We'd better start watching out for the landmarks Martin mentioned.'

'I see a river,' Rosemary observed. 'And that might be the bridge he told us about.'

They crossed a modern concrete bridge over a river greatly swollen by all the recent rain. 'Yes!' crowed Laura. 'There's the crooked postbox, and the wrought iron gates. I think we've arrived.'

'Wow!' breathed Rosemary, as she turned in through the gates. Ahead of them was a stunningly lovely old house, built of mellowed brick, covered with ivy and surrounded by mature beech trees.

'Double wow,' echoed Laura. 'That really is something.'

Slowly, with the river running alongside them, they approached Abbotslea and its neglected Elizabethan garden.

In The Lamb, several Lyvedon residents were gathered as they regularly did on a Sunday. The routine was to have a few drinks before dispersing to their various homes for lunch. It was the favoured time for an exchange of gossip, as well as conducting odd bits of business.

Gwynne Evans had something urgent she wanted to say to George Hamilton Teed, and the moment she arrived she headed for his table in the window. She brandished a copy of the local newspaper at him angrily. 'What's this?' she demanded. 'Where did you get this story?'

The middle-aged man regarded her calmly and invited her to take a stool across the table from him. 'Where do you think?' he smiled complacently.

Gwynne tried to steady her breathing. 'It says here,' she managed, 'that there are investigations proceeding into allegations that the Lyvedon Trust has mishandled a large sum of money.' She glared at him. 'What investigations? What mishandling? You must know there isn't a word of truth in it. I could sue you for defamation.'

'I did check,' he told her. 'I admit it's all a lot less dramatic than the story implies. And it all happened a while ago now. But—' he spread his hands in a disarmingly helpless gesture '—I didn't have anything else to fill the page.'

Gwynne made a sound expressing exasperation. 'That's no excuse for printing a story like this. You must know the Trust never gets involved in anything shady.'

'My dear,' he said, 'you are too naïve. Your precious Trust exists to serve local businesses and advise on their buildings. It has to cooperate with planners, architects, builders and property developers. Nobody can tell me that in that little mix of operators there is no shady dealing. I'm sorry you're cross with me, but take my word for it – nothing's going to come of it. It's just the sort of story people expect to read now and then, to confirm them in their prejudices.'

'It's Jim, isn't it,' Gwynne said, her shoulders slumped. 'You ran it to placate Jim.'

'Well,' Teed was maddeningly relaxed and expansive. 'Poor chap. I can't ignore him all the time, now can I?'

'You can,' she said, getting to her feet. 'And you should.'

'Not staying for a drink?' Teed said softly, to her retreating back.

The Lamb's garden extended around two sides and right across the front of the building. Gwynne passed several neighbours sitting at pub tables on her way back to the road leading to the village. 'Hey!' called a man with a small child on his lap. 'Hang on a minute. What's the rush?'

She paused, running a hand through her hair in a distracted gesture. 'Oh, Chris. Hello,' she said.

'What's up?'

'Have you seen the paper?' She flourished it at him.

'No. And that one's so screwed up, I doubt anyone could read it.' He laughed lightly.

Gwynne gave the offending *Observer* another savage twist. The little girl on Chris Stevens's lap watched delightedly.

'Calm down,' Chris advised. 'You know nobody ever takes any notice of Teed's stories.'

'It's still a disgrace,' Gwynne said. 'And it's all down to Jim Frazer. He starts all these rumours and libels. He really should be stopped.'

'We've all been saying that for years,' Chris agreed. 'Nothing's going to stop Jim. You should know that as well as I do.'

A woman joined them, with two more children. 'Hi, Gwynne,' she said. 'How's things?'

'Hi, Katy,' muttered Gwynne, with an effort.

'She's cross,' said Chris to his wife. 'We must try to divert her.'

'Oh, you,' said Gwynne with a reluctant grin. 'How do you always manage to do that?'

'It's a knack,' said Katy. 'I keep telling him he ought to give lessons.'

'But Katy – I'm right about Jim, aren't I. He does go too far. Think of the terrible accusations he's made over the years – about all of us. One of these days he's really going to touch a nerve and cause serious trouble for somebody.'

Katy nodded. 'He's a trial, I agree. If he wasn't so well connected it might be different. But with Martin to shield him, he's always going to get away with it. Our best hope is that he'll just grow old and tired and stop being such a bother.'

'And Teed doesn't print his letters the way he used to,' offered Chris. 'I can remember when there were two or three a week, making complaints and demanding action to clean up the village morals. I used to look forward to them, in a way.'

'They were pure libel. He should have been prosecuted,'

insisted Gwynne. 'And think of some of the things he said about you.'

Chris glanced at Katy, half amused, half wary. 'I prefer not to,' he said. 'Now, will you have a drink with us?'

Gwynne gave the family a quick inspection, treating each child to a smile, before shaking her head. 'No, I'll be going,' she said. 'Things to do.'

Katy watched the retreating figure. 'There goes Super-woman,' she murmured.

Chris patted her hand. 'Don't be like that,' he said.

As they were attending to their offspring, another figure approached their table. Looking at her, Katy thought for the thousandth time how very like her mother Fern Evans was. 'Was that my mum?' Fern asked.

Chris nodded. 'She's in a paddy with the wretched Jim,' he said.

Fern gathered up some empty glasses. 'I heard her shouting at Mr Teed,' she said. 'I was keeping my head down behind the bar. Did you read what he put in the paper?'

Chris shook his head. 'More of the same, by the sound of it.'

'It's wrong, though,' Fern insisted. 'Mum has a right to be cross about it. It would never be allowed in a normal place.' She stared around at the pub's customers. 'Look at them all! Like something out of the middle ages, all kowtowing to the local squire.'

Katy Stevens looked up from a conversation with one of her children. 'Don't knock it, Fern,' she said. 'It might be old-fashioned, but it's a lot better than living on some dreadful estate, or in a city where nobody knows anybody.'

'Oh, right,' said Fern rudely. 'So we all have to put up with crazy Jim Frazer and his lies, do we?' She clashed two glasses together. 'If you ask me, that man needs seeing to. Somebody ought to stop him.'

Just as her mother had done, she marched off. Chris and Katy both watched her go. Chris sighed. 'So like her mother,' he murmured.

Then Teed emerged from the bar and joined them. 'Seems you've upset Gwynne,' Katy accused him.

The newspaperman sighed. 'I know. It was mischievous of me. But the real blame lies with Jim Frazer. That goes without saying, surely. Besides, I've written to her, explaining the whole thing. She can't have seen my letter yet.'

'It sounds to me as if letters ought to be banned around here. A lot of people would feel much happier then.' Chris's little daughter wriggled off his lap and went running to the play area at the far end of the pub garden. Teed gazed after her thoughtfully. 'She's coming along nicely,' he said, as if she was a young animal. 'Might warrant a little story…'

'Don't even think about it,' Katy said. 'Bonnie has settled in wonderfully. She doesn't need to be seen as a curiosity, just because of her bad start.'

Teed was not deterred. 'Human interest,' he said. 'You going all the way to China and running the gauntlet of officialdom to give the little scrap a decent life. I can't imagine why I didn't think of it before.'

'Shut up, George,' said Chris amiably. 'Bonnie's not going to be fodder for your rag, so forget it.' He looked at Katy. 'We'd best get moving,' he said. 'Granny's going to be wondering where we are.'

Katy nodded. 'Come on then, you lot.'

Teed watched them assembling their various bits and pieces, before walking the quarter mile home. 'Granny's having them for a few days,' Chris explained. 'A nice holiday for all concerned.'

Teed merely smiled. Thanks to Jim Frazer, he knew quite a lot about the Stevens family that they didn't know he knew.

Chapter Three

Before Rosemary had turned off the engine of the Land Rover, a reception party was waiting for them. 'Must be the whole family,' muttered Laura. 'Mum, Dad, kids and dogs.'

The dogs were two large golden retrievers, obviously very well bred and in excellent health. They leapt around the vehicle and the people, barking excitedly. Laura and Rosemary scrambled out of the Land Rover, unable to take their eyes off the beautiful old house, covered with ivy. Everything about it thrilled them. It looked very well maintained, at first glance, with freshly painted window frames and colourful beds of flowers around the immaculate lawn. But Laura noted that two ridge tiles on the roof were missing, and that rogue dandelions were popping up through the gravel at the front of the house. In the wide flower borders around the lawn, she noted several more weeds peering between the bedding plants.

'Gosh, Martin, it's *heavenly*,' gushed Rosemary. 'Absolutely perfect.' Laura wondered whether her friend had noticed the subtle signs of a struggle to maintain control, and was being polite, or whether she had genuinely fallen for the overall image of a beautiful classic family mansion.

'I'm glad you like it,' Martin said, as if he'd heard the same sentiment a thousand times before. 'Come and meet

Suzanne.' He introduced his wife, a slender woman a few years younger than himself, who was wearing rubber gloves. She pulled them off to shake hands, explaining that she had just been trying to unblock one of the outside drains. When Laura raised her eyebrows at this, Suzanne laughed in self-mockery.

'Oh, yes,' she said. 'Most of the jobs land at my feet around here.'

'She's incredibly competent, you see,' said Martin, putting an arm around his wife's waist. 'We do have a handyman, but he's a bit erratic.'

'The odd-job man,' said one of the boys. 'He's an odd-job man, Dad.'

'Right,' said Martin. 'Sorry. This is Timmy,' he told the newcomers. 'And the other one is Toby. And the dogs are Jess and Cabbage.'

'Cabbage?' Rosemary queried. 'Surely not.'

'I'm afraid so,' Martin grinned. 'The boys were only five and six when we got the pups and we let them choose the names. Timmy insisted on Cabbage, so there it is. Actually, they're really called Gladwin Champion Golden Streak and Gladwin Champion Platinum Perfection. They're terribly well bred, you see, with pompous names to match their pedigrees.'

'They cost hundreds of pounds each,' said Suzanne, with a small sigh. 'Possibly the most expensive dogs in the south of England.'

Martin laughed, as if she'd made a delightful joke. 'And you adore them,' he said.

'I'd adore anything that cost as much as they did,' she muttered. 'Like a new roof, for example.'

'They're gorgeous,' said Laura, who had a great fondness for dogs, and who also automatically did what she could to smooth over a scratchy moment. 'They go terribly well with the house.'

'Don't they!' said Martin. 'When I was little, we had a borzoi, but it came to a rather nasty end, poor thing. I can't pretend I missed him much. These two are far better company.' Martin was obviously in his element as master of the manor, proud of his estate and the perfect family he'd created. He seemed full of energy and enthusiasm.

Laura caught a glance from Suzanne, meant for Martin. It contained as much exasperation as affection, as if she had long ago given up hope that he would ever really listen to her. It was a look that Laura had seen on the faces of countless wives over the years.

'Now,' Martin went on, 'let me show you the garden before we go any further. Have you sorted out some accommodation for the time you'll be here?'

'We'll need a bit of help from you on that,' said Laura. As Martin directed a quick look of alarm at his wife, Laura hurriedly explained about their camping plans. 'We were hoping you could let us have a little clearing or something in your fifty-acre wood,' she summarised.

Martin's reply was unmistakably relieved. 'Of course,' he said. 'No problem at all.' He turned to Suzanne. 'What do you think, darling?'

'I think the Dingle would be perfect.' She smiled a little sadly. 'I could even fancy it myself for a night or two.'

Martin laughed as if she'd made another hilarious joke. Laura, however, had seen the smile. 'This all looks like a huge amount of work,' she said, indicating the house and garden.

'Not to mention about two hundred Year Eights and Nines,' said Martin proudly.

'Goodness! You mean you're a teacher as well?'

'Only part time,' said Suzanne. 'It's a sort of job share arrangement with my friend Gywnne, at the local comprehensive. It probably wouldn't be allowed in most places, but things are quite relaxed out here in the sticks, and it suits everybody pretty well.' Then she lifted her head, and they all realised that a telephone was ringing somewhere inside the house. Suzanne went to answer it. Moments later she was back, holding the handset out to Martin. 'It's Jardine's clerk,' she said. 'Something about this week's case.'

Martin took the phone with an apologetic glance at his wife. Suzanne turned to Laura and Rosemary, and suggested she take them to see the garden instead of her husband. Willingly, they followed her.

The garden was several yards from the house, tucked away behind a ten-foot wall built of the same old brick. Most people walking across the lawns, or under the ornamental trees would have just assumed that the wall marked a boundary into a field or lane. When Suzanne pushed the door open and ushered them through it, it was like entering another world.

'It's *enormous*,' breathed Rosemary, tracing the line of the brick wall and trying to calculate the size of the area it enclosed.

'Not really,' said Suzanne. 'It looks big because we've cut everything down. It's actually about seventy-five metres by a hundred.'

'What's that in old money?' Laura muttered.

'Big,' said Rosemary.

'Actually – can I leave you here for a bit?' Suzanne said, glancing out through the door. 'There's something I need to do in the house.'

'Of course,' said Rosemary. 'We'll be perfectly all right. We'll shut the door after us when we've finished.'

'Thanks. There's lunch in about an hour.' She smiled distractedly. 'And I think Martin has some people coming early this afternoon.'

'It's a busy life,' said Rosemary cheerfully.

'You can say that again. We've got ten for lunch tomorrow – assuming you'll both join us? If the weather forecast's right, we can have it on the parterre.'

Suzanne trotted away, leaving Laura saying quietly, 'Parterre, eh?' She turned to Rosemary. 'Real lady of the manor, isn't she?'

Rosemary wasn't listening. She had walked into the middle of the walled garden, and was obviously imagining how it might look in a few months' time. 'What a waste to leave it like this,' she murmured. 'I bet there were gorgeous old roses, and bay trees and angelica and comfrey and—'

'Yes, yes,' Laura interrupted. 'But at least we don't have to wade through nettles and brambles and thistles up to our ears. It's good to have such a clean slate to work on.'

'There'll be a lot of digging, even so. And it'll have to be done carefully, to avoid damaging the brick paths.' She scraped a heel experimentally through a thin patch of grass, revealing a pattern of bricks. 'See. Under all these weeds, the original paths are still there. Isn't that amazing!'

Laura joined in some scraping of her own. 'Incredible!' she agreed. 'What fantastic quality, to last all this time.'

Rosemary was assessing the work involved. 'All these buttercups and dandelions will have to come out, roots and all – unless we douse the whole place in weedkiller.'

'Martin said something about providing us with some assistants, didn't he? For the manual labouring part.'

As if in answer to her remark, a man came quietly

through the garden door, standing as if in a daze. Laura saw him first. 'Oh – hello,' she said.

'Mmm,' said the man. His eyes flickered oddly from side to side. He had a strong, rather handsome face, with a sharp jawline and very closely cut hair.

Rosemary took a few steps towards him. 'We've come to restore the garden,' she said. 'Are you one of the people here to help us?' Laura suspected that they had both arrived at the same conclusion – that Martin had connections with a local institution that sheltered people with learning difficulties, and had offered work to some of them.

'I'm Jim,' said the man. 'I'm not supposed to be here. I've been banned from Abbotslea.'

'Oh!'

'Please don't tell them you saw me. I'll be in trouble with Madam if you do.'

'Well—' said Rosemary. 'We can't really— I mean, if they *ask* us, we can't tell a lie, can we? We don't know you.'

'Never mind,' said the man, and slipped silently away.

Laura and Rosemary looked at each other. 'Was that a real person or a ghost?' said Laura.

'Good question,' said Rosemary.

Lunch was mildly chaotic, with the two boys throwing food to the dogs despite Martin's pleas with them to stop. He apologised to his visitors, with a rueful, 'Not the traditional Sunday lunch, I know. Suzanne's probably told you we're saving ourselves for tomorrow, when we're having a bit of a party for the Bank Holiday.'

Suzanne spent much of the meal carrying dishes and plates to and from the kitchen, refusing help from Martin. When he did offer to do something, usually a full minute after the task was already accomplished, his wife merely shrugged and said she was fine, she had everything under control. Again Laura gave the parts of the house she could see a close scrutiny. A drainpipe fitting had come away from the wall in one place, causing water to run down the brickwork and discolour it. The dogs gave the impression that this was the first freedom they'd had for some time and the boys were undeniably unruly. Admittedly, that could indicate nothing more than their excitement at being at the start of a week's freedom from school.

Laura found herself reflecting on how much they lost because of Martin's constant need to be away from home. He obviously wanted to play a full part in all the housework, but had difficulty in keeping up with Suzanne's efficient systems. He was a devoted father, his gaze constantly resting on the two boys with naked adoration. But there, too, he was at a disadvantage. He was painfully out of touch with their current obsessions, the computer games and music they talked about, the school friends they referred to.

Laura tried to talk to the children, but got little further than establishing that they boarded at a small independent school fifty miles away. They came home on alternate weekends and enjoyed outdoor hobbies such as fishing and rugby. But they also spent a lot of time on the Playstation, and carried iPods everywhere they went.

'Typical of their generation,' laughed Martin ruefully. 'I have to force them outside sometimes. In the summer holidays it gets a bit better.'

'You locked the Playstation in a cupboard last year,' Toby reminded his father. 'That was mean.'

'Mean perhaps, but entirely necessary,' said Martin. 'You were glad of it after a few days. You'd never have caught that trout otherwise.'

'That was Gwynne's doing,' said Timmy. 'She taught us how.'

Martin seemed to flush slightly at this remark. Laura assumed he disliked being compared to somebody with superior fishing skills.

'Trout!' said Rosemary. 'How wonderful! Are they in this very river?'

'Further upstream, yes,' said Martin. 'One of the perks of my position is that I have automatic fishing rights for the whole stretch of the Mallam. Rather feudal, I suppose, but I don't take advantage of it. I let any of the villagers use it, who want to, as well. Last year we only caught one fish.'

'But a *big* one,' said Toby. 'Huge, in fact. Seven pounds, it was. It made a meal for five people.'

'Amazing,' Rosemary said admiringly.

Suzanne finally settled down to eat her own meal, with an air of weariness, but after a few mouthfuls, she seemed to revive. 'What did you think of the garden?' she asked.

'Oh, it's got fantastic scope,' said Rosemary. 'I can't wait to get started.'

'No time like the present, then,' said Martin. 'I suggest we get down to some basic strategies the minute we've finished lunch, if that's all right.'

As soon as the meal was over Rosemary took out a notebook and pen from her bag. Suzanne pulled her chair a little way from the table, and sat half-listening, and half watching her boys as they came and went amongst the trees beside the river.

Rosemary began to quiz Martin about the commission, Laura at her side. 'Do you have a precise idea of what plants you'd like? How concerned are you that everything should be exactly in period?'

Martin answered carefully. 'Box hedges marking the

different beds – which will still be discernible once you clear away the weeds. A lot of herbs; roses; and plenty of low-growing things like alyssum and lady's mantle.'

'You know your plants, I see,' said Laura admiringly.

'Oh, not really. I know what I like, as they say. And because we've got plenty of other garden space, as you can see...' he waved an expansive arm to illustrate his point. 'Well, I wanted the walled garden to be a haven, with its own distinct style.' Laura and Rosemary followed his gaze to the area in front of the house. The large lawn was surrounded by traditional borders containing tall varieties such as lupin and foxglove at the back, with lower-growing species in front of them. Laura watched as Rosemary finally registered the hogweed and buttercup growing where they shouldn't, and the ragged edging which by this point in the year should have been trimmed.

The house itself was host to a vigorous ivy, and one side boasted an old pergola festooned with clematis and wisteria. 'Because we've allowed this area to become a bit of a jungle, I thought it would be fun to retain the much more formal geometric character of the walled garden,' Martin elaborated.

'Right.' Rosemary nibbled the end of her pencil, and considered the notes she had made. 'I don't suppose you've got a drawing or something of how it would have looked originally?'

'As it happens, I have,' said Martin. 'There's a splendid old print that shows the whole layout. I'll go and have a look for it.'   He was back in two minutes with the promised illustration, showing the garden in the early seventeenth century. 'This is actually rather a precious document,' he said. 'I keep meaning to have it copied, but never get around to it.'

It was protected by a plastic envelope, the fragile paper already flaking at the edges. It was an engraving, produced by an early lithographic engraving technique with every line still as clear as the day it was made.

Rosemary studied it minutely. 'How closely do you want us to replicate this?' she asked. 'I mean – for a start, there's a wonderfully ornate sundial right in the middle of the garden. And then there must be...' she counted under her breath 'seven, eight, *nine*, separate segments, making up the whole design. And each of those has six divisions. That's an awful lot of new hedging to put in. And the effect these days would seem terribly fussy.'

Martin nodded. 'Yes, I've been thinking about that. I wondered whether we could compromise a bit, with the four corner beds as they were, but very much simplifying the others, with no hedges round them, and a small shrub in each. Does that sound feasible?'

Rosemary doodled on her pad, checking the results against the print. 'Bay trees,' she suggested. 'What about the centre of the whole garden? There ought to be a focal point. That's a sundial, isn't it?' She pointed at the print.

'Oh, yes. We must have the sundial,' said Martin emphatically.

'You want us to reproduce it?' Rosemary was dubious.

'Don't worry. It's still here. Didn't I tell you? It was only moved a few years ago. It's in excellent condition, apart from some of the base that's gone missing. We can put it back any time we like.'

'Where is it?'

'In the barn behind the house. I'll show you later.'

'Anything else we should know?' asked Laura, who generally took a back seat at the planning stages. She was, however, very good at pointing out practical impediments.

'We won't be able to estimate how long this is going to take until we know the full extent of the work.'

Martin shook his head. 'I can't think of anything for the moment,' he said.

'That chapel you told us about – it isn't on here,' Rosemary realised.

'Of course not,' said Martin. 'It was Victorian – I told you. The print shows the garden long before anybody thought of erecting such a monstrosity.'

Laura and Rosemary both noted the sudden strain in his voice. 'You really didn't like it, did you?' said Laura.

'It was always a source of disagreement,' he admitted. 'Some of the family loved it, and other loathed it. Take my cousin Jim, for example—'

'Jim!' repeated Laura. 'He must he the man we saw just now.'

Martin stared at her. 'Pardon?' he said.

'We saw a man when we went to look at the garden,' Laura said. 'We thought he might be one of the helpers you mentioned. But he said he wasn't supposed to be there because he was banned from Abbotslea. He asked us not to say any-thing, but, well – that seemed a bit out of order.'

'He told us his name was Jim,' Rosemary added. 'I hope we won't get him into any trouble.'

Martin sighed noisily. 'Oh Lord,' he said. 'I thought we'd convinced him he has to stay away.'

'Is he a problem?' Laura asked.

Behind her, Suzanne had a sound of exasperation. 'Problem? That's putting it mildly,' she said bitterly.

'So who is he?' Rosemary asked, with a nervous glance at Laura.

Martin leaned back in his chair, as if weary of the subject. 'He's my cousin. We used to come here constantly when we were boys, staying with our grandparents. Now he lives on the estate, in a cottage.'

'And he doesn't approve of your removal of the chapel?' Laura was trying to keep up.

'It isn't for him to approve or disapprove,' said Suzanne. 'Martin can do as he likes on his own property.'

Martin gave her a pained look. 'That's true, I suppose. Besides, the chapel was genuinely hideous. It might sound romantic, but believe me, it wasn't. I never liked it, even as a boy. I just woke up one morning and decided it had to go.' His face was flushed, and he gave an awkward little laugh.

The discussion was interrupted by the return of Timmy and Toby, breathless from their exercise. They flopped on either side of their mother, who put a quick hand on each shiny head. 'You shouldn't rush about so soon after lunch,' she told them, rather belatedly.

'How far from here is Jim's cottage?' asked Laura.

Martin replied, after a moment's calculation, 'It's about half a mile, but he still seems to think he has the right to wander about the house as if he owned it.'

'Half a mile, and that's still your land?' Rosemary said. 'Gosh!'

'It's mostly rented out to local people, of course. It doesn't really feel like ours any more. Although it doesn't seem to bring in much income,' he added ruefully, with a glance at Suzanne.

She widened her eyes, as if to point up a gross under-statement. 'Abbotslea itself is incredibly expensive to maintain,' she said. 'People look to us, you see, to keep it unchanged.'

'And pass it down to me,' said Toby, importantly. 'I'm the firstborn, and I get to inherit it all.'

Laura looked at him thoughtfully. She had never actually considered the implications of the age-old system of inheritance in Britain. Then she looked at Timmy, beside his brother. If anything, Timmy was the more robust of the two, with a look of keen intelligence and humour. Toby already carried an air of complacency about him, as if the world would always deliver anything he needed, without much effort on his part.

'I see,' she said, and could not resist adding, 'But your father looks good for a while yet. A bit like Prince Charles – you might have to wait until you're seventy before you inherit anything.'

'That's right, young man,' said Martin.

'But you were only twenty-nine when your father died,' said Timmy, looking worried.

Suzanne reached out and patted her younger son's head. 'Poor Grandad was never in very good health,' she said. 'And he didn't really look after himself very well. Your daddy isn't like that at all.' She gave Martin a look that seemed to be assessing his durability.

'So this Cousin Jim,' Rosemary persisted. 'He didn't inherit anything? What does he do for a living?'

Martin laughed cynically. 'Nothing at all, I'm sorry to say. He spends a lot of his time writing inflammatory letters to the local paper.'

'Oh?' Laura blinked a little at this. 'How peculiar.'

'And infuriating,' said Suzanne. 'He watches people, and invents libellous stories about them. It's extremely annoying for practically everybody in the village, especially as he justifies it all by claiming to be "The conscience of the village".'

'And does the newspaper print them?'

'Very rarely,' said Suzanne. 'Although there's something

in this week's edition that I bet was sparked by Jim.'

Martin shot her an enquiring look. 'Is there?' he said. 'I didn't know about that. What does it say?'

'I'll fetch it,' said Suzanne, and went into the house. She was back moments later with the paper. She flipped through until she reached the right page, and spread it out before her husband. 'See,' she said, stabbing at a column with an angry forefinger. 'Poor Gwynne must be furious.'

Martin scanned the piece, muttering a few words to himself. '"Mismanagement…questions to be asked…a law unto itself…" This is outrageous. Teed ought to know better than to run stuff like this.'

'I agree,' said Suzanne. 'But he'll say it's in the public interest, or some such nonsense.'

Martin's eyes were still on the newsprint. 'I suppose he doesn't actually say anything defamatory,' he concluded. 'I mean, in the true legal sense. It's all allegation and innuendo.'

'As usual,' snapped Suzanne.

Martin folded the paper and pushed it away. 'Well, the best thing is just to try and ignore it.'

Rosemary picked up her notepad. 'Have we finished?' she said.

'Not quite,' said Martin. He went on to talk through the purchase of all the plants they would need. 'There's a wonderful stall in the Long Horton market that sells all the old plants that would have been in the garden originally. It's run by a chap called Bernie. He's got a nursery as well, where you'll find just about everything you need, especially the herbs.'

Rosemary was making copious notes. 'It'll be a big job,' she warned him. 'All those fiddly little hedges to be put in, and the paths marked out at exactly the right angles, even with the simplified version.'

'Well, as I said, I've got you some assistants,' said Martin. 'I think you'll find they speed things up dramatically.'

Their discussion had taken the best part of an hour. Slowly, Martin got out of his chair and gestured encouragingly at Laura and Rosemary. 'Now we'd better go and have a look at the Dingle before the next visitors arrive,' he said.

'OK,' Laura stood up expectantly. 'I've been looking forward to this.'

Martin gave her an appraising look. 'You really are sure you want to camp, are you? There's a nice little hotel just outside the village. I'm sure they'd have a room for you.'

'We're sure,' said Laura firmly, ignoring the look of anguish that Rosemary threw her.

'Come on then.' And he marched them across the lawn and along a path beside the river for three or four minutes. Then he stopped, and pointed to a level area of mossy grass surrounded by trees. 'How does that suit you?' he asked.

The two gazed around in delight. 'It's like fairyland,' said Laura. 'I bet there'll be owls at night.'

Rosemary uttered a stifled groan. 'Not to mention foxes and bats and a million creepy-crawlies,' she said. 'Please, Laura, have a heart. Martin says there's a hotel. Can't we—?'

'Far too late now,' asserted Laura. 'It's all decided.'

Rosemary sighed. 'At least the river's nice,' she conceded, looking down the sloping bank to where the Mallam flowed swiftly over a bed of large rocks.

'It's in full spate at the moment,' Martin nodded. 'It's quite dramatic when it's like this.'

'Beautiful,' said Laura. 'Perfectly lovely. And I suppose we can make good use of it?'

'Definitely,' Martin confirmed. 'You can use the water for washing, and even for making tea. It's very pure.'

The river was fifteen or twenty yards distant, down a gentle slope. It flowed rapidly, making quite a noise. There was a fallen tree at one edge of the clearing, with ferns growing on it. Dappled sunlight filtered through the branches overhead.

'Absolutely perfect,' Laura breathed again. 'Thank you very much.'

Martin glanced at his watch. 'That's good. Now I must get back to the house. They'll be here any minute now,' he said.

'Who?' asked Laura.

'Wait and see,' he smiled. 'I suggest you come with me, and make their acquaintance.'

Chapter Four

It was just before three o'clock when a minibus came into view, drawing to a halt on the gravel in front of the house. Martin went to greet the driver, beckoning Laura and Rosemary to follow him. The retrievers bounced excitedly alongside.

Four men got out of the vehicle. One wore a uniform that Laura recognised as that of a prison officer. The other three were in ordinary clothes, but had armbands stitched onto their sleeves.

'Welcome to Abbotslea,' said Martin. 'It's good of you to come back for another stint.' He turned to Rosemary and Laura, explaining, 'This isn't their first time here. They did some work for me last month.'

The officer nodded amiably at Martin and then addressed Laura and Rosemary. 'Cyril Coutts at your service,' he said, extending a hand to each in turn. 'Let me introduce my charges. Huxton Rymer, George Marsden Plummer and Rupert Waldo. All quite prominent in their fields, I might add.'

'Oh?' Laura looked more closely at the men. 'In what way?'

'Sorry – that'll have to wait until another day. This is just a short visit to assess the job and how long you're likely to want us.' Mr Coutts smiled apologetically. Then he addressed Martin, 'When would you like us to start work?'

Martin raised an eyebrow at Rosemary, before saying, 'I should think tomorrow, if that's all right. Let me show you what's involved.'

Dumbstruck with surprise at this development, Laura and Rosemary followed the group of men into the walled garden. The men had obviously been there before. They stared at the site of the demolished chapel, muttering between themselves.

'They took it down for you!' Laura realised.

Martin gave a brief nod. 'That's right,' he said.

Laura detected, yet again, a peculiar atmosphere whenever the old chapel was mentioned. Martin's face would flush and he generally tried to change the subject. She resolved to find out just why it caused him such discomfort.

The three prisoners expressed confidence that they could supply whatever assistance might be required, and Mr Coutts made it clear that he would be on guard at all times. 'Don't worry,' he twinkled at Rosemary. 'They're not a bit dangerous.'

'I wasn't worried,' she assured him. 'They look like very nice chaps.'

'They'll tell you their stories, I have no doubt, while they're here,' he said. 'Embezzlement more or less covers it, but each has his own particular speciality.'

'They're from an open prison then?' Laura asked.

'That's right,' said the officer. 'Bleakmoor Grange.' He turned to Martin. 'We'll have to discuss some of the practicalities, sir,' he said. 'Especially after last time.' Martin grabbed the officer by the elbow and urged him a few paces before resuming the conversation in a low tone.

Rosemary and Laura made a discreet withdrawal despite

a strong feeling of curiosity. 'Last time?' Laura mouthed. Rosemary pulled a conspiratorial face. There was no doubt in either mind that it would be a priority to discover just what had happened.

'The next job will be to put the tent up,' Laura said, rubbing her hands in eager anticipation. 'I don't suppose it'll take long.'

'You haven't lost the instructions, have you?' Rosemary entertained a moment of hope, with the lure of a warm soft hotel bed still at the forefront of her mind.

'We won't need them,' Laura breezed. 'I can remember how it all went.'

An hour and a half later, things were somewhat different. Rosemary's jaw ached from having to suppress sarcastic remarks, as Laura persistently tried to attach bracepoles and flaps and pockets and eyelets in a coherent sequence. The instructions had evidently been translated from the Chinese by a young schoolchild. ' "Insert small end of pole A in eyehole of large tent piece (see diagram) until full. Bring section X into conjunction with flap and fasten with stud." ' Rosemary read these lines for the fourteenth time, in a voice full of despair. 'It doesn't *mean* anything,' she wailed. 'It's gibberish. Laura, we'll have to give it up before it gets dark. We can go to that hotel Martin told us about.'

'Nonsense. There has to be a logic to it,' Laura persisted. 'We must have started in the wrong place. Look – if we thread the pole through *here*, and then bring that piece over like *this*…' she matched action to words, and for a moment things seemed promising, but then the same problem as before reasserted itself. The pole refused to thread any further, leaving a large section of uselessly flapping material with nothing to support it.

'Oh, drat the thing. I give up.' Laura threw it down and stared frustratedly at the tangle at her feet.

'Hooray!' Rosemary rejoiced. 'I thought you'd never give in. Come on.' She started down the path towards the Land Rover.

'Don't be ridiculous,' Laura called after her. 'We'll have to go and ask somebody to help, that's all.'

Rosemary paused. She knew from experience that she was not going to be able to get her way until Laura was thoroughly beaten. 'Right,' she said. 'I'll give you half an hour. If that tent isn't erected and fit to sleep in by then, I'm off. That's my final word.'

Toby and Timmy were throwing sticks for the dogs on the lawn when Laura reached them, somewhat out of breath.

'Where's your father?' she asked them.

They shook their heads blankly. 'Don't know,' said Timmy. 'He was here a bit ago.'

'Well, we need him. We can't seem to get our tent up properly.'

Toby dropped the stick he was holding and gave Laura a scornful look. 'Is that all? Come on, Timmy.'

They loped along the path to the clearing with Laura trailing behind them. The dogs ran joyfully ahead as if knowing where the boys were heading.

It was like magic. In a deft display of teamwork, Toby and Timmy threaded, connected, pegged and zipped until the tent stood squarely on the mossy grass in all its majesty, with almost ten minutes to go to Rosemary's deadline. Not content with that, the boys proceeded to construct a campfire, complete with ring of stones to confine the embers and a neat edifice of poles from which to hang a cooking pot.

'There!' said Toby, when they'd finished. 'We were only waiting to be asked, you know. We'd have come and helped you hours ago if you'd said.'

When the boys had gone, Laura produced two torches for later in the evening, as well as two inflatable airbeds and two sleeping bags. 'Here,' she said generously. 'I'll do yours for you, if you like.'

Rosemary was making herself at home on her side of the tent. She zipped and unzipped the various flaps, marvelling at the versatility of the whole arrangement. 'Thanks,' she said. She sat down. 'There isn't really anywhere for bugs to get in, is there?'

'Not unless they can work a zip,' panted Laura, pumping away at the inflator. 'Is this thing going up at all?'

'It's coming along very nicely,' Rosemary encouraged. She switched on her torch and started playing with it. 'This ought to be bright enough to read by,' she noted. 'You did think of everything, didn't you.'

'I tried,' gasped Laura. 'Here. This should do.'

Rosemary took the bed and stretched out on it. 'Amazing!' she said. 'It's really comfy. Now we just have to cook a bit of supper and then we can get to bed.'

Laura sat back on her heels. 'You've changed your mind, then, have you? About camping, I mean.'

Rosemary tilted her head. 'Just so long as the weather holds up, it might not be too bad,' she conceded.

'I never dreamed it would be so difficult to get the tent erected. It's all a bit of a *hassle*, isn't it.'

'That was just teething troubles,' Rosemary said. 'Next time, we'll get it done easily.'

An hour later, they were in their night clothes and occupying their individual compartments of the tent. 'Hey!' Rosemary called. 'Did you hear that?'

Laura was wrestling to remove a sharp stone that threatened to puncture her bed. She was working it along to the edge of the tent, through the groundsheet, but it was a slow business. The salty packet food they'd eaten was giving her severe indigestion, as well. 'What?' she said.

'An owl. Hooting somewhere across the river. It's a lovely romantic sound.'

'Oh, good,' said Laura. 'Drat.'

'What's the matter?'

'I knelt on a stone. A different stone. Why have I got them all?'

'I think I've got one or two, but I've been working round them. I put my clothes on top of the worst one.'

'Oh.' Laura abandoned her task and lay down on the airbed, inside the sleeping bag. Everything seemed to bounce. She rolled on to her side, which was better, but somehow not the exact position she usually adopted in bed. When she rolled back, the sleeping bag performed an evil twist, cocooning her like a well-swaddled baby. Eventually she realised she had over-inflated the bed, so it had no give. Irritably, she sat up and fumbled for the cunningly concealed bung, and the clever valve arrangement that was designed to make it as hard as possible for air to escape.

'What are you doing?' called Rosemary.

'Don't ask,' groaned Laura, as she finally released the pressure, only to find that too much was escaping. Quickly she replaced the bung and lay down again on the now flaccid mattress. It was all right, she told herself. It was *fun*. She switched off her torch and tried desperately to get to sleep.

* * *

At seven-thirty the next morning, Rosemary was lazing on her airbed listening to the river sounds close by. Birds were doing their morning chorusing, adding to the music of the countryside. 'Heaven,' she murmured happily, before a twinge in her back reminded her that camping also had some disadvantages.

She allowed herself another half an hour before remembering that she and Laura were expected to make a start on the garden, in spite of it being a Bank Holiday. Everyone had agreed that having arrived at Abbotslea it would be foolish to waste a day. Besides, the men from the open prison were expected to work, regardless of what the calendar might say. She rolled off the airbed and pulled on a cardigan, before slipping outside and down to the river. On the way she grabbed a billycan to collect water for morning tea.

The river was still flowing very fast, the water a reddish brown from the soil washed along from further upstream. There were massive rocks strewn along its course, which might offer stepping stones in dryer times. Anybody attempting to cross it in such full spate would be asking for trouble.

And then she saw him, only a few yards away. A man was standing on the largest rock in the middle of the river, the water rushing around him. He was stock still and seemed to Rosemary as if he was waiting for something. Almost immediately she recognised Jim, the man from the garden the day before. He was staring around himself in the same unfocused way, conveying a disturbing sense of vagueness. 'Hey!' Rosemary shouted. 'Get off there. It's dangerous.'

Afterwards, she found it difficult to describe exactly what happened. He didn't jump or slide or lose his balance.

He didn't dive or step into the water. Somehow he just folded up and let the water take him away. Rosemary watched in a state of paralysed horror as his sleek head twirled past her in the murky rushing water and onward down to the bend in the river. She almost felt the impact as he was slammed into one rock after another. It was all over in a dozen seconds. For the same length of time again, she struggled to convince herself that it had really happened. There was nothing to indicate that the man had ever been there.

Finally, she managed a strangled scream. Dropping the billycan, she dashed back to the tent, calling for Laura, who did not appear. Rosemary tore back the flap of the tent and blundered into her friend's section. 'Wake up!' she squealed. 'Laura – something terrible just happened.'

Chapter Five

Martin and Suzanne Frazer woke slowly in their enormous ancestral bed, where generations of Frazers had been born and a few had also died. Suzanne had insisted on a new mattress for it when she had first come to Abbotslea, but most of the room had been left unchanged. A vast mahogany wardrobe stood against one wall and the carpet was finest Persian, dating back well over a century.

Suzanne's first thoughts on waking were concerned with the forthcoming lunch. Martin had suggested a barbecue, which he would orchestrate himself. That had been a very tempting idea until she remembered the previous occasion when he had got the timing wrong and people had waited hours for the first piece of meat to appear. 'So I'll go and buy one of those newfangled ones that do all the work for you,' he had offered.

'We can't possibly afford it,' Suzanne had argued. 'You know there isn't any spare cash. Not now we've got to replace the guttering. As well as paying these women to do the Elizabethan garden.'

'They're far cheaper than most landscape gardeners,' Martin had said mildly.

'I don't doubt it,' she said. 'But they still cost money.'

'Darling, we really aren't as hard up as all that. You're worrying needlessly, as usual.'

She had looked at him with her accustomed blend of affection and frustration. It was true that he earned a good salary, and her own income from teaching was a healthy contribution. Money, she wanted to explain to him, wasn't really the point.

'The fact is, though,' she had summarised, 'we can't justify getting a fancy new barbecue.'

'OK, then.'

'And that means I'd rather play safe and do the cooking indoors.'

In truth, Suzanne found cooking one of the more satisfying of her many tasks. She enjoyed being a hostess, having a lot of people filling the place with chatter and laughter, especially the friends she had invited this time – people she had known since before the boys were born; people who would avert their eyes from the cracks and weeds and wonky gutters. She lay on the fine linen sheet, staring out of the window at the blue sky, listening to the rushing sound of the swollen river and making her plans.

It seemed to take hours for Laura and Rosemary to alert the Frazers, tell the story, summon the police. But when Rosemary next looked at her watch, it was only nine-fifteen. Beside her stood a police officer, who Martin had introduced as Constable Donald Stuart from the local station, the two men evidently well known to each other. He was staring into the rushing river. 'We're searching along the whole length of it, of course,' he was saying. 'Although there's one stretch where it goes through dense woodland. That might be tricky.' He looked at her. 'This happened once before, you know – three or four years back. A homeless chap, fell in just a little way down there...' he pointed towards the village, '...and washed up in the estuary three days later.'

'Dead?' croaked Rosemary.

The constable nodded. 'It's the rocks that do the damage, you see. Especially when it's in full spate like this.'

'You don't think there's much hope for him?' Rosemary asked.

The policeman shook his head. 'It doesn't look very good. The water's so murky, it'd be hard to spot somebody. But we'll do everything we can. We've got all the local lads out already. And Martin knows the river so well, he'll show them the places where it's easier to get a footing and climb up the bank. There's a chance Jim's lying exhausted but alive somewhere.'

'Did you know him?'

'Jim Frazer? Oh, yes. Everybody knows Jim. Not that he's exactly popular. I probably shouldn't say it – but if he hadn't fallen in like you say he did, there's plenty that would have liked to push him. If ever a man invited violence, it was Jim.'

'Well, nobody pushed him,' said Rosemary, screwing her face up painfully at the memory.

'Suicide, you mean?'

She nodded uncertainly. 'I suppose it must have been.'

The morning acquired an unreal aspect as the search for Jim proceeded in vain. Phone messages flew back and forth, all essentially saying 'No news.' Rosemary found herself feeling very wobbly from the shock of what she had seen. 'It was so *strange*,' she repeated to Laura. 'One minute he was looking me straight in the eye, and the next he was whirling down the river without a struggle. I can't stop thinking about it. I'll never get that face out of my mind.'

'Work's the best therapy for you,' said Laura decisively. 'Come and make a start on the garden.'

Rosemary sighed. 'OK,' she agreed. 'It's not as if there's anything else to do. But oh, Laura – that poor man! I don't care how annoying he was, nobody should be allowed to get so miserable that they do – what he did.'

'It's odd, though, isn't it,' said Laura. 'When Martin and Suzanne were talking about him yesterday, they didn't give the impression he was depressed or at risk of doing away with himself.'

'They probably didn't realise,' said Rosemary. 'People often don't.'

The two boys had inevitably been involved in the events of the morning. Rosemary had noticed them standing wide-eyed and pale when the police car had swept up to the house. While Rosemary was being questioned, Laura had made it her business to be with the youngsters, explaining what the procedures would be. 'I used to be a police-woman, you see,' she told them, greatly to their fascination. Toby had wondered whether Jess and Cabbage might be recruited in the search for their uncle, which Laura acknowledged might be a great idea. 'Although they didn't really like him,' added Timmy.

'Didn't they? Why not? He seemed quite nice to me when I saw him yesterday.'

'Dad's trained them to chase him,' said Toby with a frown. 'He isn't supposed to come here, unless we invite him. Timmy and I think that's quite mean. Mum says he's a big nuisance and he makes her nervous. She locks the door to make sure he stays out of the house.'

'Goodness!' said Laura feebly, wondering at this peculiar family. 'Well, I expect they'll find him any time now, without needing the dogs.'

'Yeah,' said Toby, sounding very unconvinced.

In the garden, Rosemary began methodically assembling her tools. She still looked very pale and preoccupied, and Laura decided it would be best to let her recover gradually. She went to the area where there were still obvious signs of the former chapel. 'We'll have to dig these foundations out,' she said.

'The prisoners will, you mean,' said Rosemary.

Laura paced out the dimensions. 'It must have been very tiny,' she said. 'I can't help thinking it deserved to stay.'

'Well, you're wrong,' came a voice behind her. She turned to see Suzanne standing in the doorway of the garden. 'It was an eyesore. It should never have been allowed in the first place.'

'No planning regs then, I suppose,' said Laura.

'Don't *you* start,' said Suzanne, rather crossly.

Laura's eyebrows rose. 'What did I say?'

'You reminded me of Jim, going on about planning permission. He was insanely keen on keeping the chapel.'

Rosemary, hearing this, walked up to Suzanne. 'Was he?' she said, her eyes fixed on the other woman's face. 'Was he upset enough about it to kill himself?'

Suzanne took a step back, putting her hands up defensively. 'You don't know what you're saying,' she protested. 'That's close to implying that Martin drove him to suicide because he demolished Jim's precious chapel.'

'Well, it does seem a shame,' said Laura, as usual trying to soothe both the others. 'But surely nobody would kill themselves over a ruined building.'

Suzanne seemed to have a sudden change of heart. 'Jim was capable of anything,' she said bleakly. 'I just didn't like to hear anybody blaming Martin for his death.'

She began to walk out of the garden. Rosemary and Laura stared at her departing back. 'Well, that's told *us*,' muttered Laura.

But Suzanne had not finished with them, after all. She turned in the doorway, a tense smile on her lips. 'Don't mention the chapel to Martin, if you can help it,' she said, with real appeal in her voice. 'He's got enough to worry about.'

'He isn't back yet, then?' Laura said.

Suzanne shook her head. 'He'll be frantic. He won't give up searching until they find the body.'

Rosemary winced. 'That policeman said there was still a chance he could have crawled out onto the bank,' she said.

'We'd have heard by now if that had happened,' said Laura, hoping she wasn't being tactless. 'It must be a ghastly shock for all of you.' She looked round, at the soft blue sky, and the fresh leaves on the ancient trees between the house and the river. It was not a scene that fitted with misery and suicide.

'Yes.' Suzanne gave herself a little shake. 'I should go and find the boys. They'll be upset.'

'Were they fond of their uncle?'

Suzanne's eyes hardened. 'He wasn't their uncle,' she snapped. 'He was their father's cousin.'

Laura wondered why such a detail should matter so much. 'Sorry,' she said. 'I'm still trying to get to grips with your family tree.'

Suzanne smiled feebly. 'That's all right,' she said. 'It isn't exactly my family, anyway. Although, as it happens...' she sighed, and seemed to lose the thread of what she was about to say.

'Yes?' prompted Laura.

'Oh, well. As it happens, Martin and I are connected. We come from the same ancestral stock, as you might say if we were cattle. If you're interested, I can show you. We've got genealogy back to the thirteenth century. Can you believe that?'

Laura had a sense that Suzanne was thinking of Jim and how he too had been a branch of this same family tree. A branch which had grown crookedly, perhaps, with no offshoots of its own – but still a loss to be mourned. 'Yes, I can believe it,' she said gently.

But Suzanne had already gone, walking stiffly towards the driveway, where she expected her husband to reappear.

Rosemary had been distracted by her own turbulent thoughts as Laura talked with Suzanne. She was struggling to convince herself that Jim would be found and rescued before the river could dash his brains out on the rocks. She walked around the walled garden, methodically planning where the new beds would be, and what initial preparation would be required. The two parts of her mind operated independently, the garden and the would-be suicide both claiming her attention. There was none left over for the women apparently chatting near the garden door.

By mid-day they had made little noticeable progress. 'I'm hungry,' Laura realised. 'We never had any breakfast.'

Rosemary frowned. 'Wasn't there supposed to be a lunch? With people?'

'Goodness, so there was. Poor Suzanne – she seems to have an awful lot to cope with.'

'You surely don't feel sorry for her? She's got the life that most women would die for.'

Laura jingled one of her earrings thoughtfully. 'It's mostly image, though – don't you think? Scratch the surface and the whole thing looks more like an endless list of maintenance jobs than a life to be envied.'

'I'm not sure you're right,' said Rosemary. 'The fact remains, she seems to have forgotten she's having people here for lunch.'

'And that's bad news for us,' grinned Laura. 'We might have to have another packet of sausage and mash.'

They pulled off their gardening gloves and left the garden. There was no sign of activity. 'Where are the boys, I wonder?' said Laura.

As she spoke, a couple came into view, walking up the curving drive towards the house. They seemed to be very interested in the river, walking close to the bank and directing their gaze at the water. 'They think they might see the body,' said Rosemary. 'Look at them!'

'Human nature,' said Laura. 'You can understand the fascination. Let's go and meet them.'

There was no doubt that the visitors had heard the news. The woman's eyes were wide as she gazed enquiringly at Laura and Rosemary. 'Who are you?' she said.

'We're restoring Martin's Elizabethan garden,' said Laura, holding out a hand. 'Laura Thyme and Rosemary Boxer.'

'Hi,' said the man, taking her hand. 'We're Chris and Katy Stevens. We weren't sure we should come – whether Suzanne still wanted us. It's true, then – about Jim? What a terrible thing.'

Laura nodded, and together they approached the house.

Suzanne was with her sons on the area that had been designated the 'parterre' at the side of the house. It was a large square patch, paved in a design that gave Rosemary a sudden new idea for the layout of the walled garden. 'But it's not strictly a parterre at all,' she whispered to Laura. 'More a rather fancy patio.' An old wisteria had been trained up supports on one side of the square, but the rest was open to the sun. Sturdy wooden seats were arranged around a large table.

'Katy!' shouted Timmy, running to greet her. 'Where's Jasper? And Freddie?'

'Gone to stay with their granny for a few days,' Katy told him. 'I'm missing them already.'

'And Bonnie?' said Timmy warily, looking past them as if expecting to see the little girl in their wake.

Chris laughed. 'And Bonnie,' he confirmed. Timmy's relief was palpable.

'Suzanne,' Katy began. 'We heard the news. You must be feeling so…' she gave a little shrug to indicate that words had failed her.

Suzanne made a visible effort. 'Oh!' she said. 'My God! You've come for lunch. I forgot all about it.'

Katy made a soothing gesture. 'It doesn't matter. We can go away again. Or better still, let me help.' Her voice had acquired a low hypnotic tenor. Laura felt as if it was washing over her like warm scented oil. A look at Rosemary suggested she was feeling something similar.

'No, no.' Suzanne shook her head. 'Heavens! What must you think?'

'Come on, Sooz,' said Chris. 'Never mind the food. We wanted to see if we could help somehow. We didn't realise you had these good ladies here.' He indicated Laura and Rosemary, who were hanging back rather awkwardly.

His wife continued her calming instructions. 'Come with me, Suzanne,' she ordered. 'Chris, stay here and be sociable. Everything will be all right.' The words were ordinary enough, but the indefinable something in her voice seemed to have everyone in her power. Suzanne obediently moved into the house, and Chris gave a rueful shrug at Laura.

'You're doing the garden?' he repeated. 'About time too. Now the chapel's gone—' he stopped, and cocked his head with a grimace that suggested he feared he'd said too much.

Laura watched him closely. 'What about the chapel?'

Chris shrugged with exaggerated carelessness. 'Nothing. Just that poor old Jim was so fond of it. It seems a bit tactless to talk about it, that's all.'

'Poor old Jim,' said Rosemary distantly. 'I keep hearing those words.'

'Rosemary saw him fall into the river,' Laura explained. 'She's still trying to get over it.'

'He didn't *fall*,' muttered Rosemary. The other two looked at her, but didn't say anything.

'So what do you do?' Laura asked Chris, forcing a brightness into her voice.

He responded with similar heartiness. 'I illustrate book covers. No two days the same, which is how I like it.'

'I can imagine,' agreed Laura. 'It must be ever so interesting.'

He examined her face for a few seconds. 'Yes,' he said. 'It's good fun most of the time.'

'And Katy?' asked Laura.

'Ah! Well, Katy is another of the village superwomen. They seem to breed them around here. She works as an anaesthetist at the hospital in Westover. She also supplies remedies for friends and neighbours, that she concocts herself. And we've got three young children.'

'I'm impressed,' said Laura, wondering whether he'd left something out. Katy Stevens had struck her as a woman with a great many sides to her.

Suzanne emerged then from the house, carrying a tray of glasses and a bottle of white wine. She smiled vaguely at everyone and let Chris take the tray from her.

'There's Gwynne!' Toby suddenly shouted, from where he and his brother had been playing with the dogs on the lawn. 'And Fern. Mum – they've *all* come. I knew they would.'

Two women were walking up the drive, in very much the same fashion as the Stevenses had. They too seemed to be magnetised by the river. Suddenly, behind them a car appeared. 'Daddy as well!' crowed Toby.

Mortified by her poor performance as a hostess, Suzanne hurried back to the kitchen. Katy met her in the doorway, her face a study in serenity.

Rosemary and Laura examined the new arrivals, now standing hesitantly beneath the wisteria. 'Hello!' Laura said, rather heartily. 'We're here to restore Martin's walled garden. I'm Laura and this is Rosemary.'

'Gwynne and Fern Evans,' said one of the women. At first glance they seemed to be sisters, very much alike to look at. But then Laura noted how the younger one showed signs of being much less sure of herself, responding to Toby's clamour with obvious relief. The girl went off with the Frazer boys, and Rosemary moved away, rather aimlessly. 'My daughter,' Gwynne explained to Laura. 'She's eighteen.'

'And you were only twelve when you had her,' said Laura. 'At most.'

'No, I was twenty, actually,' Gwynne corrected, seeing

nothing to smile at in the flattering comment. 'It's true, is it – about Jim?'

Laura felt suitably reproached for her flippancy and nodded. 'It's a terrible business,' she said. 'Rosemary saw the whole thing. I was still dozing in the tent, when I heard her shouting.'

Chris Stevens was speaking quietly to Rosemary, sitting with her on one of the wooden benches. 'She looks shell-shocked,' Gwynne observed.

'She is,' Laura agreed. 'It's really knocked her off balance.'

'She ought to ask Katy for a remedy.'

'Oh?'

'It's a little sideline of hers. She prepares homeopathic concoctions for various emotional upsets.'

Laura raised her eyebrows. 'Yes, Chris was just talking about that. She's qualified, is she?'

'I guess she knows what she's doing.' The words sounded like a warning to Laura, and she said nothing more on the subject.

Martin Frazer finally disentangled himself from his sons and joined the group. 'Lunch!' he groaned. 'You were all invited to lunch. We completely forgot.'

'It doesn't matter,' Gwynne assured him, her eyes on his. 'I am so sorry, Martin. About Jim. Have they – I mean, is he…?'

'Not a sign of him,' Martin sighed. 'There isn't much hope now, I'm afraid.'

Gwynne moved closer and gripped Martin's arm tightly. 'I can't believe it,' she said huskily. 'Jim's been part of our lives forever. It just isn't possible.'

Martin put a hand briefly on her shoulder. 'I know,' he said.

Laura watched the intimate moment with interest. Noticing her scrutiny, Martin smiled. 'Gwynne and I go back a long way,' he said easily. 'She was the first girl I ever kissed.'

'And he makes sure he tells everybody he meets,' Gwynne added. 'I never know whether to be embarrassed or not.'

Laura smiled uncertainly, and directed her gaze at Fern, who was still giving all her attention to Toby and Timmy. 'I see,' was all she said.

The impromptu lunch was consumed in an atmosphere of shock and swirling emotion. Toby and Timmy went from a rather manic effort to force the adults to behave normally to a sudden subdued anxiety. They looked from face to face, nudging each other now and then and whispering. Laura felt sorry for them as the full impact of what had happened sank in. Although she still could not quite understand Jim Frazer's role in the family and the wider community, it was plain that everyone felt bad about his disappearance.

Rosemary was making a big effort to be sociable. Chris Stevens had remained at her side, his manner warm and reassuring. He asked her about her ideas for the walled garden and just how she'd come to Martin's notice. Watching him across the table, Laura felt he was not especially affected by the events of the morning. He seemed to be struggling to repress a natural jollity, that could be glimpsed in his twinkling eyes and ready smile.

Leaning over to Katy, Laura asked her about the remedies she supplied. 'Gwynne thought Rosemary might benefit from one of them,' she explained. 'She's had a nasty shock.'

Katy smiled. 'Absolutely,' she said. 'You should come

over and collect it this afternoon. We don't live far away.'

Laura was struggling to get a sense of this woman, who worked at a responsible post where people's lives depended on her, while at the same time possessing a quiet force which seemed to emanate from her like magnetism. At least she felt it was a force for good. Suzanne looked a lot calmer after spending a few minutes in Katy's company.

Laura was also wondering whether Rosemary could be persuaded to take one of Katy's remedies, when it had such unclear provenance. 'I'll try,' she said. 'I'm not sure whether I'll be able to get away. We're supposed to be working, you see.'

'On a Bank Holiday?'

Laura nodded. 'We want to get cracking while the weather's nice,' she explained. 'And we never like to waste any time.'

'Are you staying at The Lamb?'

Laura shook her head and explained about the camping. It sounded slightly silly to her own ears, as she tried to convey enthusiasm for the outdoor life. 'It's a brilliant tent,' she finished. 'Really state of the art.'

Martin was restless throughout the meal. He took over from Suzanne in carrying bread and cheese and fruit out from the kitchen, tripping over Jess and dropping a bowl of apples. He jumped violently when the house telephone rang, running in to answer it – only to emerge a minute later saying it was George Hamilton Teed, wondering if there was any fresh news.

'He ought to know better than bother you at a time like this,' said Gwynne crossly. 'That man really gets on my nerves.'

'He'll miss Jim, though,' said Chris. 'He relied on him for most of his stories.'

Everybody seemed to freeze for a moment, causing Laura to catch Rosemary's eye and widen her eyes in a silent expression of curiosity. Then Martin spoke. 'Teed hasn't used any of Jim's letters for months,' he said.

'Oh, but he has,' Gwynne corrected him. 'That piece last week about the Lyvedon Trust came from Jim, even if it wasn't on the letters page. I tackled him about it yesterday.'

'I showed it to you yesterday, remember?' Suzanne said to Martin.

'We can't be sure it had anything to do with Jim, though,' he insisted stubbornly.

Gwynne threw him an impatient look. 'Well, I'm sure,' she said. 'It's obvious. Teed should be ashamed of himself.'

Chris broke the prickly silence. 'Forget it, Gwynne,' he pleaded. 'It's only another bit of Jim's mischief, when all's said and done.'

Martin slapped the table. 'And it doesn't matter now, does it,' he said loudly. 'Jim isn't going to write any more letters, so you can all rest easy from here on.' He glared accusingly at one person after another.

'All very well for you, old chap,' muttered Chris. 'He wasn't going to drop you in it, now was he? However badly you treated him, Jim remained devoted to his beloved cousin Martin.'

'It wasn't as simple as that,' Martin protested.

'No, because you treated him so badly, he committed suicide,' came a light voice from behind him. He spun round to see Fern looking down at him.

Again there was a frozen moment, as everybody seemed to wait for a furious voice from the sky. Brave girl, this one, thought Laura.

Suzanne stood up. 'I've had enough,' she said. 'I can't take any more of this.'

Nobody tried to stop her as she stumbled into the house and slammed the door. Martin reached out and took Fern's arm for a moment. 'You're right,' he said huskily. 'I feel dreadful about it. But I never for a moment thought—' he blinked hard and rubbed his nose. 'Poor old Jim.'

Chapter Six

Monday afternoon passed slowly, with Martin belatedly informing Laura and Rosemary that he had postponed the arrival of the three prisoners until the following day. 'It would be too complicated, the ways things are,' he said tiredly.

'Of course,' Laura agreed. 'We'll carry on with digging out weeds and marking out, then, and that sort of thing.'

Gwynne and Fern had not left with the others. Fern was playing with the boys, and Gwynne was obviously trying to give support to Martin. She had followed him into the garden, and stood looking around with an expression of nostalgia. 'Remember when we played in here?' she murmured. 'You, me and Jim.'

Martin grimaced. 'I remember,' he said. 'Happy times. Poor old Jim. I'll never understand exactly what went wrong.'

When they'd gone, Laura gave Rosemary a close scrutiny. 'It's all very odd, isn't it,' she ventured. 'The way they talk about Jim. I can't understand it.'

'He must have been a bit disturbed,' said Rosemary. 'Maybe he was mentally ill. I've been getting that impression. They were fond of him, but he made them uncomfortable. He did look strange when we saw him in here yesterday.'

'Are you feeling better now?' Laura asked. 'You look it.'

Rosemary twitched her shoulders as if throwing off a heavy weight. 'Yes, I'm over the worst,' she said. 'I'll be fine tomorrow. It helped hearing everybody talking about it. It sort of diluted the shock, seeing them all react more or less the same as I did.'

'Except that Chris bloke. He didn't seem to care much.'

'He's nice, though. And if I've got it right, he's another one who grew up around here and knew Jim as a boy.'

Laura rubbed her temple as if to try and disentangle some of the threads. 'It's not easy to sort them all out, is it. Oh, I forgot to say. Katy Stevens does some sort of remedy for shock. She said you could have some if we go and collect it.'

Rosemary blinked. 'Remedy? Is she a doctor?'

'An anaesthetist, apparently. But this is a sideline. It sounds as if she makes it herself.'

Rosemary shook her head. 'I don't need any New Age nonsense. I'd be better off nibbling at a bit of feverfew. *Much* better off – I know feverfew works.'

'Oh, well,' Laura shrugged. 'Let me know if you change your mind.'

They saw the Frazers again later in the afternoon, as they finished work and headed towards the Dingle. Toby and Timmy spotted them and ran after them, calling them to wait. The dogs were nowhere to be seen.

'Dad says would you like to come to the house for a cup of tea,' said Toby. 'He wants to talk about the garden. He's got to go away again tomorrow, you see.'

Willingly, Laura turned back, assuming Rosemary would follow. But her friend was sitting on a large rock, a few feet from the river's edge, staring into the water.

'Hey!' Laura said gently. 'Wake up.'

'Oh,' Rosemary sighed. 'Sorry.'

It was a perfect early summer evening. The sun was on the front of the house, turning the brick to a vivid crimson, and making the new leaves of the surrounding trees glow as if luminous. 'Look at that!' breathed Laura. 'Isn't it stunning.'

'Lovely,' said Rosemary.

Martin ushered them into a well-proportioned room with large windows looking out on the back garden, which was mainly in shadow. 'This is officially the morning room,' said Martin. 'It gets the early sun.'

There was no sign of any tea. 'I'll fetch Suzanne,' Martin said. 'I think she's feeding the dogs.'

Suzanne appeared before he had a chance to summon her, carrying a laden tray. Deftly she distributed cups and small cakes. 'I really am so sorry about lunch,' she said. 'I feel such an awful fool.'

'Don't say that,' Rosemary urged. 'It made me feel much better, knowing somebody else was as traumatised as I was.'

Martin gave her a sympathetic look. 'Are you better now?' he asked.

'Well – I keep thinking I am, but then it washes over me, all over again. And I feel so *tired*, which is ridiculous, because I slept perfectly well last night.'

'Shock does that,' said Laura knowledgeably. 'You should have let me get some of that remedy from Katy.'

Suzanne made a noise like a snort. They all looked at her. 'Don't waste your time on that rubbish,' she said. 'Katy's remedies are a joke.'

Martin cleared his throat. 'Come on,' he chided her. 'Half the village swears by them. You can't just dismiss it like that. She's done a proper study of it – when she was in China she took a whole course.'

'Right,' said Suzanne sarcastically. 'Six whole weeks of flim-flam.'

Laura tried to be diplomatic. 'It's a Chinese system then, is it, that she uses?'

Martin frowned. 'Well, not exactly. It's based on homeopathy, which is European, but she found a few new plants that she says have excellent uses. You'll have to ask her if you want details.'

'She seems to be a very powerful presence,' Laura said tentatively. 'That hypnotic voice. It gave me the feeling she could make me do anything if she tried.'

'It's just a party trick,' said Suzanne.

'But—' Laura wanted to remind Suzanne of the way Katy had calmed her down, but couldn't find a way to say it.

Martin seemed to know what she was trying to say. 'She does have an effect on people. She had a way with Jim, as well. She tried quite hard to stop him being so erratic and angry.'

'Did it work?' asked Rosemary.

'Not so's you'd notice,' said Suzanne. 'Besides, she gave up some time ago, when she realised he was libelling her along with everybody else.'

Rosemary caused a distraction then, as a biscuit crumb went astray, making her cough loudly for a few minutes. When she was able to breathe again, she began a new subject. 'You really are going to Leeds tomorrow, then?' she asked Martin.

He groaned. 'You won't be surprised to hear that I couldn't persuade Mr Jardine to spare me for another day or two. I phoned him half an hour ago and practically begged him.'

'The man's a monster,' said Rosemary angrily.

Suzanne smacked her hand on the table. 'My feelings entirely,' she said. 'I told Martin he ought to just say he's ill, but he won't.'

'I'd have to have at least three broken bones, or a notifiable disease, before he'd take any notice,' said Martin. 'But it's only for one night. I'll be back before dark on Wednesday.' He looked at Suzanne. 'And I can be here for part of tomorrow. He doesn't need me until the end of the session, and then for the whole of Wednesday morning.'

Then Laura reminded Martin that they were there to talk about the garden and what he wanted them to do in his absence. Resolutely, he outlined the next stages of the project. 'Remember you're to go down to Long Horton tomorrow morning and talk to Bernie. I told him a while back that I was going to restore the garden, so he won't be surprised. He knew the gardens here as a boy. His father was my grandfather's under-gardener, in the good old days. He'll greet you with open arms. You've got a free hand to select whatever you think will work. Herbs, roses, grasses – you choose.'

Rosemary's eyes brightened at this. 'That sounds great!' she enthused. She went on to quiz him about the exact degree of authenticity he was aiming for, prompted by his mention of grasses. 'As far as I know,' she said, 'the Elizabethans didn't use ornamental grasses. But they're tremendously popular today, with a lot of new ones coming in.'

'Use them,' he said. 'They'll look great and have a softening effect.'

'What about the sundial?' asked Laura. 'We ought to have it in position before we do anything irrevocable. Is it terribly heavy?'

Martin pulled a face. 'Exceedingly heavy. It was a stupid mistake ever to move it. I took it into my head to reposition it on the front lawn, where everybody could see it. But Suzanne wasn't sure, and after we'd got it out of the garden, we could never really work out the best spot for it. And there were never enough people to shift it, anyway. The odd-job man's a law unto himself, for a start. Every time I thought I'd got enough men together to move it, he'd go missing. He's a good worker when he's here, but we never know when that's going to be. Suzanne's taken to hiding his tools, so he can't go off on other jobs when he ought to be here.' He laughed at this piece of subterfuge. 'That's typical of my wife. She has all sorts of tricks up her sleeve to make sure Abbotslea gets what it needs.'

Behind him Suzanne gave a modest little smile, before offering more tea.

Martin walked with them part of the way to their tent. 'You will be all right, won't you?' he said. 'There was some mention of rain on the forecast, but not until tomorrow, I believe.'

'The tent's waterproof,' said Laura. 'Or supposed to be.'

'We'll be fine,' said Rosemary. 'It's much more comfy than I'd ever have thought possible.'

At her shoulder Laura gave a soft sigh at the prospect of another night spent trying to adapt to the whims of the airbed. At least, she resolved, she would make sure that stone was out of the way before she settled down for the night.

'And you'll go to Long Horton early in the morning, will you?' Martin's casual question did not conceal the sense that this was an instruction. 'You can't miss it. Just follow the road through Lyvedon and carry on for twelve miles or so. It's well signposted. Actually, it's quite a pleasant little town. Gwynne works there two days a week at the Lyvedon Trust.'

'The Lyvedon Trust is in Long Horton?' Laura repeated carefully.

Martin laughed. 'Sounds silly, put like that. The Trust is a charity that acts as a sort of advisory service to small businesses and farms in the area, especially as regards their properties. My family set it up, so we got to christen it. Gwynne's a wizard when it comes to dealing with planners and the media. She can whip up a campaign to save some crumbling medieval cowshed before you can whistle.'

'So what does she do on the other days?' asked Rosemary.

'Oh, I thought Suzanne had already explained that? The two of them work at the local comprehensive, teaching part-time.'

Rosemary shook her head, annoyed with herself. 'Of course she did. I'm sorry. I'm afraid I'm finding it a bit difficult to concentrate.'

Martin gave her a reassuring pat on the arm. 'I know,' he said. 'It's a strain for all of us. Not knowing where he is makes it worse. Let's hope…well…maybe in a day or two…'

'That's right,' said Laura, with a hint of briskness. 'Tomorrow's another day, and all that.'

Martin and Rosemary both looked at her as if she'd gone slightly too far. Then Martin smiled. 'You women,' he said. 'Suzanne and Gwynne are the same. Never put off your stride for long, holding everything together, doing six things at once.'

Laura caught a hint of inferiority in his voice. 'Don't undervalue yourself,' she said firmly. 'All that travelling, and putting up with Warwick Jardine for days on end. That's real dedication, if you ask me.'

Martin laughed. 'Well, yes. I must admit it isn't always easy. And it's constantly at the back of my mind that I should do more here. That's why it's so good that we're tackling the walled garden at last. It really feels like progress. Suzanne's been talking about it for years.'

'Well, we're pleased to be able to help,' Laura said. 'Aren't we, Rosemary?'

Rosemary had been walking a few steps behind them. 'What? Oh, yes.'

Conscious that Martin had plenty of demands on his time, Laura nonetheless felt there was much more she wanted to ask him. Her natural curiosity had given rise to countless questions about the village and the great mansion that seemed to have retained a feudal control, as if in a time warp.

'Have you got time to tell us a bit more about this place?' she asked him. 'It's obviously got a huge amount of history. Your family's been here for most of it, I would guess.'

'That's right,' Martin agreed. 'Lyvedon and Abbotslea are really all part of the same settlement. The houses in the village were occupied by our workers originally. It's grown quite a lot since then, of course, but we try to keep a lid on expansion. It might sound selfish, but everyone agrees the place is worth preserving in much the state it is now.'

Laura diplomatically refrained from arguing the point, but she was very much aware that there were plenty of different viewpoints to that of a man owning a large private estate in prime English countryside. She didn't want to pick a fight with him, in any case. Martin was a pleasant man, with no obvious vices, and she had no wish to upset him by mentioning housing shortages or modern values.

'And so many people seem to have spent their whole lives here,' she went on.

'The ones you've met, yes. They're all old friends of mine, and of each other.'

'Amazing,' sighed Laura. 'But even you won't be able to stop progress forever. It looks to me as if Suzanne realises that rather more clearly than you do.'

Martin's chin rose defiantly for a moment at the implied criticism. Then he relaxed and smiled. 'So she keeps telling me,' he agreed.

'Sorry,' Laura said. 'That was rude of me. I think you've done a great job here – both of you.'

'It's mostly Suzanne,' he conceded. 'She works miracles.'

'That's because she grew up knowing how to manage a huge house and garden,' Laura summarised. 'To the manor born, so to speak.'

Martin nodded. 'Something like that,' he said.

They had been sitting on a fallen tree close to the tent, their eyes mostly on the flickering water. Rosemary seemed to be more relaxed, sitting back, propped up by her arms. After a few moments of silence, Martin stirred and made his excuses. 'I'll see you tomorrow,' he said. 'Don't forget we've got the workers coming – probably about nine-thirty.'

After he'd left, Rosemary got up and began to walk slowly around the Dingle, examining it in detail – the tent squarely pegged on the rising ground above the river, and the campfire neatly waiting to be lit. 'It seems different, somehow,' she said. 'More sinister.'

'Nonsense,' said Laura robustly. 'It's exactly the same as

we left it.' She gave Rosemary a look. 'You're not going to have the vapours, are you?'

'I might, if I knew what they were.' She sat down again, on a stone beside the cold fire circle. 'But actually, no. I'm going to make a list of suitable plants for the garden, and then read my book for a bit. You can be Quartermaster again, and get the supper ready. That market sounds good, don't you think?'

Laura nodded. 'But I won't come with you. You'll probably need all the space you can get in the wagon, and I'd better be here to greet the labour force.'

'Fine,' said Rosemary.

Only a little while later, they realised that Suzanne's tea and cakes had ensured that they were far from hungry. It was six o'clock, with another two or three hours of daylight still to come.

Before they could decide on what to do with the time, a man came along the riverbank towards their clearing. 'Invader,' muttered Rosemary. 'Who on earth can he be?'

'Good evening ladies,' the man said. 'Would you be the two garden experts here to help Martin?'

'That's right,' said Laura, sufficiently familiar with village life not to be surprised at his knowledge. 'Laura Thyme and Rosemary Boxer.'

'Delighted to meet you. I'm George Hamilton Teed, editor of the *Lyvedon Observer*.'

'Ah!' said Laura. 'We've heard about you.'

He chuckled. 'All bad, I expect.'

Laura evaded the question, and turned towards the river. 'Do many people come strolling along here?' she asked. 'Martin did say something about his woods being open to people from the village.'

'He's very generous with his property,' said the

newspaper-man, apparently in all sincerity. 'But no, not a lot of people take advantage of it. Most of them are too busy. Speaking personally, I like to find a quiet spot for some fishing, one day a week.'

Laura pursed her lips. 'On the other hand, this is the spot where a man disappeared into the river only this morning, and you're a journalist,' she observed.

'And that looks like a camera bag,' said Rosemary, who had been quietly listening. She waved an arm at the river. 'Nothing much to see now. A photo isn't going to capture anything that happened.'

'But maybe the water remembers,' said the man. 'Maybe there's some kind of trace still lingering.'

Rosemary shivered. 'Don't!' she pleaded. 'I've got to sleep here tonight.'

He blinked at her. 'Excuse me?'

'Fine powers of observation you have,' said Laura. 'Look!' She pointed at their tent. 'That's our home for the rest of the week.'

'Well, you've got the weather for it,' he said. 'Though I gather it's liable to rain by Friday.'

Rosemary shook her head. 'We've had enough rain for the time being,' she said.

'The river certainly thinks so,' he nodded. 'This is two or three feet higher than it would normally be in May.'

'All the better to drown in,' said Rosemary darkly. 'Is that what you mean?'

He met her eyes, and something seemed to pass between them. Rosemary shivered again, and wrapped her arms around herself. 'It's just a river,' she said, as if to convince herself.

'Of course it is,' Laura endorsed. 'No need to start imagining things.'

'Of course not,' said Mr Teed, in a voice that carried little conviction. 'Now I'll be getting along. Delighted to make your acquaintance.'

They watched him go, Rosemary with a strange expression. 'He knows something,' she said. 'Something about what happened here.'

'You know who he reminds me of?' said Laura. 'With his deep slow voice and weird comments.'

'Who?'

'Katy Stevens.'

Trying to break Rosemary's agitated mood, Laura insisted they get a few minutes' exercise by walking down the drive to the road and back. 'What's the point?' grumbled Rosemary. 'We've only got to come back here for supper.'

'It'll help work up an appetite. And I want to send this card to Matthew. It's his birthday on Monday. What kind of a mother forgets to post her son a card?'

'It'll be awfully early.'

'Never mind. Better early than late.'

It only took five minutes to stroll down to the red post box on a pole, which Martin had described as a landmark, to help them find Abbotslea. The pole listed quite seriously and the box had a special printed notice attached to it, advising that it would only be emptied on Tuesdays and Fridays henceforward, and anyone with more urgent mail should proceed to the collecting box in George Street.

'How peculiar,' said Laura. 'I'm sure that contravenes any number of official regulations. But I suppose it should still arrive by Monday.' She popped her son's card into the box, where it landed with a hollow *plop*.

'They're trying to prolong its useful life, I suppose,' said

Rosemary. 'If it was opened every day, it would collapse in no time.'

'Then they ought to replace it with a more stable one,' said Laura.

The box stood close to the great gates of Abbotslea, and the two assumed that it would only be used by the Frazers, in any case. 'I wouldn't be surprised if it doesn't even get emptied twice a week,' said Rosemary.

They went to bed when the light faded, at about nine-thirty. Laura prepared tomato and basil soup, followed by an ambitious plate of scrambled egg and bacon. The fire burned cheerily, and the bacon sizzled. 'That was extremely delicious,' Rosemary announced as she finished. 'I'm most impressed. I feel a lot better than I expected to.'

The river sounded less ferocious, after a second warm dry day, and Rosemary fell asleep much more quickly than she had anticipated. Laura gained victory over the airbed and the stone, only to realise that a small buzzing insect was in the tent with her. It could only be a mosquito and it was certain to bite her. They always did. And then the place would itch for two or three days and she would scratch it and make it worse. Mosquitoes were generally quite easy to catch and squash. She remembered an epic night in Italy where the body count had reached well into double figures in the morning. But this one was cunning. And it was pitch dark. If she switched on her torch and started flapping, she'd wake Rosemary. So she burrowed deeper into her sleeping bag and tried to pretend it wasn't there.

Chapter Seven

Rosemary set off for the market with mixed feelings. The challenge of recreating the walled garden was one she ought to be relishing. The sun was shining and the big house of Abbotslea cast its friendly shadow over the sweep of gravel, as Rosemary drove the Land Rover slowly across it. The long drive down to the wrought iron gates was bordered for much of the way by laurels and lilacs and other large shrubs which had obviously been in place for centuries. A line of lime trees replaced the shrubs as she approached the gates, and always the presence of the river was impossible to ignore.

Once in the lane leading to the centre of Lyvedon, the landscape changed. The river dived off to the south, only to curl back again, forming a protective loop around the settlement. The geology was such that the river was forced to twist and turn, as well as plunging downhill. 'Unusual,' Rosemary murmured, as she tried to glimpse its course. In her experience, rivers generally flowed downhill in a relatively straight line. The buildings had been cleverly positioned to avoid any risk of flooding, many of them standing on walls that rose above the riverbank. In many places sturdy bulwarks had been built against the force of the water. All of which, she realised, would make any search for a person in the water seriously complicated.

The road to Long Horton was narrow and twisting, with high hedges and sudden wonderful views. She bowled along quite cheerfully, anticipating the purchase of a lot of new plants as one of life's great pleasures.

The town, when she finally reached it, was busy. Parking space was reduced by the presence of the market, but she found a slot in a small side street not far from the market square.

Stalls overflowed the square into the streets radiating from it. Crowds of people, swollen by schoolchildren on their half-term holiday, moved slowly from one stall to another, while traffic tried to get past and stallholders shouted their wares.

Rosemary lost all sense of time and urgency. She examined cheap clothes, second-hand books, handmade pottery, fresh vegetables and gadgets for slicing hardboiled eggs. By the time she caught sight of the unmistakable plant stall that Martin had described, the sun had disappeared and it was threatening to rain.

Back at Abbotslea, Laura was preparing to greet the three prisoners and their warder. They arrived at nine-thirty, looking eager for work. Laura supposed it must be something of a treat for them to get a change of scene and be given something constructive to do. The door of the garden was firmly closed behind them. Their warder, Mr Coutts, had brought a folding chair with him, which he ceremoniously placed close to the door. For the first time, Laura considered the implications of working with three convicted criminals, who might well have escape in mind. Would the necessary restrictions and security procedures make their task of restoring the garden a lot more complicated?

Martin had followed the group into the garden, and gave a short speech. 'These gentlemen will be here for one week only,' he began. 'Mr Coutts is responsible for them and will maintain the proper precautions.' He gave the convicts an apologetic glance. Laura understood that it seemed rather rude to suggest that such respectable-looking men might attempt to abscond or commit further crimes while on his property. But all three prisoners smiled forgivingly and nodded their heads. Looking at each face in turn, Laura found herself warming to them already. They were rascals, she had no doubt, but the fact that they were in an open prison suggested there was no great harm in them.

'Well, better get to work,' Martin continued, rubbing his hands together briskly. 'You'll need tools, of course. Laura, perhaps you could come with me. Suzanne's given me the key to the toolshed,' he explained. 'Which, I might tell you, is a very special privilege. When we first got married, there were hardly any proper tools here. Suzanne's father bought us a fabulous collection as a wedding present and she treats them like the crown jewels.'

Laura smiled patiently, wondering whether there'd be a decent wheelbarrow amongst the treasure. Martin led the way to the shed and unlocked the door. Inside there were several shelves of equipment, including a hedge trimmer, garden spades and forks, chisels, screwdrivers, trowels, rakes. There was a large pegboard with a host of gadgets hanging from it, their shapes drawn out, to indicate where they should go. 'Not bad,' said Laura admiringly. 'Does anybody ever get to use them? Surely most people who work here would bring their own?'

'If they do, we try to persuade them to use our things. Better quality altogether. But Suzanne makes sure nothing ever goes missing.'

Another pointer to Suzanne's dedication to Abbotslea, thought Laura. She scratched the mosquito bite on her cheek thoughtfully. 'We'll need nearly all these,' she said, indicating the collection of garden tools. 'And maybe a hammer of some sort to drive in the pegs for marking out the new beds.' She looked round again. There didn't seem to be a hammer.

Martin conducted a quick search. 'The hammer lives here,' he said, pointing to a place on a board, showing the outline of the tool. 'I wonder where it is. I bet you that odd-job man's gone off with it.' He pulled a face. 'Suzanne's going to be furious with him when she finds out. He isn't allowed to take anything away with him.'

'Well, there's a mallet here, look,' said Laura. 'That's actually better suited to the job anyway, now I come to think of it.'

Together they loaded the equipment into a large sturdy wheelbarrow and took it all back to the garden. 'Do you want me to sign for it?' Laura asked jokingly. 'If it's all so precious?'

Martin shook his head. 'It's not as bad as it sounds,' he smiled. 'But I will just mention to Mr Coutts that he needs to be sure none of it walks at the end of each day.'

'They don't look like petty thieves,' she noted, looking at the prisoners. 'If they're from an open prison, I imagine their crimes were rather more subtle than that.'

'That's true,' said Martin. 'I think you'll have some fun finding out from them exactly what they did. I haven't forgotten what your previous profession was.'

She scratched the bite again, and gave him a nostalgic sigh. 'It seems a long time ago now,' she said. 'But I must admit I can still take an interest in anything to do with police work.'

Martin gave her an uneasy look and started to say something, when Suzanne could be heard calling for him from the house.

'Martin? Telephone!' she shrilled.

Laura felt her usual flicker of irritation at the way telephones so regularly interrupted conversation – especially, it seemed, here at Abbotslea.

But Martin seemed almost relieved. 'Coming,' he called, and ran off without a backward glance.

Left with the four men, Laura wasted no time in satisfying a question that had niggled at her since Sunday. Cornering Mr Coutts close to the garden door, she asked him, 'What happened when you were here before?'

He looked at her blankly. 'Sorry?' he said.

'You said something to Martin. "After the last time". What was it?'

'Oh, that!' He gave a forced laugh. 'It was all to do with that Jim chap – the one who's gone and thrown himself in the river. Can't say I'm surprised.'

'So what happened?'

'He wasn't happy about Mr Frazer taking down the old chapel. He accosted one of my men about it. Got a bit nasty for a minute or two. We'd been a bit slack with the security, I'm sorry to say.' He was speaking in quick bursts, glancing around to ensure that nobody could hear him. But Laura had the impression that he was keen to tell the story. She raised her eyebrows encouragingly.

'It was Huxton Rymer who took the brunt of it.' He tipped his head towards one of the prisoners. 'Not a man to cross, as it happens. Burns slow but steady, if you understand me.'

'What did Jim do to him?'

Mr Coutts narrowed his eyes. 'Called him a lot of bad names. It surprised all of us, how much he knew about everybody. Screamed at him loud enough to be heard three villages off.'

'But it wasn't *his* fault the chapel was demolished.' Laura tried to imagine the scene. 'The prisoner's, I mean.'

'That's right. But he wasn't going to mouth off at his cousin, was he? Old Huxton just got in the way. Not that he felt any better for knowing that.'

Laura held up a finger. 'You mean, Jim never directly criticised Martin?' She remembered other comments to this same effect. 'Why? Was he afraid of him?'

Mr Coutts shook his head. 'I think it was more that he loved him,' he said quietly. 'Worshipped him, even – man and boy. It broke his heart to see that old chapel come down. And his cousin knew it.'

'He knew, but he went ahead with it anyway?'

Mr Coutts just gave her a look.

Martin's call was from the police at Westover – the sizeable town situated at the mouth of the river Mallam. It came at the same moment as Rosemary was parking the Land Rover in Long Horton. 'We've found a body, sir,' came the voice of a young policewoman. 'If you don't mind, we think you ought to come and have a look.'

'Is it him?' Martin demanded.

'We can't say, sir, until you've made a formal identification.'

Saying little to Suzanne, Martin flew to his car. He drove the twenty miles to Westover in eighteen minutes, his mind deliberately blank. He had seen bodies countless times before in his capacity as local Coroner, as well as those of his parents, tidily tucked into satin-lined coffins.

This, he knew, would be very different.

They had done their best. Mud had been wiped away, and eyes and mouth firmly closed. But it was nasty, all the same. His cousin's familiar features were discoloured from abrasions apparently caused by the rocks in the river, and one large contusion on his temple had altered the whole shape of his face. He stared for a long time, noticing the old cord jacket he had given to Jim five years ago or more. Thank goodness, he thought, for that jacket.

'Yes, that's Jim,' said Martin.

'You're sure, sir? It isn't always easy…'

'It must be him. That's his jacket.'

The policeman shifted uneasily from one foot to the other. 'Sir?' he said softly.

Martin made a great effort. 'It's his face,' he said, with a firmness he did not feel. 'It's my cousin.'

'Could we have his full name, please, sir?' said the policeman, apparently satisfied at last.

'James Anthony Frazer.' Martin also supplied date and place of birth and current address, automatically, without even having to think.

The formalities were over very quickly. Martin did not ask for any medical details, eager to get away from the place.

But the police officer had more to say. 'Very rapid progress from Lyvedon,' he said. 'Never known one manage it in less than two days.'

'All that rain,' said Martin. 'It's two feet deeper than usual.'

'Right, sir. That'll be it, then,' agreed the man.

'There'll have to be an inquest, of course,' Martin remem-bered. 'That'll be awkward – I'm the local Coroner.'

'One good thing about a quiet area like this,' said the officer. 'There won't be much of a delay on that. This is the first sudden death we've had for a fortnight. In most places it's a six-week wait for an inquest these days. With any luck this one can take place right away – soon as the pathology report comes in.'

Martin wasn't listening. 'We'll have to find a locum Coroner,' he said. 'I'm too closely involved to do it.'

'Leave it with us,' said the young man. 'That'll be our problem, not yours.'

He was thanked for his time and his businesslike approach before he left. The return drive to Lyvedon and Abbotslea took longer, as he struggled with a mass of pent-up thoughts and feelings. Memories of his boyhood with Jim and the inexorable slide towards disaster that had followed. He wondered whether anybody had been taking care of Jim's animals since he had disappeared. He couldn't summon up much concern for them. There was always some energetic woman in the village who took charge of that sort of thing.

The shower over Long Horton was sudden and sharp. Umbrellas instantly materialised, making an impenetrable sea of coloured nylon between the stalls. Rosemary joined the general rush, unfolding a small brolly from the depths of her bag. Movement through the market became much more difficult and she felt a need to escape to a calmer spot. She turned back, heading for a narrow alleyway at one corner of the market square which might provide some shelter.

She stood under an overhanging gable while the rain slowly abated. A lot of people, she realised, had made a dash for their cars and had gone home, their browsing spoilt for the week. The pavements were suddenly much less crowded. She remembered the reason why she was there, and headed towards Bernie's plant stall.

It was halfway down the southern edge of the square, taking up a double space. Not only was the stall itself crammed with seedlings and bedding plants, but the pavement all around was filled with a profusion of healthy-looking specimens, which looked as if it included almost everything on her list.

She made her way towards it, crossing the open square, between two lines of stalls. She glanced at them as she went, their colour and variety impossible to ignore. A face flickered across her vision, but initially she took little conscious notice of it. She felt cold, suddenly, and irritated by the rain. If it didn't stop, the work in the garden would be interrupted.

There it was again: a sharply etched jaw, with a shadow on it from a few days' stubble. Eyes that were gazing away to the man's left, where he seemed to be planning to cross the road. This time, Rosemary took more notice. It was a face she had seen before, very recently. A face she associated with shock and sadness and trouble.

Suddenly, the eyes met hers, and in that split second she knew exactly who he was. It took all her breath away, paralysing her thoughts as well as any movement. And, it seemed, something similar was happening to the man. He reared back as if abruptly confronted by a rattlesnake. Putting a hand up to cover all but his eyes, he ducked and turned and ran away.

Rosemary was left silently mouthing to herself.

Jim. That was Jim!

Chapter Eight

In the Stevens household Katy and Chris were finding it strange without their children. 'Freedom!' Chris yodelled as he went into the bathroom.

Katy did not respond. She was holding the lotus position for an additional five minutes, feeling the need to prolong her morning yoga routine. Thoughts of Jim Frazer filled her mind and she had difficulty in calmly assimilating them, stacking them in a tidy corner of her mental filing cabinet. The combination of yoga and meditation could be very powerful, she had discovered. It brought everything into its correct order, and strengthened her for the day ahead. It partly explained her talent for influencing the people around her, enabling her to maintain focus even through the most chaotic times.

But Jim's face persistently floated past her mental gaze, despite all her efforts. Jim Frazer had escaped somehow, turning the tables and managing to alarm her more than anybody had for a long time. How had she, with her acute sensitivity, let him gain such a hold over her? How was she going to find peace, knowing the dreadful thing he had written about her to George Hamilton Teed?

Over breakfast she tried to share her feelings with Chris. 'I can't stop thinking about Jim,' she began.

Her husband ran a hand through his grey-flecked beard.

'Don't get in a state about it. The truth is, Jim's been a lost cause for years. If you look beyond the emotion and the shock, what's happened might even be for the best. He wasn't ever going to find happiness, let's face it. It's a bit brutal, I know, but as I see it, nobody loses anything by his death, and quite a few have something to gain. Imagine life without all those maddening slurs on our character. You have to admit it's like a cloud lifting.'

Katy nibbled at her toast, chewing slowly. 'You think we're better off without him?'

'I think the whole village is better off without him. If you ask me, he woke up that morning, took a good hard look at himself, and came to the same conclusion. I mean – what did the future hold for him?'

'It feels all wrong to be talking like this. Somebody ought to have rescued him.'

'Easier said than done.'

'Yes,' she said urgently. 'Maybe. But not impossible. Look at Bonnie. She's proof that anybody can be saved.'

Chris shook his head. 'Not at all. She was a baby when we found her, and she responded to being loved and kept safe. Jim was a grown man who had chosen the path of bitterness.'

Katy heaved a sigh. 'It isn't that easy. I would think you'd know that.'

Chris flushed at the implied criticism. 'Don't forget I've known Jim all my life. I watched him change when his grandpa died and his cousin's father inherited the estate. We all sympathised with him. It was blatantly unjust. It made Martin uncomfortable, knowing he'd got such an undeserved advantage, simply from an accident of birth. But it didn't justify the attacks he made on all and sundry. Poor Suzanne, for one. He made her life a misery, you know he did.'

Katy still felt painfully mixed up. 'We could have got him all wrong. I wonder, now, whether we overreacted, just as Suzanne probably did.'

Chris sighed. 'A bit late for that. But at least it looks as if he remained loyal to Martin.'

'Displacement,' said Katy knowledgeably. 'It occurs to me that his real grievance must have been with Martin, from the start.'

Chris reached over, and rubbed her upper arm, in a favourite gesture. 'That may or may not be true, my love, but there was no help for it. You can't change the rules of inheritance with impunity – they work, unfortunately. If you divide everything equally every time somebody dies, you'd end up with no great houses, no flourishing businesses, even.'

'You'd end up with fair shares for everyone. The great houses can go to outfits like the National Trust, accessible to everyone.'

Chris blew out his cheeks. 'You think the National Trust would care for Abbotslea the way Suzanne Frazer does? She gives her personal attention to every brick of that place. It's her whole life.'

'Yes,' said Katy with a sigh. 'And she knows that when Martin dies, it all goes to Toby, with not one of those precious bricks for Timmy, just because of another accident of birth. And anyone can see already that Timmy has more feel for the place. He's far more suited to being a local squire than Toby is.'

'Same as Jim and Martin,' Chris nodded. 'I admit that fate seems to have other ideas quite a lot of the time.'

'Well, I hope they've learned a lesson from this terrible business with Jim.'

'In what way?' Chris wondered. 'What can they do?'

'Make proper provision for Timmy. Find a worthwhile career for him, divert his attention to something else.'

'Right,' said Chris sceptically. 'I suspect that's another thing that's a lot easier said than done.'

Rosemary knew he had seen her looking at him. He had been waiting for a gap in the traffic and moved hurriedly across the road, seconds after her sighting of him. She let out a strangled cry and fought with people and umbrellas in an effort to push between the cluttered stalls and follow after him. It was like a nightmare, where you can't move in any direction. The point of an old woman's brolly almost took her eye out as she pushed her way between the stalls. When she looked around again, there was no sign of Jim.

She did not give up. He couldn't be far away and she was determined to find him. It felt as if her very sanity depended on it. Only she had seen him go into the river. Now she was the only witness that he was still alive. She had to touch him, speak to him, to assure herself that he was real.

But she couldn't find him. She circled the market square three times, as well as the side streets. The rain stopped as abruptly as it had started and the umbrellas disappeared. It was getting late and she had work to do. Feeling dazed she went back to Bernie's plant stall and introduced herself. She was panting and flushed, causing Bernie to look at her curiously.

'Sorry,' she gasped. 'I've just had a very unsettling experience.'

'What? Seen a ghost?' he asked jovially.

'Exactly that,' she told him with a shudder. 'A dead man walking.'

The stallholder was plainly out of his depth. He glanced around the market square as if to assure himself he'd find

MEMORY OF WATER 99

support if this madwoman started to do anything alarming.

Rosemary took a deep breath. 'Never mind,' she said. 'I suppose it's good, really. I mean – if he isn't dead after all.' She gave him a watery smile. 'I need some plants, anyway. They're for Martin Frazer and the Elizabethan garden at Abbotslea.'

The man's face relaxed, and he held out a long-fingered hand for her to shake. 'Well, glory be!' he exclaimed. 'I never thought he'd get around to it.'

'Martin said you'd have most of what we need,' she explained, with a huge effort to focus on what she needed to say. 'Plus fertiliser and other things. Can I put in an order?' She examined his stock, forcing herself to pay proper attention. Slowly the range of his wares began to impress her. 'These are wonderful!' she told him. 'I haven't seen such old varieties for years.'

'My dad was a seed collector,' Bernie explained. 'He started back in the twenties, when a lot of the older things were still flourishing. I've got my own nursery, with all you're likely to need. This is only a fraction of it.' He beamed proudly. 'I was beginning to think young Martin was never going to get around to restoring that garden. You'll be wanting a few dozen ramblers for the walls as well, I shouldn't wonder.'

Rosemary hadn't considered the edges of the garden, for which she now reproached herself. The mellow brickwork would soak up the warmth of the sun and provide shelter from the wind. Rambling roses trained along it would quickly present a fabulous display. 'Of course,' she said.

Bernie directed her down a maze of small streets to a point where he could help her load the first batch of plants into the Land Rover. It took them nearly twenty minutes, and when they were done, the vehicle was crammed with foliage like a moving forest. Rosemary put the vehicle into reverse. 'I can hardly see out,' she said, feeling weak and incompetent.

'Use your mirrors,' he suggested. 'And I'll see you again next week. I'll bring you a selection of roses, and have a hunt for some comfrey.'

Rosemary hesitated. 'I think I've changed my mind about comfrey,' she confessed. 'It's too…' she groped for the word.

'Butch?' offered Bernie.

She nodded. 'Something like that,' she agreed. 'It certainly isn't delicate, and I don't much like the flowers.'

'Fine,' he said. 'I'll hold back on the comfrey.'

What a nice man he was, she thought, as she started back to Abbotslea. He had, for a few minutes, almost made her forget that she had seen a man who was widely assumed to be dead. But now it all rushed back at her, making her feel shivery again. Except, she assured herself, there had to be an obvious explanation. Jim was alive, and his family would be so delighted. She had to hurry and tell Martin the good news. Only as she got closer to Lyvedon did she start to wonder how people would react. Had there not been, just below the surface, a sense of relief that Jim was gone? Would they wholeheartedly welcome the news that he was alive and well after all?

And why, she wondered, had he been lurking in distant Long Horton, instead of announcing himself to his family and friends, and calling off the police hunt for his body?

Gwynne Evans had elected herself as the 'energetic woman in the village' to take charge of Jim's livestock. She had quietly walked over there early on Tuesday morning, before she had to be at the office in Long Horton. The birds and animals all rushed frantically towards her, as if they hadn't seen a human being for days.

The four hens were confined to a fox-proof run, with a little house for roosting and laying. When Gwynne threw a dipperful of corn to them, they darted at it like mad things. Looking in the nesting boxes, she found ten eggs, which suggested that nobody had collected any for at least two days and probably three. But she was not familiar enough with Jim's routines to be sure. It was possible that he didn't collect eggs every day – and if he had been depressed enough to kill himself, he could well have been in no fit state to attend to his animals.

The two goats had a small paddock at their disposal, with a covered area for bad weather and chilly nights. There was no sign of anything edible, and their plaintive bleats conveyed severe hunger. There was no water in their trough, either. 'You poor things,' Gwynne crooned to them. 'We'll have to find you a new Daddy now, won't we.'

She knew that if Fern had her way, they'd end up adopting the goats themselves, if not the hens as well. Fern had often visited Jim's beasts when she was younger, braving his unpredictable moods and showing a genuine interest in his oddly childish hobbies.

She doubted she'd have time to find new homes for the creatures before the end of the week. Gwynne had plenty of energy, but was often short of time, living a complicated existence with two jobs as well as a vigorous involvement in village life.

Like Chris and Katy Stevens, Gwynne had very mixed feelings about Jim's death. She had sometimes felt he singled her out for special vituperation because she had rejected his advances in their early years. Not until she had escaped to university and teacher training, taking her little daughter with her and enrolling as a mature student, had she managed to convince him that she really wasn't ever going to marry him. Like a stuck record he had endlessly accused her of preferring Martin to him, of plotting to get rid of Suzanne and claiming Martin as her rightful husband.

She had tried a range of different responses, but none of them had any effect on him. She tried assuring him that she had no wish to marry anybody, and he had replied, 'Only because you can't have Martin,' with a cruel sneer that Gwynne pretended not to see. She had struggled to convince him that they had all three of them been children when the idea had first taken root that she and Martin were in love. 'It's different now,' she insisted. 'We've all grown up.'

But Jim had not grown up – that was the problem. For him, they were all still in their teens, and emotions were running as high as ever. And there were still some good times. The earlier Jim still existed, despite his more recent bitterness and misanthropy. She never quite gave up hope that he would change back one day to the softer gentler version of himself.

When she eventually returned to Lyvedon with her teaching qualification, she found with relief that he had given up hope of changing her mind – but he had not forgiven her for the hurt. Although she tried hard to ignore his innuendoes, she knew what they were, and what effect they had on people hearing them. She had seen the looks from people in the village, which seemed to say *We don't believe – of course we don't. And yet...* The same thoughts were directed at others, she knew that. Jim had made mischief on a wide front, casting doubt on the most blameless of lives. He had real skill at finding the vulnerable spots, accusing people of things that *might* be true. Things they could have had difficulty in disproving, if they'd ever been called upon to do so. But the worst thing for Gwynne was the constant desire to win his friendship. She wanted him to like her, to approve of her and abandon his sniping nastiness. Like many others in the community, she remembered him as a boy and yearned to rediscover the Jim he had once been.

Driving to Long Horton, her mobile went off in her bag on the passenger seat. Despite strong temptation, she did not answer it. Knowing her luck, she thought, she'd be caught by some roadside camera and would lose her licence. Whoever it was could leave a message.

She listened to the recorded message as soon as she had parked the car in her own reserved space. She heard Suzanne Frazer's voice in her ear.

'Gwynne – they've found Jim's body already, down at the weir. Martin's identified it. And he's going away again today, would you believe it? Can you come over later on? I need somebody to talk to.'

Gwynne sighed. Suzanne was her friend, and had been for years, but sometimes the demands she made felt excessive.

She opened up the office and methodically sifted through the letters that had been waiting for her. Almost all of them were from the Council Planning Office, but one was from a regular contributor to their funds and another was from George Hamilton Teed, belatedly advising her that he had decided to use a few lines from a recent letter sent by Jim Frazer. Looking at the date of the postmark, she tried to calculate whether he had written it before or after her attack on him at The Lamb. Slightly to her embarrassment, it seemed to have been before. Why hadn't he tried to defend himself, she wondered irritably. If she'd seen this letter she might not have been so angry with him.

Inevitably she found herself thinking again about Jim. He had often felt like a disease in the heart of Lyvedon. And now he was gone, it was almost as if someone had come along and issued a magical healing remedy to the sickness that he had generated.

At the same time as Rosemary was looking into the face of the vanished Jim only two streets away from Gwynne's office, Laura was getting to know the three prisoners detailed as garden labourers. They were all eager to tell her their story, all the more so when they realised that she had been a police officer herself. This came as something of a surprise to her, expecting that they would have less than positive feelings towards enforcers of the law.

'Oh, no,' Huxton Rymer protested. 'We've every respect for the rule of law. I was a Member of Parliament as it happens.'

Laura ransacked her memory and came up with a half-forgotten scandal to do with a forged signature and a hugely valuable diamond necklace accepted from a foreign head of state and passed to Mrs Rymer, who wore it shamelessly until questions began to be asked. 'Well, well,' she murmured, wishing Rosemary was there to share the discovery. 'How much longer do you have to serve?'

'Five months, three weeks and four days,' he said promptly. Laura laughed, thinking that criminals seemed to have improved somewhat since her day.

The most promising of the three from a gardening point of view was George Marsden Plummer. He was a burly man, who looked as if he had grown up in the open air and knew how to operate a spade.

'Mine's an insurance fraud,' he said before Laura could

find a polite way to enquire. 'It seemed innocent enough the first time, but I have to admit I got rather carried away. I always like to see a good fire, you know. My warehouse burned down, I'm sorry to say. Very careless of me, that was. I blame my father, at least partly. He was a farmer, as it happens, and we always had a lot of hay and straw stacked about the place. You can't imagine how straw will burn after a dry spell.' His eyes grew wistful and Laura took half a step back. She could almost smell the smoke.

The third man was slight and poorly muscled. He had rather protruding eyes and a delicate boyish mouth. Laura thought she'd seen the face before, but had no idea where. He caught her quizzical gaze. 'Telly, love,' he said. 'Celebrity chef. Maybe not your cup of tea – I had the early afternoon slot, aimed at bored housewives.'

'Sorry,' smiled Laura. 'I've always made it a rule never to watch television before six in the evening.'

'Good for you, lovey,' he said, with a roll of his eyes. 'You must have glimpsed one of my trailers, possibly. I can see you recognised me.'

'So, how…?' The question remained a delicate one.

'Tax fraud,' he said sadly. 'There were spin-offs, you see. Invitations to speak, product endorsements, books, magazines. It's the penalty of fame these days. And I just lost control of the documentation.' He shrugged helplessly. 'Mind you, they've all been ever so kind to me. Prison's nowhere near so bad as they want you to think. Except for the food, of course.' He shuddered.

It was half past eleven when everyone finally converged on Abbotslea. Martin was met by a white-faced Suzanne as he climbed out of his car. Laura had been speaking to her and stood nearby.

'Is it him?' Suzanne asked faintly.

He put his arms around her, more for his own comfort and support than for hers. 'Yes,' he said, his voice muffled by her hair pressed against his face. 'Yes, it's Jim. He's dead. It was difficult to identify him, but I'm sure it was him.'

Rosemary's arrival went unnoticed for a few moments. She climbed down from the Land Rover and stared at the stiff-looking group on the gravel in front of the house. She could make no sense of it, her mind already full from her own bewildering morning. But whatever was going on, Martin and Suzanne looked as if they could do with cheering up, and she had just the news that would do it.

'Hello!' she began, trying to attract their attention.

Laura stepped forward and intercepted her. 'Not now,' she hissed.

'But—' Rosemary began to feel a chill deep inside her. 'I want to tell them something,' she finished, still watching the couple as they continued to cling together.

'It can wait,' Laura insisted. 'Come with me, and give them some privacy.'

'What's happened?' Rosemary asked, in a whisper. 'Tell me.'

Laura led her a short distance away before replying. She spoke in a calm voice, like an adult explaining something unpleasant to a young child. 'Martin's just been to Westover and identified the body. It's definitely his cousin Jim. They fished him out of the river early this morning, at the weir.'

'No!' Rosemary gasped. 'Oh, God, no.' She looked wildly at Laura. 'It isn't possible. I've just seen him, alive and well in the market.'

Chapter Nine

Martin went in search of Laura and Rosemary half an hour later. He was busily making plans for the coming days, finding the best way to cope with what had happened lay in practical matters. It was working remarkably well. Suzanne, however, was taking longer to recover. He had never seen her so pale or so lost for words.

Laura heard him coming along the riverside path as she made coffee on the campfire. 'Don't say anything to him,' she warned Rosemary.

Rosemary frowned. 'Why not?'

Laura struggled to be diplomatic. Her friend was obviously deluded in her belief that the man she'd seen was Jim. It was not really surprising, Laura thought charitably, after the shock of witnessing him getting swept away by the river. But it would be very unwise for Rosemary to share her delusions with anybody in the Frazer family. 'Because you can't be certain,' she said carefully. 'It would only cause more trouble. Give them time to get over the worst of it, OK?'

Rosemary nodded dumbly, her eyes on Martin, who gave a rueful smile at their little settlement. 'You could use our kitchen, you know,' he said. 'Suzanne won't mind you boiling a kettle and having some of our coffee.'

'Thanks,' said Laura. 'I must admit this is taking an awfully long time.'

He turned to Rosemary. 'I see from the Land Rover that you found Bernie,' he said.

For a moment she looked at him blankly, before nodding. 'Oh, yes. He's got some brilliant things,' she said tonelessly. 'I'm going back next week for another lot. I left him a list.'

Laura felt she should say something about the discovery of Jim's body, but somehow it had all been covered already, the day before. In many ways the events of the morning were just an inevitable confirmation of what everyone had expected, and she was worried that if his name was mentioned now, Rosemary would feel impelled to reveal what she had seen in Long Horton.

'We've got plenty to keep us occupied,' she said, instead.

'Good, good,' said Martin, still watching Rosemary. Then he seemed to give himself a little shake. 'To be honest, I've come to ask you a favour, if that's all right.'

'Fire away,' Laura invited.

'Well, the thing is, Suzanne's in rather a state since Jim's body turned up and isn't too happy about my going off again.' He looked awkward. 'I know we gave the impression we couldn't put you up, initially, but...'

'So what does Suzanne want?' Laura prompted him.

'She asked me to see if you'd be prepared to sleep in the house tonight, just while I'm gone. I should be back by bedtime tomorrow. She'll cook you a supper as well, unless you've got other plans.'

Laura pulled a face and reached for a packet of dried mashed potato. 'I think this was to be our meal this evening, along with something called Chicken Shreds in Spicy Sauce. You bung the whole lot in one pan and add water.'

Martin merely raised an eyebrow.

Laura fingered the mosquito bite on her cheek yet again. 'Just for one night, you said?'

'That's right. You can be back here tomorrow night. I'd hate to spoil your fun permanently.'

Rosemary gave Laura a reproachful prod. 'What she means is – thanks very much and we'd be delighted,' she told Martin. 'And don't feel you have to hurry back on our account.'

The light mood only lasted a few moments. 'Was it awful at the police station?' Laura finally asked, unable to stay off the subject any longer. 'I mean – you don't have to talk about it, of course. But – well – we're good listeners if you want to.'

Martin sighed. 'Poor old Jim. He thought of himself as a victim all his life, one way and another. But he never did much to help himself.' He looked back towards the big house, the roof just visible through the trees. 'It wasn't fair, I know. But neither was it reasonable to blame me the way he did.'

Laura caught Rosemary's eye, urging her to stay silent. Martin had a sudden thought. 'Oh, yes – Rosemary, the inquest will probably be this week. Thursday, most likely. As soon as they've done the post-mortem this afternoon, and have a definite cause of death, they'll confirm it. You'll be called as a witness, of course. I hope that won't be a problem for you?'

Without waiting for a reply, he spun on his heel and started back along the path. 'Suzanne says seven o'clock – OK?' he called over his shoulder.

Rosemary and Laura were left to assimilate his information. 'Inquest?' Rosemary croaked. 'They'll ask me to testify on the Bible, won't they? To say I saw Jim Frazer drop into the river.'

'You know,' Laura said thoughtfully, 'you keep using different words for how he got into the water. "Fall", "jump", "drop". What *did* he do, exactly?'

'A bit of all those. He just – sort of – let himself slide in, a kind of shallow dive, I suppose. I can't get any closer than that to how it was.'

'It sounds deliberate.'

Rosemary nodded. 'It was deliberate, sort of. He bent his legs and leaned forward, and then he was in the water. I think it took his feet out from under him. He was standing on a big rock that was half out of the river, but sometimes there'd be a surge that came higher.' Rosemary clasped her hands together. 'Oh, I don't want to have to go through it in front of a Coroner and a jury. I'll sound stupid.'

'No you won't,' said Laura.

'I will if I tell them I saw the man alive and well this morning in Lyvedon market.'

Laura gave her a considering look. 'I won't mention it if you don't,' she promised.

Fern Evans was working a double shift at The Lamb, as she had been for some weeks past. Against her mother's advice, she had insisted on taking a year out after her A-levels, and now it was May and she'd got virtually nothing to show for it. Gwynne had given up making suggestions about working holidays in New Zealand or Tanzania and accepted that her daughter's true motive was insecurity about leaving Lyvedon. She had a place at a university a hundred miles away, starting in September, and her earnings from the hotel were really beginning to mount up. 'Oh, well,' Gwynne had conceded, 'I must admit it's nice having you around for a while longer.'

Fern had lived in the village almost all her life, except for an absence of four years while her mother got her degree, which had begun when Fern was five. She regarded most of the inhabitants of Lyvedon as honorary aunts and uncles. Even the man who was in fact her father behaved more like an indulgent uncle, most of the time. Her parents had never married, and had parted company quite amicably when Fern was six months old. Now he had a wife and children, leaving Fern and Gwynne to make their own lives.

She knew it was an old-fashioned existence in many ways, and that she could not stay hidden away forever. Mostly she was looking forward to the life of a student, meeting new people and testing her own abilities. 'You'll be fine,' Gwynne repeatedly assured her. 'You'll have all the boys running after you. I just hope you won't go overboard, making up for the quiet life you've had.'

Fern had winced. Boys – or rather, men – were still a delicate subject for her. 'Oh, *Mum*,' she said.

The people who stayed at The Lamb were mostly middle-aged couples who were on walking or bird watching holidays. The unspoilt nature of the area, with the river and the wooded hills, attracted visitors who enjoyed quiet pursuits. They did not often attempt to engage Fern in conversation, taking her for a typical teenager, but when she shyly informed them about the best places to see a kestrel or wood pipit, they revised their assumptions about her.

Mr Hamilton Teed – as he preferred to be called – had always been a good friend to her, and despite recent conflict, a friend to her mother as well. She looked forward to her chats with him when the bar was quiet. For a man, he was a terrible gossip, and after he'd had a few pints of best bitter he would tell her things about the people of the village that she knew she ought not to be hearing.

'How do you know all this?' she often asked him.

But he would only tap the side of his nose and murmur, 'I *am* a journalist, my dear. Journalists have a special knack of finding things out.'

Fern thought she knew where most of his stories came from. Everybody knew that Jim Frazer dreamed up stories about the people around him, and then wrote his fantasies down in colourful letters that were despatched to the *Lyvedon Observer*'s office. But the uncomfortable part for Fern was that she knew for a fact that some of the things Teed told her were true – and they were meant to be kept secret.

Teed came in now, positively rubbing his hands with satisfaction. 'Heard the news?' he demanded of Fern and the two other people in the bar. They all shook their heads. 'Jim Frazer's been found, down at the weir. They've got him at the mortuary now. According to my source' – he gave a smug little smile – 'the inquest's going to be Thursday morning. Too late for this week's paper, unfortunately. Still, I've got enough for a tasty headline, even so.'

Fern tried to take a steadying breath. She hadn't expected there to be such a world of difference between Jim being seen falling into the river, and his actual dead body turning up. 'He's really dead, then?' she said. 'Jim Frazer's dead.'

'That's what I'm telling you, pet. It's going to shake things up around here and no mistake. A lot of people breathing easier, for a start. Until they all start wondering which of them had the strongest reason for wanting him out of the way.'

The people sitting at one of the bar tables looked at him

in astonishment. They were strangers to Lyvedon, and Fern could see them wondering what kind of a place they'd come to.

'Isn't that slander or something?' she said to Teed. 'Do you mean somebody persuaded Jim to kill himself? Don't forget that woman actually *saw* him. She'll testify at the inquest. You need to speak to her before you spread such revolting rumours.'

'I would if I could,' he protested. 'But Martin Frazer's got her walled up in that garden of his. I did see her on Monday, with her friend. They're sleeping in a *tent*, would you believe? Anyway, they weren't saying very much.'

'What did you want her to say? She saw Jim go into the river, yesterday morning. And now they've found his body. End of story.'

Teed narrowed his eyes, and shook his head. 'Not a bit of it,' he argued. 'Since when has it been possible for a body to get from Abbotslea to the weir in twenty-four hours?' He gave her a searching look. 'Think about it, my lovely. You'll see I'm right.'

Fern tried hard to ignore the implication. She knew the river every bit as well as Teed did and had entertained similar thoughts herself. But only for brief snatches, before pushing them away. 'Well,' she said lightly, 'unless that woman was dreaming or deliberately lying, that's the only explanation, isn't it?' she said.

'I'm not so sure about that,' said Teed, reaching for his pint of Best.

Laura's liking for the three convicts increased with every hour she spent in their company. Mr Coutts, too, was turning into a firm friend, as he sat contentedly on guard at the door of the garden his face turned towards the sun.

He had brought a copy of the local paper with him, as well as a magazine entitled the *Ferret Fancier*. As his charges worked, he concentrated on his reading, only raising his gaze now and then to check that all was as it ought to be.

Rosemary's mood swings were becoming a central element in the work. She would utter deep sighs every now and then, stopping work to stare over the garden wall, scratching her head, clearly reliving her sightings of Jim Frazer over and over again. Laura had accepted, with profound frustration, that there was very little she could do to persuade her friend that the man at the market had to have been somebody else. Once the inquest was concluded, she hoped the whole business would be over with and they could enjoy the restoration of the garden without the cloud of confusion that was currently hanging over them.

It was with mixed feelings that she anticipated the evening in Abbotslea with Suzanne. The topic of Jim was sure to be foremost in their conversation, and Rosemary's bewilderment was unlikely to be assuaged. And, she feared, it would be hard to go back to the tent after a night in one of Suzanne's spare rooms.

Cautiously she worked her way to Rosemary's side. 'You won't tell Suzanne about – you know. What you saw in the market. Will you?'

Rosemary heaved another sigh. 'I suppose not. Why – do you think it'll upset her?'

'Something like that,' Laura nodded. 'We don't want to raise false hopes that Jim's still alive, do we?'

'He isn't.' Rosemary's voice was flat. 'Martin has seen his body.'

'In that case, we don't want Suzanne to start wondering if something weird might be going on. It'll only frighten her. Until we can either forget the whole business, or work out exactly what has been happening, we should keep it to ourselves. Don't you think?'

'What about the inquest?' Rosemary's face was drawn with worry and inner conflict. 'What on earth am I going to say?'

'Face that when you come to it,' Laura advised.

Laura had told Rosemary, the previous evening, about the altercation between Jim Frazer and Huxton Rymer, during the demolition of the chapel. 'He's another one who isn't going to shed any tears over Jim's death, then,' Rosemary had commented. 'The list seems to get longer all the time.'

'Laura!' came the voice of Rupert Waldo. 'We've finished preparing for the new hedges now. What'll we do next?'

'Wow – that was quick!' Laura turned to Rosemary. 'Should they tackle those foundation stones? We need plenty of good muscle power for that.'

'S'pose so,' said Rosemary wanly.

Laura led her little gang to the site of the chapel, giving the whole area a close scrutiny. 'There isn't much left to do,' she observed. 'You'd never get away with such shallow foundations these days.'

'Definitely not,' confirmed George Marsden Plummer. 'Even a farm barn would get more footings than this. Still, lucky for us, eh? We can lever up those flagstones in no time. Nice things, they are too. Martin can sell them to a reclamation outfit. Make a tidy penny, they will.'

Laura noticed the wistful look on his face. 'You've been involved in reclamation, have you?' she asked.

'Just dabbled, now and then,' he admitted. 'Not really my line – but I can turn my hand to most things. You have to these days,' he added.

For the first time, Laura wondered what a person would do with a dismantled Victorian chapel. There'd be windows and roofing materials and a whole mountain of stonework. 'Does anybody know what Martin did with the stone from the chapel?' she asked.

Huxton Rymer snorted. 'We certainly ought to. George and I and Martin's odd-job man spent about three weeks carting it into the woods.'

'What?'

'That's right. We loaded it into a van, a few bits at a time, and the odd-job man drove it through the woods. There's a rough track that connects with the back road,' he explained vaguely. 'Then the poor bloke unloaded it all again. I dare say Martin's just waiting for the right moment to dispose of it.' George made a strange noise at that point, a kind of throat-clearing, and Huxton Rymer fell silent.

Rosemary, however, began to take more interest. 'You know, I keep getting a funny feeling about that chapel. Every time it's mentioned, people turn shifty. Even Martin seems to have a guilt complex about it.'

'With good reason,' said Huxton Rymer. 'He never should have taken it down. And there's me getting all the stick from that cousin of his. Another couple of weeks and he might have got his way.'

Laura's eyebrows went up. 'How do you mean?'

'Jim was trying to get it listed. Then it would have been safe from demolition – preserved forever, as like as not.'

'So Martin demolished a building that was liable to have a preservation order put on it?' Laura tried to catch Rosemary's eye. 'That's a serious matter.'

Rosemary kicked idly at a mound of soil. Her thoughts were obviously somewhere else.

'What are you thinking?' Laura asked her.

'About Jim,' said Rosemary predictably. 'He must have really loved the chapel.'

Huxton Rymer snorted. 'Don't waste your sympathy,' he told her. 'The bloke was a nutter. The chapel was a ghastly bit of rubbish that should never have been built in the first place.'

'If you say so,' said Rosemary, gloomily. 'But it's my belief that Martin feels worse about it than any of you realise.'

Firmly, Laura changed the subject. She looked at Rosemary's foot, still jabbing at the mound. 'What *are* all these mounds, anyway?' she asked. 'Look – there's lots of them.'

Waldo answered her. 'I've been wondering that myself,' he said. 'I think somebody's been digging. See, there are holes beside all of them. Might be some kind of soil analysis, do you think?'

'Martin never said anything about that,' Laura noted. 'It's as if someone has been searching for something. They're mostly in this small area, look.'

Nobody seemed very interested, and within five minutes the work had resumed, marking out the paths and areas for planting.

Not another word was said about the chapel.

Gwynne finished her duties at the Trust in good time. Her usual hours were ten till three, two days a week. That was more than enough to keep abreast of the various conflicts over development projects and business rates, to make the Trust's position crystal clear on all the different issues, and to maintain a detailed diary of all the decisions and arguments that comprised the Trust's role. She had made seven phonecalls, despatched ten emails and written four letters, as well as receiving two visitors who wanted to consult her about their prospects of starting up new ventures locally. She gave her full attention to the work, quoting minor subsections of the Planning laws from memory and rallying bodies such as the Chamber of Commerce and the Commission for Architecture and the Built Environment to her support. It was mentally stimulating, but also tiring.

Only when she was halfway back to Lyvedon did she clear her head enough to think about recent events at home.

She went first to her cottage, to change out of her work clothes and drink a pot of tea. The exhaustion slowly receded, leaving a satisfied sense of a job well done.

Fern was not at home, despite it being the gap between her shifts at The Lamb. She went in at ten every morning to clean the rooms and get the lunch tables set up. Then she served drinks through the long opening hours in the middle of the day, finishing at three. The second shift started at six, and went on until the last meal was consumed, which was usually shortly before ten in the evening. The routine was firmly established by this time, and Gwynne knew she would miss it when Fern left home for university in four months' time. She was counting down the weeks, trying to persuade herself that it would be a positive change in her life. She would be free to come and go without answering to her daughter. She could go away on some travels, perhaps. She could get a Life.

But Fern had been her constant companion for the past eighteen years. The imminent separation was already causing her sleepless nights, and sudden cold panics. Without her child, she was not at all sure who she might turn out to be. Finding herself at a crossroads – or was it a watershed? – in her life was both exciting and frightening. None of her relationships had worked out for very long because she had been so busy with her daughter. But now it would be different.

It was true that the village people needed her – she had made sure of that. It was Gwynne who drove people to hospital appointments, and ensured they had suitable care when they came home again. It was Gwynne who helped the elderly with their applications for benefits and payments of bills. Both Fern and Suzanne accused her of being an unofficial citizens' advice bureau, a charge she did not deny. 'Somebody's got to do it,' was all she would say. But she knew, deep down, that it was all a pale substitute for a real partnership, for a special Someone who would always be there, caring about her, and being cared for in return.

Martin had probably left Abbotslea by now, she surmised, although she couldn't remember whether he was going to Manchester or Leeds or even Nottingham. It was never the same place twice and there seemed little point in trying to monitor his movements. The important thing was that Suzanne found it hard living with a man who was so frequently away. Gwynne privately thought that she would make more of an effort to welcome him when he did come home, in Suzanne's place. She might even try to go with him once in a while, when he had a long case in some distant city. 'I can't do that,' Suzanne had protested, when she had once suggested it. 'What about the dogs? Not to mention a little matter of a teaching job.'

'I'll watch out for the dogs,' Gwynne had offered. 'And you know we agreed to cover for each other at school if the need arose.' But the idea had never got any further. Gwynne hadn't pushed it. In some dark part of her, she took some satisfaction in knowing that Martin's wife was making only an average sort of success of their lives together.

She left a note for Fern, saying 'Gone to Abbotslea. Come along later if you like. I'll probably be there till about eleven.'

Then she set out on the familiar short walk up to the big house. A walk she had done hundreds, perhaps thousands of times from her earliest days. Initially, Martin and Jim had only been there in the school holidays, for a week or two at a time. Then, when Martin's father had died, only a year after Martin married Suzanne, a new generation set up home in Abbotslea. Gwynne had held back at first, but when Toby had been born, and Martin had asked her to keep a friendly eye on Suzanne, the two women had become friends, and Gwynne regarded the house almost as a second home. Fern had delighted in the little boys, even babysitting them when she was old enough. When Timmy had started school, Suzanne had felt constrained to find some outside work, and the idea of sharing a full-time teaching post with Gwynne arose almost casually over a bottle of wine one evening. The coincidence of their very similar qualifi-cations, combined with the undoubted influence they both held in the community ensured that the Head of the comprehensive embraced the idea with no objections. Only Martin's insistence that Toby and Timmy attend an independent school sometimes made things awkward.

Gwynne got to the house just before seven. She walked in without knocking, and found Suzanne stretched out on the sofa, a large glass of red wine in her hand. There was a savoury smell coming from the kitchen.

'All right?' Gwynne asked, eyeing the wine.

'Get yourself a glass,' Suzanne said, lazily indicating the bottle on a side table.

Gwynne did as invited, and settled down in one of the armchairs. 'Hard day?' she said.

'You got my message, I take it? Jim's officially dead now. Martin saw the body.'

'Was he upset?'

Suzanne tossed her hair out of her face. 'Oh, I don't know. Yes, I imagine he was. You know Martin – so unemotional.'

'He's not really,' Gwynne said mildly. 'He's got plenty of feelings just below the surface.'

'Oh, I know. But just once, I'd like to hear him scream and shout, to let it all out.'

'Like you?'

Suzanne pouted. 'Are you saying I'm a drama queen?'

'Not at all. You're the perfect English lady most of the time. You just like life to be a bit more exciting than Martin does.'

'He thinks one of Jardine's stupid fraud cases is the most excitement a person can wish for. He comes back *glowing*, sometimes. Anyone would think he'd been with another woman.'

Gwynne put down her glass and leaned forward angrily. 'He would *never* do that,' she said emphatically.

'Oh,' flounced Suzanne. 'I know he wouldn't. He's far too well behaved. The perfect husband.'

'Well – isn't he?'

Suzanne looked around the room. 'Yes, he is,' she said quietly. 'I know how lucky I am. I'm just in a funny mood, that's all. I got really panicked earlier on – when I couldn't get hold of you on the phone. I've asked those women to stay in the house with me tonight. They'll be here in a minute, I expect. They're eating with us as well.'

Gwynne's first thought was that her own presence was rather superfluous, in that case. She would have preferred to have stayed at home, with her own thoughts about Jim, and Lyvedon, and what might happen next.

But she did her best to greet them warmly when Laura and Rosemary arrived. They all assembled in the kitchen, where Suzanne quickly produced a large meal for six. 'I wish you wouldn't always assume you have to produce lavish meals for people every time they drop in,' Gwynne said to Suzanne, who pretended not to hear her, as she gathered up cutlery from a drawer.

'Does she?' Laura murmured, unable to conceal her anticipation.

'You mustn't think yesterday was typical,' Gwynne said. 'She was so thrown by what happened, she forgot all about lunch.'

'Yes, we know,' said Rosemary, slightly impatiently. 'We were all thrown, me especially.'

'Yes, of course you were,' soothed Gwynne.

Toby and Timmy ate with them and it was a pleasantly relaxed meal, taken around a big pine table at one end of the large kitchen. 'We nearly always eat in here,' Suzanne said. 'I hope you don't mind the informality.'

Laura laughed. 'Compared to a camp fire, this is Buckingham Palace,' she said.

The boys disappeared to their rooms the moment the meal was over, with orders from Suzanne not to make a noise and to go to bed by nine-thirty. Laura wondered whether she would go up and tuck them in, or even read to them. It must be strange, she reflected, having them away at boarding school so much of the time. The home routines would have to be re-established over and over again. But Toby and Timmy both appeared to be well-adjusted happy children and she was not inclined to criticise.

It was interesting to observe the relationship between Suzanne and Gwynne. Together they loaded the used crockery into a slightly battered-looking dishwasher. The two seemed to be good friends, with no undercurrents that Laura could discern. Or not until it came to the subject of Martin's cousin. 'I fed Jim's animals this morning,' Gwynne said. 'They were terribly pleased to see me. I ought to go over again this evening, I suppose, and make sure the hens are shut in.'

Suzanne looked at her. 'How long are you going to carry on with that? They'll have to be sold or destroyed or something, won't they?'

'Oh no, that's all decided,' said Gwynne airily. 'The hens can come here, and the goats are going to live at The Lamb. I'll only have to go over to Jim's a few more times, until we can get them moved.'

Suzanne stared at her. 'When in the world did all that get decided?'

Gwynne laughed. 'It only took a couple of phonecalls. No big deal.'

'I'm not sure I want hens here.'

'Yes you do. They'll be very decorative. They can help in the walled garden – can't they?' she asked Rosemary and Laura, who both smiled bemusedly.

'It's always you, isn't you,' said Suzanne. 'Coming to the rescue.'

Gwynne smiled. 'They say that's a bad character defect, don't they. Compulsive caregiver, isn't that the jargon for it? I guess I'm too old to change it now.'

'And why should you?' put in Laura before she could

stop herself. 'People like you keep the wheels running. We'd be sunk without you.'

Rosemary snorted. 'Nice mixed metaphor,' she said. Gwynne's peal of laughter sounded forced to Laura, as if born of relief.

Laura felt some relief herself that Rosemary had finally joined in. She had been quiet through the meal, answering questions, but not initiating any of the conversation. She livened up slightly when Gwynne began to reminisce about the walled garden, emphasising how delighted she was that Martin had finally found somebody to restore it. 'I hope there'll be dozens of climbing roses all round the walls,' she said, with a girlishly romantic expression. 'All scented, of course. Just imagine it on a summer evening, with great drifts of colour and the sundial back where it belongs.'

Her last words were drowned by a sudden loud clatter from the dishwasher. It sounded as if a piece of metal had broken loose and was careering around inside the machine. 'Dratted thing!' said Suzanne. 'The basket's come adrift again. All the knives and forks get tossed around. Let me switch it off.'

'No sign of a new one yet, then?' said Gwynne.

'Not until we've had the roof fixed, paid the school fees and…' she looked at Laura and Rosemary '…and got the garden finished.'

An hour passed quite easily, with only occasional shouts audible from upstairs. 'They're playing some sort of computer game,' said Suzanne. 'I often wonder how parents managed before computers.'

Laura caught Gwynne's eye and thought she detected a suppressed response, along the lines of 'They read to them, or played with them, or took them out to watch badgers at twilight.'

But then Suzanne surprised her. 'Time to go and quell them,' she said, getting up. It was exactly half past nine. 'I'll be twenty minutes or so, probably. I'm reading them *The Silver Sword* and we've only got this week to finish it.' She laughed. 'I know they're a bit old for bedtime stories, but it's something of a tradition. And it's a wonderful story. I never get tired of it.'

'That's lovely,' said Laura. 'Lucky boys.'

Left with Gwynne, there was a moment's silence. 'I gather you won't be going back to your tent tonight?' Gwynne said.

'No,' said Laura. 'Martin asked us if we'd stay in the house, because Suzanne was upset. Only for one night, until he gets back.'

'I see.' Her expression was distinctly sceptical.

'I think he might have thought we would be nervous as well,' said Rosemary. 'After all, Suzanne's got the boys, and there's no suggestion that there's anything to be scared of.'

'No,' said Gwynne. 'Of course there isn't. And you survived last night perfectly well, didn't you?'

'Perfectly,' said Laura stoutly. She fingered her bite again, finding that it had almost disappeared.

Despite their brave words, all three jumped when the kitchen door suddenly opened. Gwynne was the first to recover. 'Oh, Fern!' she said. 'You're early.'

The girl nodded. 'Not much custom this evening.'

'You can come and help me see to Jim's hens, then. They'll need to be shut in.'

Fern smiled. 'I've just done it,' she said. 'I thought you'd forgotten. I took the short cut along the river from The Lamb. The moon's lovely already.'

'You see,' said Gwynne to the others. 'Fern's not scared.'

'Scared?' said Fern. 'Why would I be? I've been walking through these woods at night since I was about ten. I know every inch of them.'

'You'll miss it when you go to college,' said Gwynne.

'Which is why I'm making the most of it now. But it won't be the same without Jim,' she added sadly. 'He and I would often bump into each other out there and stop for a chat. I feel awful now, the things I used to say about him. I never really meant it.'

'I know,' said Gwynne softly. 'We all feel like that.'

'I saw him on Friday, never guessing that would be the last time,' Fern went on. 'He was at the postbox, dropping in a letter. I told him it wouldn't be collected till Tuesday, but he said there was no hurry.'

'Not another of his stupid letters to the paper?' said Gwynne.

'I don't know. Probably. If it was, it just shows how dotty he was. He could have walked to Teed's office in ten minutes and saved himself the stamp.' Then she grinned. 'But I know why he did it. He wanted to keep the postbox in use, and not give the authorities an excuse to have it taken down. I used to wonder if that was the real reason he wrote all those letters. I mean – they were all to Teed. He never wrote to anybody else.'

'And Teed should have known better than to encourage him,' snapped Gwynne. 'I could not believe it when I saw what he'd put in last week's paper.'

'Don't start that again, Ma,' pleaded Fern. She looked at Laura and Rosemary. 'I bet you've heard it already.'

Laura made a diplomatic face. 'Gwynne did mention it,' she said. 'And it seems that Jim made insinuations about other people as well.'

'All the time,' sighed Gwynne. 'It was the cross we all

had to bear, where Jim was concerned.'

'Can we have the hens, Mum?' said Fern suddenly. 'There's plenty of room in the back garden.'

Gwynne shook her head. 'I'd rather not,' she said. 'When you've gone, I'll be free to come and go as I like. I might decide to take foreign holidays or go hill walking in Scotland. I don't want to be tied down by livestock. Anyway, I've already told Suzanne that she's got to have them.'

Fern gave her a reproachful look, but before she could answer, Suzanne came back from reading to her boys. She greeted Fern and made her some coffee. Shortly afterwards Fern and her mother went home, leaving Laura and Rosemary wondering what time they ought to head for bed. Suzanne hadn't yet shown them their room, so their overnight bags were still sitting in the hall near the foot of the stairs.

A phonecall interrupted Laura's hesitant suggestion that they should go up. Suzanne made no attempt to answer it. 'The machine can take it,' she said. 'I can pick up if it's important.'

Suzanne's own voice could be heard giving the usual invitation to leave a message. Then Martin spoke. 'Hi, love. I've arrived. The roads were clear for once—'

Then Suzanne picked up the receiver and unselfconsciously conducted a five-minute conversation with her husband, telling him she was fine, the boys were fine, Laura and Rosemary were there as requested and she'd had a really nice evening.

She didn't ask him about his own evening, except for a polite enquiry about the drive to Leeds. When she asked him what time he expected to be home, the reply clearly wasn't to her liking. 'That's terribly late,' she complained. 'The boys will be asleep.'

Moments after the phonecall ended, she escorted her guests to their room. It was at the back of the house, large and tastefully furnished. Twin beds were covered with generous duvets, and the moon shone in through the window, until Suzanne closed the curtains, standing at the window for a moment, looking out onto the moonlit grounds behind the house.

'It's very kind of you to keep me company,' she said. 'It's not like me, really, but I suddenly seemed to lose my nerve. Of course, Martin overreacted, but I'm glad he did.'

'So am I,' said Laura, with considerable emphasis. Although she would rather die than admit it, the prospect of returning to the tent was less appealing every time she thought about it.

Chapter Ten

Wednesday was devoted to vigorous work in the garden, with scarcely a break. The weather was mild, but cloudy, and Mr Coutts spent the day repeatedly scanning the sky for some signs of the return of the sun. The prisoners dug trenches at the further end of the garden, marking out two of the new beds, and putting in several of the plants that Rosemary had acquired the day before. By lunchtime, the design was already starting to emerge, and questions about paths and whether or not to create a softening to the overall effect with more beds at the sides of the garden were being discussed. The prisoners were not shy in expressing their opinions. Huxton Rymer, the former MP, favoured them with his views on the simplified beds planned for the gaps between the large triangular ones they were working on. He paced it all out, calling for everyone to stop what they were doing and watch him.

Rosemary was everywhere with a long metal ruler, checking for symmetry. Over and over, she said, 'This is such a big area! We can afford to make these central beds really bold.' The subdivisions that she had talked over with Martin were causing her some difficulty. 'They mustn't look fussy,' she said. 'But if they're too big, the effect won't be right at all.'

Almost all the work was taking place at the lower end of the garden, furthest from the door and the site of the old chapel. The day before had seen the job of removing the remaining foundation stones completed, and they were neatly stacked along the wall beside the door and Mr Coutts's canvas chair.

After a few strenuous hours, Rosemary straightened up and scanned the whole garden. Her attention was again snagged by the series of small mounds, several more of which had recently been uncovered when Rupert had moved some sheets of galvanised iron. 'They can't be molehills, can they?'

'Of course not,' said Laura. 'But I don't suppose we'll ever know who made them. Somebody's going to have to fill them in, though, aren't they?'

They had been informed by Suzanne that there would be sandwiches and soft drinks provided for themselves and the prisoners at one o'clock. 'I should have organised the same thing yesterday,' she apologised. 'But...well...'

'Don't be silly,' said Laura. 'You really don't have to feel we need feeding, when you've got so much else to think about.'

'It's just today,' Suzanne admitted. 'Usually the prisoners bring their own packed lunch, but I like to make something special for them now and then.'

Greatly to Mr Coutts's delight, the sun came out for a few minutes just as they ended the morning shift.

Laura and Rosemary filled their plates with a selection of top quality sandwiches, and went in search of a quiet spot. One of the retrievers appeared and flopped panting at Rosemary's feet.

'Poor Cabbage,' said Laura. 'She looks terribly hot. The boys must have been exercising her a bit too strenuously.'

'How can you tell which one it is? They look identical to me.'

'Oh no,' said Laura. 'This one's got longer hair on its neck, and the tail doesn't curve up so much. And she's got a much gentler expression. They're not the same at all when you really look.'

Rosemary nibbled a smoked salmon sandwich, without any show of appreciation. 'It feels like a lull before the storm,' she said. 'I've managed not to think about Jim all morning – but it can't last.'

The prisoners were given sandwiches inside the garden, with Mr Coutts distributing them scrupulously. 'They're nice chaps, aren't they,' said Laura.

'Mmm? Who?'

'The prisoners,' Laura said patiently.

'I'm not too sure about that George. Arsonists always make me nervous.' Laura had repeated verbatim the stories of each of the prisoners, dwelling especially on how she had reacted when George had explained himself.

'We'd better keep an eye on him,' Rosemary said.

Laura laughed. 'He hasn't much opportunity to set fire to anything inside a walled garden,' she said. 'Let's hope he's had some aversion therapy while he's been in custody.'

Rosemary made a sceptical face. 'Unlikely, don't you think?'

'It was a joke,' sighed Laura. 'Although they ought to have provided some kind of group work, which might have helped.'

George Hamilton Teed was feverishly rushing to catch the midday deadline for the *Observer* with his dramatic piece about Jim Frazer. He did not go into his office, but remained at home composing the story and then sending it electronically to the printworks at Westover. Then he considered putting in a few hours in the office, situated in the Lyvedon High Street, in case anybody wanted to drop in for a chat. This seldom happened, since the great majority of his 'chats' took place in the bar of The Lamb. He sometimes had to admit to himself that the office was an expensive luxury that he might well have to give up before long. It was part of a converted coaching inn, with a beautiful courtyard between the building and the street where the coaches had once turned around. Other local businesses had premises there, and he would have no difficulty in disposing of his section. He used it as the official postal address, and a place to store the files, which went back well over a century to when the *Lyvedon Observer* had been a substantial and well-respected newspaper. His habit was generally to be there all day Friday, making an early start on the following week's material and deciding which weekend activities he would attend in pursuit of copy.

Wednesday afternoon and evening were almost always free time. His work was over for the week, the presses rolling in Westover, producing the paper for first thing the next morning. He wouldn't even go to The Lamb that evening, where he was sure to get drawn into local gossip. He would pursue his other passion, whatever the weather and whatever his mood.

The River Mallam was only moderately good for fishing, but Teed knew all the best places. His father had introduced him to them when he was six. He would sit motionless for hour after hour, watching the setting sun throw its rays across the flickering water, and let his mind go blank. He could feel it doing him good, calming and refreshing him after the trivialities of village life that beset him the rest of the time. He loved Lyvedon and its residents – he had even been rather fond of poor Jim Frazer – but he liked his own company best.

He had been mainly truthful when he had told the gardening women he was checking the fishing potential on their stretch of the river. It had been several months since he'd gone that way, lulling the canny old trout that lurked there into a sense of security.

Taking his rod and bait and folding stool, he set out for the stretch of river a mile away, through the woods belonging to Abbotslea. There was no hurry – the fish didn't really rise until the heat of the afternoon was gone. Martin had given him a lifelong licence to fish in whichever part of the river he wished, and he would work out, early in the week, exactly where he would head for on Wednesday afternoon.

The news about Jim had affected his choice in a way he found rather surprising. He felt an aversion to sitting on a bank overlooking a point where a dead body must have swept past only two days earlier. He knew it was foolish – the water was not the same water that had carried the body – but he still didn't like the idea. Only a brief appraisal of the other options convinced him that his reluctance had to be overcome. Besides, despite his determination to remove his journalist hat for the rest of the day, he was still a newshound – and the Abbotslea woods might just have something interesting to reveal, if he kept his eyes open.

He used the same path that Rosemary and Laura used to reach their tent. He stepped briskly through the Dingle, hoping he wasn't disturbing anybody, noticing that the tent remained just as it had been the previous evening. He had also meant what he'd said about the water retaining some strange kind of memory of what had taken place.

Something so significant surely had to make a mark, disturb the elements that had swallowed up the wretched Jim Frazer. While not exactly expecting to see a ghost, he would not have been unduly surprised to detect some kind of *shimmer* on the air, or a distant echo of Jim's last cry.

But there was nothing. He pressed on through the woods, to a point where the path met a small road, which crossed the river on an old bridge. The road looped down from a farm away on a rising hill to the right, crossed the river via a very solid stone bridge, dived through the dense Abbotslea wood and rose again to link with the back road to Lyvedon, a mile or so distant. The bridge was sturdy enough to take substantial traffic – which was fortunate since it was the only access for the farm. It also provided a route for the Frazers, taking them from the house to Jim's cottage, and a small back road beyond that. Teed was fond of the bridge and the dense woodland that grew close by and gave shade to the deep pool where the trout like to lurk.

He had almost reached his goal. Just another hundred yards, through the coppiced area, where the old hut used by the coppicers still stood, looking as if it was regularly maintained, even now. Perhaps the alders were still sometimes harvested for the timber that could be turned to charcoal. He made a mental note to find out just what went on in this part of the wood – it might make a nice little story one day.

A movement caught his eye as he looked at the hut. The windows were dusty and the light was unreliable under the trees. But he could have sworn he'd seen a face, peering out. A man's face, it was.

Teed went to investigate, peering in through the murky glass. Inside there was a wooden chair and a brazier visible, as well as some coils of rope. He could see no sign of a man, nor anywhere a person could hide. Shrugging at his own foolishness, he walked on.

Inside the hut, the man slowly got to his feet. He had been lying full length on the floor below the window, pressed tightly against the wall. Nobody could have seen him, he promised himself. He was quite safe.

Martin was pleased to find his case concluded well before the anticipated time. The evidence that Warwick Jardine had produced had been so unarguable that the prosecution had virtually collapsed. There had not even been any need for a debriefing afterwards. But there was one small matter that Jardine needed to discuss.

It was quickly completed, on the walk back to the car park. Martin had done his best to be suitably grateful, as the news was presented to him so condescendingly. 'Well, that's great,' he had managed. 'We'll be honoured.' Inwardly he sighed, thinking of the implications. 'Now, if there's nothing else, I'll get home. Suzanne will be happy I'm back so soon.'

It was still a long drive, and he'd be lucky to make it by eight. He phoned Suzanne to give her the revised schedule. 'Could you tell Rosemary the inquest is tomorrow?' he asked her. 'Ten o'clock in the Lyvedon meeting house. There's something else she ought to know, but I think that's best saved for the morning. See you soon, darling.'

In his head, he still heard Jardine's parting words. 'I'll see you tomorrow then, Frazer.'

'Well, that was short and sweet,' sighed Laura, as she and Rosemary trudged along the riverbank to the Dingle, at the end of their day's work. 'Pity Martin's Leeds case was so brief.'

'Oh, I'm quite happy to be back,' said Rosemary. 'Hello, tent. Did you miss us?'

'Maybe he'll get delayed. Maybe Jardine will keep him overnight after all, in one of his famous changes of mind.'

'Of course he won't. He promised Suzanne he'd be back before dark. What's the matter with you? We're home.'

With an effort Laura agreed. 'You're right,' she said. 'Home sweet home.'

But Rosemary's good cheer was also rather forced. Suzanne had given her Martin's message about the inquest the following morning, and she was dreading it. The only course of action seemed to be to try and forget all about it, throwing herself into preparing the supper and then making more sketches and lists for the garden. She rooted through the box that Laura had filled with provisions, and organised a hopelessly ambitious meal.

'You can't have all that,' Laura objected. 'There'll be nothing left for the rest of the week. Besides, there isn't room for more than one pan at a time over the fire.'

They bickered comfortably about it, until Laura eventually took over the cooking as usual.

The time seemed to pass quickly, and as darkness fell they heard a car engine and the crunch of gravel. 'There you are,' said Laura. 'Martin's home.' The excited barking of the dogs con-firmed her words. 'Now Suzanne will be happy,' she added.

Chris and Katy Stevens were still finding the house disconcertingly quiet, that evening. With none of the normal bedtime routines to attend to, they found themselves at rather a loss. 'I'm not sure I like this,' said Katy. 'Four nights is too much of a good thing.'

When the phone rang, they both scrambled to answer it.

Katy won, and found herself listening to a torrent of complaint from her mother. In the background there were howls from protesting children.

'For heaven's sake, Mum – what's going on?' Katy demanded.

'Bonnie can't find her Cuggie. Jasper has cut his finger and Freddie insists you packed the wrong underpants. Frankly, Katy, I think we've all had enough. Is there any chance you could come and fetch them back again tomorrow?'

Katy's voice slowed and deepened, as she told her mother to fetch Bonnie to the phone. 'Let me deal with her,' she said.

Speaking to Bonnie in the same altered voice, she easily persuaded the child that everything was perfectly all right, that lost things were quickly found again, that sleep was a wonderful thing, and that they would all be together again the day after next.

Chris listened with his usual admiration. He had often tried to achieve the same effect himself, with very little success. Katy had a natural talent that few people properly appreciated. It was hardly too strong to say she hypnotised them, convincing them that her suggestions were the most obvious and worthwhile courses of action, that there was nothing to fear, and little point in arguing. Sometimes he thought she wasted it. If she wanted to, she could probably rule the world, simply by the power of suggestion.

Bonnie having been put right, Katy proceeded to work the same magic on her two sons. Each one had his difficulties dispersed and his mind set to rest. The plan was for them to remain another whole day and night, with the eventual reunion on Friday.

Chapter Eleven

At midnight, Rosemary still hadn't managed to get to sleep. Suzanne had passed on the message from Martin at five and she had been shaking ever since. Now, she gave up trying to sleep and switched on her torch. 'Laura?' she hissed. 'Are you awake?'

Silence. Rosemary knew it was selfish of her, but she felt a terrible need to talk. Since she had told Laura about the man in the market, the subject had hardly arisen again. The garden work had been an effective distraction for them both. But now she could think of nothing else.

She switched the torch on and off several times, directing it towards Laura's section of the tent. Perhaps that would waken her, without Rosemary having to do anything more obvious. When nothing happened, she was not surprised. Laura always slept like a stone.

Finally, she crawled through to her friend and shook her. 'Wake up!' she said. 'Laura, please wake up.'

With a startled flurry of movement inside the sleeping bag, Laura finally came to life. 'What?' she slurred. 'Warramarra?'

'I can't get to sleep,' Rosemary whined. 'I'm so scared about tomorrow.'

'Errgghh,' groaned Laura, peering at her watch. 'I only

dropped off about an hour ago myself. The sleeping bag kept trying to suffocate me.'

'I'm sorry. I'll be all right in a bit. I just need to talk it through. Sorry,' Rosemary babbled. 'What I'd really like is a cup of tea, but I suppose that's too much of a palaver.'

'Yes it is,' said Laura. 'But there's some beer, I think.'

'Beer?' It was the first Rosemary had heard of it.

With enormous patience, Laura wriggled out of the sleeping bag and shuffled out of the tent, where a large plastic box held their provisions. She came back with two bottles of beer. 'I hope we can get the tops off,' she grumbled. 'I can't find an opener.'

Rosemary delved into the pocket of her jacket, and produced a jangling collection of keys and other gadgets. One of them lifted the tops off the bottles with ease. They settled down on Laura's airbed, and Rosemary confessed all her worries.

Laura did everything she could to calm her. 'The inquest is really only a formality,' she insisted. 'The Coroner has to be satisfied that the cause of death is fully established. It'll all be over by lunchtime.'

Rosemary was not mollified. 'But what will I *say*?' she wailed. 'The truth, the whole truth and nothing but the truth. That means I have to say I saw Jim in Long Horton, at the same time as Martin was identifying the body. It will either make Martin look like a liar or me like a nutcase.'

'The most likely explanation is that you simply saw a different man, who looks like Jim,' said Laura.

Rosemary shook her head. 'I saw him as large as life only a few feet away. It was undoubtedly the same man that I saw fall into the river. And the one we saw in the garden when we first arrived here. I can't have been mistaken.

Everything about him was the same.' She put her head in her hands and squeezed hard. 'I must be going mad,' she moaned.

Laura rubbed her shoulder gently. 'Let's assume that isn't the explanation,' she said calmly. 'Which means we have to think of something else.'

'Like what?'

'Well, there seems to be some confusion of identity. The one certain fact is that Jim Frazer is dead. Martin doesn't doubt it and he's known him all his life.'

Rosemary frowned. 'What if Martin lied? The police in Westover won't have known Jim. What if Martin falsely identified him?'

'It's possible,' Laura agreed slowly. 'But why would he do that?'

'And how could he get away with it?' Rosemary said. 'With the inquest and everything.'

'It wouldn't be too difficult, actually. Nobody will question it at the inquest – it'll just be assumed. And at the funeral it's sure to be a closed coffin, because of the injuries. No other near relatives to interfere. It is possible.'

'But terribly unlikely. Martin's such a nice person. He wouldn't get involved in anything so underhand.'

'He might be protecting somebody.'

'Wait!' Rosemary pleaded. 'My head's hurting. Let's go back a step. The man I saw falling into the river is still alive. Let's start from there.'

Laura held up a hand. 'And we have no certain proof that he was Jim,' she realised. 'He just *said* he was.'

'Yes! So the dead man probably *is* Jim. Which means Martin is acting in perfectly good faith.'

'OK,' said Laura. 'But there is still something peculiar going on, isn't there?'

'I don't know,' Rosemary squeezed her head again. 'I feel very strange.'

'It's all probably a silly coincidence. The man you saw in the river was just teasing you for some reason. Showing off. Just a local idiot trying to impress.'

Rosemary frowned. 'No, that won't work. Everybody says *Jim* was the local nutter. It's much more likely that I didn't really see the same man after all – maybe there are dozens of Frazer cousins in the neighbourhood, all looking alike.'

'Except the man we saw looked nothing like Martin,' Laura observed.

'True. But it's still possible, if Jim has the Frazer features and Martin doesn't.'

Laura nodded doubtfully, while Rosemary rushed on with her enticing new theory. 'Don't you see? It could work. The simple explanation would be the right one, then – we saw Jim in the garden, then I saw him jump into the river and now Martin's identified his dead body. That would all be completely beyond question if I hadn't gone to the market.'

'But you did, and now it isn't,' said Laura. 'Because you know perfectly well that you were absolutely sure it *was* the same man. And you think he saw you, as well, and was panicked. So there definitely is something suspicious about the whole thing.'

Rosemary moaned. 'You're not making me feel any better.'

'I'm doing my best. And I think we should both get some sleep. We'll be wrecks in the morning, otherwise. Just try thinking about the garden. We'll have to spend the afternoon catching up. Once the inquest's over, everything's going to be nice and normal and we can get the job finished by the middle of next week.'

'Right,' said Rosemary doubtfully. 'I'll try. Sorry I woke you up.'

'That's OK,' said Laura generously.

Martin escorted Rosemary and Laura to the quaint old meeting house at the lower end of Lyvedon's High Street. 'It's rather small, but we're not expecting many people,' he said. 'I've conducted quite a few inquests here in my time as Coroner.'

Rosemary stared at him. 'You're the Coroner? But—'

'Not today, of course,' he said. 'In fact, I've been meaning to tell you—'

He was interrupted by the arrival of a large Daimler sweeping up to the door of the building. Laura had to jump out of the way. 'Watch out!' she called. Then she saw the driver. 'Oh, my stars!' she gasped. 'Look at that paintwork!'

Warwick Jardine QC emerged from the mottled vehicle, looking brisk and busy. 'Pretty little village you've got here,' he said to Martin. Then he turned to inspect the women, in his customary condescending manner. He and Rosemary recognised each other at the same moment.

'You!' they said in unison.

Rosemary was the first to grasp the implications. 'You're the Coroner?' she said.

Martin took her arm. 'You mustn't speak to him before the inquest,' he urged. 'Come with me.'

They sat on a bench outside the main room for a few minutes, Rosemary still thunderstruck by this new twist to events. Where before she had been nervous and torn as to exactly what she ought to say, now she was almost paralysed. Laura spoke to her in a low urgent voice. 'It's perfectly all right,' she said. 'He has to conduct everything properly. Try to forget who it is, and just think of him as a man doing a job. Come *on*,' she entreated. 'It really isn't that bad.'

Rosemary took a deep breath. 'No,' she said. 'You're right. He's just a puffed-up windbag. And he hates me. He'll be impatient and unsympathetic.' She clenched her fists. 'So I'll just say what they expect me to, and leave it at that.'

'Good,' said Laura. 'Now I think it's time to go in.'

The room was only half full. Chris and Katy Stevens sat beside Martin, with Fern and Gwynne in the row behind them. Eight or ten other villagers had turned out to witness the unusual proceedings in their midst, most of them looking as if they were anticipating something satisfying. George Hamilton Teed sat with a notebook in his hand and a camera by his side. A man in a suit sat at the front, beside Constable Stuart – the police officer who had responded to the original call from Abbotslea when Jim went into the river. 'That's the pathologist,' said Martin, pointing to the man in the suit. 'The one who did the post-mortem.'

Everything happened with dignified ceremony. Constable Stuart recounted his observations on the riverbank and the evident distress that Miss Boxer showed at what she had witnessed. No, nobody else had observed the deceased fall into the river. He, Constable Stuart, had also been present when the body had been discovered at the Westover weir, at seven-thirty a.m. the following day, Tuesday. Mr Martin Frazer had been informed, as next of kin, and he had made a formal identification of the body as that of Mr James Anthony Frazer. The said Mr Martin

Frazer was present at the inquest if this fact were to need further verification. Yes, he had been slightly surprised at the speed with which the body had travelled, but the river had been in full spate which no doubt explained it. Furthermore, he had obtained signed statements from three residents of Lyvedon to the effect that Mr James Frazer was a man of eccentric habits and gloomy demeanour. He was widely known to be resentful of his lot in life and to shun human society. It was Constable Stuart's strong impression that nobody was unduly surprised at what had happened.

A murmur of agreement rippled through the observers on the benches at the back of the room.

The Pathologist gave a dry little report, to the effect that he had found many contusions on the body, in particular the unprotected head and hands. The cause of death had certainly been one of these blows, and not drowning. There was no water at all in the lungs.

'Does that not surprise you?' asked the Coroner.

'A little, Your Honour,' said the Pathologist. 'It suggests that a fatal blow to the head occurred shortly after the deceased found himself in the water. However, given that the river was of no great depth, it is perfectly plausible that he was unable to get his footing, but did succeed in keeping his nose and mouth out of the water for some time, before the fast current dashed him against one of the many rocks. A reasonable assumption is that the especially violent contusion on his temple was what killed him. A close examination of the tissue surrounding the blow confirms this as the probable cause of death. The skull was badly damaged at that point.'

'Thank you,' said the Coroner. Nobody took up his offer of further questions to the witness.

Then it was Rosemary's turn. She was asked to confirm her name and address and reason for being at Abbotslea. 'Would you tell us, please, in your own words, what took place on the morning of Monday 27th May,' came Jardine's frosty instruc-tion.

Rosemary cleared her throat. When she spoke, her voice emerged tight and high. 'I was collecting water for our morning tea.'

'From the river?' came the Coroner's disbelieving interrup-tion. He glanced briefly around the room, eyes wide, as if to suggest that they were dealing with a very odd and possibly insane person.

'That's right. We were camping.'

'Very well. Continue.'

'When I saw a man standing on a large stone in the middle of the river.'

'Standing on a stone,' repeated the Coroner, as if this was another piece of bizarre fantasy.

'Yes. He looked at me, and then he just – well, *dropped* into the water. He was whirled away in a few seconds, around the bend in the river.'

'And you can confirm for us that that man was Mr James Frazer?'

'Well…' Rosemary hesitated.

Laura felt her insides turn to ice as she willed Rosemary to act normally, knowing how unlikely that was.

'Well?' said Jardine.

'Well, I am sure he was the man we saw on Sunday, who told us his name was Jim.'

'Please explain.'

Rosemary haltingly described the encounter in the walled garden, and the man's odd behaviour. 'It was the same man,' she repeated.

'Thank you,' said Jardine. Laura exhaled with relief. Rosemary could stop there, her integrity intact. She tried to catch her friend's eye, and convey with a silent jerk of the head that it was over and she could step down.

But Rosemary was looking at Martin Frazer with a strange expression. Then she scanned the room, as if searching for someone.

'Actually…' she began, her voice very low.

'I beg your pardon?' barked Jardine.

'Actually, I think I should just mention that I believe I saw the same man again, the following day.'

The room erupted in a buzz of bewildered gasps. People looked at each other, as if to check they'd heard correctly.

'What?' Jardine rapped. 'What did you say?' He fixed her with a look full of outraged contempt.

'I was at the market in Long Horton on Tuesday morning, and I saw him. It was the same man. I was only a few yards away from him.'

The Coroner closed his eyes, and took a long steadying breath. His fingers drummed threateningly on the table in front of him. 'You are telling this inquest that you saw Mr James Frazer, *alive*, on the morning that his cousin Mr Martin Frazer, was identifying his *dead body* in Westover?'

'Perhaps I was mistaken,' whispered Rosemary.

'Miss Boxer, it seems to me that you have some kind of compulsion to interrupt and pervert legal proceedings, wherever you encounter them,' said Jardine, slapping the table. 'And perhaps you could now stand down and desist from wasting our valuable time.'

He sat in angry silence for a few moments, watching Rosemary make her way back to her seat. Then he asked Martin Frazer to come to the stand. 'I regret to have to do this,' he told his colleague. 'But in the circumstances…' he nodded to the clerk, who stepped forward to take Martin through the oath. Then Jardine asked him, 'Are you absolutely certain that the body you were called to identify in Westover mortuary on Tuesday morning was that of your cousin, James Anthony Frazer?'

'I am, Your Honour,' said Martin.

'Thank you,' said Jardine. 'No more questions.'

He drew a deep breath and solemnly pronounced his findings – that Mr James Anthony Frazer took his own life on the morning of Monday May 27th while the balance of his mind was disturbed.

It was as if Rosemary had suddenly shown symptoms of the Black Death, as the meeting house emptied. Almost everybody ignored her completely and gave her a wide berth. But a smaller subgroup approached her with furious expressions and accused her of making trouble. This group consisted of Fern Evans, an elderly woman Rosemary had never seen before – and Martin Frazer, who said little but merely repeated, 'What were you trying to *do*?'

'Sorry, sorry,' Rosemary repeated wretchedly. 'But I had to say it. I took an oath. "The whole truth", you see. Those words kept echoing in my head.'

'Leave the poor woman alone, for heaven's sake,' came a rescuing voice. 'She's obviously not deliberately making waves.'

It was Chris Stevens. His bearded face carried its usual warm smiling expression, which he directed at Rosemary. 'Come and have some lunch with us,' he invited. 'You'll feel better for it.' His gaze extended to Laura. 'You too, of course,' he added.

'Thanks,' they said together.

'We'll take you to The Lamb. It's about a quarter of a

mile away. The walk'll do you good,' he said. 'It's another nice day.'

Before they could set out, they heard the *clunk* of a camera shutter, and realised George Hamilton Teed had just taken a photograph of them. He did it again, as they looked directly at him. And then two more times.

'Hey!' Laura protested.

'That's all, ladies. Many thanks,' said the newspaperman with a grin. 'You'll see yourselves on the front page of next week's *Observer*, unless I'm much mistaken.'

Laura spluttered for a moment, before accepting the inevitable and following Chris and Katy.

Laura and Rosemary had not yet seen The Lamb, and they gave it an approving inspection as they approached. 'Another historic Lyvedon building,' said Laura.

Chris chuckled. 'It was in fact the local slaughterhouse, until about a century ago,' he informed them. 'Some people still say they can hear the ghostly echoes of the terrified beasts, on a quiet night.'

'Oh, don't,' Laura shuddered. 'That's awful.'

Chris shook his head. 'Not really. It was all quite small scale and remarkably humane, as I understand it. Besides, the build-ings where the business was done have all gone now. What you see is the home of the slaughterman and some new additions.'

'And some rather splendid gardens,' said Laura.

Rosemary gave them her automatic professional scrutiny. 'Not bad,' she decided. 'I like the escallonia. It must look wonderful later in the year.' She was referring to a long thick hedge of the shrub, bordering the road. 'Unusual for a pub,' she continued. 'And the fuchsia's pretty good, too.'

'You're prattling,' said Laura under her breath.

'Sorry,' said Rosemary.

They sat at a table in the garden at the front of the building. 'Our usual, as it happens,' smiled Chris. 'Funny how one falls into these habits without ever meaning to.'

It was still rather early for lunch, so drinks were ordered, and then they seemed to slump, released from the tensions of the morning. When Fern arrived for her midday shift, she glanced at them and then swept past without a word. 'Oh dear,' said Rosemary. 'She's terribly cross with me.'

'She's a bright girl,' said Katy. 'She worked out the implica-tions ahead of everybody else.'

'Implications?' queried Laura.

'If what you say is true, then Jim might not be dead. It throws a very odd light on Martin. It makes him look – not quite suspicious – but not as squeaky clean as everybody thinks he is.'

'Jim is dead,' said Chris. 'If he wasn't, someone would have seen him by now. Jim was no hermit – he roamed the length and breadth of the village. I imagine just about everybody saw him practically every day.' He looked at Rosemary. 'But he would never have gone to Long Horton. For a start, he hasn't got a car – how would he get there? For another thing, he didn't like crowds. A market would be torture to him. So the probability is that it wasn't Jim Frazer you saw.'

Katy sniffed reproachfully. 'I'd say certainty, not probability,' she said.

'Who was it then?' demanded Rosemary. 'Has Jim got a double?'

'Not that I know of. I'm afraid I'm as bewildered as you are. It's a mystery. But let's try to forget about it now. After all, it doesn't really matter. Jim's dead, the inquest found that he took his own life. It's tragic and shocking, and done with now. Let's talk about something else.'

Laura seized the opening eagerly. 'Tell us about your children,' she invited. 'Are they still at their gran's?'

Katy nodded. 'We're fetching them back tomorrow. I think everybody's had enough of a good thing. I'm missing them dreadfully and my mother sounded seriously frazzled when I spoke to her last night. She thinks Bonnie's starting a cold, too. She'll be needing some remedy.'

'Ah, yes,' said Laura, remembering Katy's offer on Monday. 'I suggested Rosemary try some, but she said she was feeling better. Didn't you?' she prompted her friend.

'Homeopathy, is it?' Rosemary asked. 'Do you have some-thing for a bad case of insanity?'

Katy leaned towards her. 'Is that how you feel?' she asked, in a voice full of concern. 'Poor old you.'

'Pretty much,' Rosemary admitted. 'I mean – I saw a dead man, as large as life. There's no satisfactory explanation for it, so I must be mad. Simple.' She laughed mirthlessly.

'I do have a remedy for feelings of loss of control, being overwhelmed, that sort of thing.' She rummaged in a large bag and produced a small bottle with a rubber bulb in the top. 'Try some of this,' she invited. Rosemary gave the bottle a wary look.

'Do you make them yourself?' asked Laura.

Katy nodded. 'I do, as it happens.'

Rosemary frowned. 'Don't you need a licence for that sort of thing?'

Katy laughed. 'In fact, no. As far as the law is concerned, all I give anybody is water. Not many people realise what powerful stuff that is.'

'Don't get her started,' warned Chris with a crooked

smile. 'Katy has theories about water that might sound a bit wacky on first acquaintance.'

Katy acted as if he hadn't spoken. Her eyes seemed suddenly deeper, fixed probingly on Rosemary's face. 'Here,' she uncapped her bottle and held it in the air. 'Please try it. Just three drops on your tongue. Let me do it for you.'

With a despairing look at Laura, Rosemary obeyed, opening her mouth like a baby bird for the drops.

'It doesn't taste of anything,' she reported.

'It'll do the trick, you'll see,' said Katy, with calm conviction. 'Keep the bottle, and have some more at bedtime.'

Chris interrupted. 'We're back to the same subject,' he objected. 'I want to talk about my work.' He parodied a spoilt child, making them laugh.

'Go on, then,' said his wife. 'I'm just popping in for a word with Fern. She looked as if she could do with a bit of attention.'

Chris looked at Laura. 'As it happens, I had another motive for bringing you over here,' he confessed. 'I've been wanting to talk to you again, ever since I saw you on Monday.'

He went on to talk vaguely about his work as an illustrator of book covers. When Laura asked him whether he'd done any seriously famous ones, he listed five or six bestselling titles, none of which she or Rosemary could remember having seen.

'They're a bit out of your area of interest, I imagine,' he said. 'I tend to favour gothic horror, and the more violent thrillers. But I'm highly versatile. Now, the thing is…' and he went on to explain that he was looking for a model for an urgent commission. 'The book's called *The King's Last*

Mistress,' he said. 'And I believe yours is the very face and figure I'm looking for.'

Laura flushed with excitement. 'Really?' she breathed. 'Surely not!'

'Trust me,' he assured her. 'Now, when can you come?'

Laura looked at Rosemary. 'Sometime at the weekend, maybe? Do you work at weekends?'

He frowned. 'Not if I can help it. But if that's all you can manage – well, fine. I was hoping for this afternoon, but...' he shrugged.

Laura felt bad at his obvious disappointment. 'The garden, you see,' she said. 'We have to be there all day.'

'What time do you stop?'

'We'll have to work late this evening, to make up for missing the morning. I could come tomorrow, if you like.'

'All right then,' he said. 'Make it five-thirty or six. That'll be perfect. We should be back from collecting the kids by four or half past. Katy can give you some supper afterwards, if you like.'

'That's very kind,' said Laura, feeling as if she'd agreed to something that might turn out to be more than she'd bargained for. 'But I wouldn't put her to that trouble, straight after getting the children back.'

Martin was waiting for them when they got back to Abbotslea after lunch. Laura glanced at her watch. 'Is he annoyed that we've taken so long, do you think?'

'Annoyed, yes. But I don't think it's because we're late.'

'Oh, there you are,' he said to Rosemary. 'Now, about this morning.'

'Martin, I don't know what to say. I told the truth, that's all. I didn't mean to cast doubt on your integrity, or anything like that. But the fact is, something doesn't add up, and I can't just pretend that it does.'

Laura gave her friend an admiring look. She certainly seemed to have recovered dramatically. It was tempting to think Katy Stevens' remedy might have worked after all.

'I don't understand what you mean,' said Martin.

Rosemary squared her shoulders. 'I mean, Martin, that I can't bring myself to believe that the man I saw in the river is dead.'

Laura had a sudden thought. 'Have you got a photo of Jim?' she asked. 'That would resolve things, once and for all.'

Martin bridled even more. 'Things *are* resolved,' he shouted. 'Jim committed suicide. The inquest proved it. Look—' He was quickly calm again. 'If it helps you to believe it, feel free to go to Jim's cottage and search his desk. There might be a photo there.' He threw a key down on the table. 'That's for his front door. If you go through the woods a little way, past the Dingle and then over a stone bridge, the cottage is three or four hundred yards on the right.'

'OK,' said Rosemary, still holding her ground. 'Thank you. We'll do that.'

George Hamilton Teed was deeply puzzled. As he wrote up his report of the inquest, making as much as he could of the drama at the end, he struggled to make sense of what the Boxer woman had said. If he was to do full justice to the story, justifying the anticipated place on the front page of next week's paper, he had to have an angle that would avoid libelling anybody, while at the same time making it clear that this had been no ordinary inquest.

He started with the statements about Jim Frazer's character, embellishing them to depict a tormented soul, racked with resentment at the unfairness of his birth. Born to the younger Frazer brother, he had watched his cousin inherit the huge Abbotslea estate, leaving nothing but a ramshackle cottage for Jim. Teed indulged in a few lines on the law of primogeniture still unchanged from feudal times.

He drew attention to the presence of the two ladies who ran a business entitled 'Rosemary & Thyme' whereby they improved, or even sometimes created, unusual gardens, as well as dealing with problems of disease or neglect. They were currently restoring the Elizabethan walled garden at Abbotslea, he explained, assisted, he understood, by a small group of prisoners from Bleakmoor open prison on day release.

'And then came the dramatic revelation in Miss Boxer's testimony,' he wrote. *'Under oath, she claimed to have seen the deceased man alive and well in Long Horton market on Tuesday morning. The morning after he had tumbled into the river Mallam before her very eyes. Was she deluded? Under severe pressure from the Coroner, she admitted that she might have been. Her claim did not alter the finding of Suicide.'*

Teed sat back in his chair. It still didn't make any sense. Unless – he remembered the face at the window of the little hut, the previous afternoon. It had been so indistinct, he could not identify it. And when he'd looked in, there had been nobody. If *he* could see a ghost – an impossible thing surely? – then why not Miss Rosemary Boxer too?

Chapter Twelve

Work on the garden was proceeding very well. The prisoners had been industrious throughout the morning and almost all Rosemary's purchases from Bernie's market stall had been put in place, fertilised and watered. Halfway through the afternoon, Suzanne appeared, apparently on a tour of inspection.

Nervously, Rosemary waited for some reproach about her statement at the inquest. Suzanne had not been present, but there was no doubt that she had heard all about it from Martin. But the reproach never came. Instead there was admiration for the progress in the work and a suggestion as to the positioning of the climbing roses. 'I have a list of my favourites,' she said, producing a sheet of paper with several named roses. Rosemary raised her eyebrows. Suzanne certainly knew something about the subject.

'I expect Bernie will have most of these,' she said.

'Oh yes, he has,' said Suzanne confidently. 'I know for a fact.'

'While you're here, can we ask about the sundial?' said Laura. 'It would help if we could have it brought in fairly soon. Otherwise, we might not leave the right sized gap for it.'

'And you'd risk crushing things when you drag it into

place,' Suzanne nodded. 'I'll get onto it.' She frowned. 'It's times like this when we need the odd-job man.' She sighed theatrically. 'I'll give him a piece of my mind when he does show up again.'

'Not to worry,' said Laura. 'We've got four strong men at our disposal here. Not to mention Martin.'

Rosemary nudged her. 'I don't think you can count Mr Coutts,' she whispered. 'He doesn't seem to think he's here to work.'

Laura waved a dismissive hand. 'He will if I ask him,' she said.

Rosemary laughed. 'You sound like Katy Stevens,' she said. 'She seems to have faith in the power of suggestion as well.'

When Suzanne had gone, Laura blew out her cheeks. 'Well, she's bounced back, hasn't she? Really on the ball this afternoon.'

'Relief, I suppose. Getting it all sorted – at least according to Martin. After all, it doesn't affect her directly, anyway. She can just get on with her life as if nothing much has happened.'

'Which is exactly what she seems to be doing,' said Laura.

At the end of her shift, Fern loitered, reluctant to go home. The landlord noticed her hesitation and put down his glasscloth. 'What's up, kid?' he asked. 'No home to go to?'

She shrugged. 'There won't be anybody there. I don't really want to be on my own.'

'You're upset about Jim? Is that it?'

'More or less. That woman, saying she'd seen him on Tuesday. How *dare* she?'

Rob had heard the whole story from his customers

during the lunchtime session. He had a professional interest in the matter, as well, being a Special Police Officer, permanently on standby for any local emergency and taking a turn on the rota for neighbourhood 'visits of reassurance' – a recent development intended to persuade the community that they were being watched over by benign officers of the law.

'Why does it bother you so much? The poor lady must have made a mistake. It's easy enough. After all, she doesn't know anybody around here.'

'Then she should have kept her mouth shut,' insisted Fern. 'What did she hope to achieve?'

Rob shrugged. 'Maybe she just thought she should tell the truth as she sees it.'

But Fern was not pacified. 'It's so unpleasant for Martin,' she went on. 'People are going to wonder. Teed's sure to put it in the paper, making a drama out of it.'

'The next paper's a whole week away. It'll be old news by then.'

'Yeah.' Fern sighed. She couldn't tell him exactly what was bothering her. She couldn't reveal to anybody that she could in fact suggest an explanation for what Rosemary had said at the inquest. And it was an explanation that would throw doubt on everything, including the conclusion that Jim Frazer had killed himself.

'Poor Martin,' said Laura, not for the first time. 'He really seems to be hurt.'

Rosemary gave an irritable twitch. 'I know he is, but it's not my fault. He's in such a superior position around here, it's difficult to avoid the conclusion that he knows about everything that goes on. And that means that if there's been a switch of identity somewhere, he's got something to do with it. Anyway, I'm going to take him up on his offer to have a look at Jim's cottage. If it was a bluff, then I'm calling it.'

'When?'

'As soon as we're finished here. You don't have to come, if you don't want to. You can light the campfire and get the supper started.'

'No way!' Laura protested. 'I'm coming with you.'

They found the cottage reasonably easily, despite taking a short detour to admire the calmer reaches of the river above the old bridge. 'It must be spooky here sometimes,' said Rosemary. 'All these trees and not a sign of human habitation. You can just imagine wolves and bears, can't you?'

Laura pointed at the ground. 'Plenty of human activity, look.' There were tyre marks leading down a track beside the river, as well as signs of considerable traffic crossing the bridge itself. 'And the wood thins out just over there,' Laura went on, pointing to the opposite bank. 'That must be where the cottage is.'

She was right. Jim's home was in a cleared area, with only a few surviving oaks providing some shelter. There was a small paddock containing two goats, and a stoutly made hen run. 'Ahhh!' Laura sighed, when she saw the goats. 'Aren't they adorable!'

She leaned over to pet the animals, only to pull back when one caught hold of the cuff of her jacket and started tugging it. 'They look hungry,' said Rosemary. 'Didn't Gwynne say she was feeding them?'

'They're fine,' said Laura. 'Just playful.' She tried again, and the goat submitted more graciously to her attentions.

Rosemary produced her key and unlocked the front door of the cottage. Immediately she was in the main living room, which was furnished with a shabby sofa, a large table and two upright chairs, a huge old bureau and a small bookcase. There were several model planes hanging from the ceiling, and two large displays of almost-dead flowers in vases, one on the table and one on the windowsill.

She went directly to the desk and tried the flap. It opened at her touch, revealing a jumble of notepaper, envelopes, carbon paper, pens, paperclips and sticky tape. There was also a balsa wood aeroplane tucked into one of the pigeonholes. Something about the disorder made Rosemary think it was the desk of a person who had intended to come back to it. Not, in other words, someone who was planning to kill themselves. Even a man like Jim Frazer would surely have made some attempt to tidy up first – and perhaps even leave a note for his cousin?

Opening the drawers below the flap, she found a hoard of toys dating back some decades. Trying to calculate Jim's age, she realised that some of these things would have been out of date even when he was a child. Carefully she lifted out a model steam engine that reminded her vividly of one that the little boy next door to her had played with in the early Sixties.

Stacks of old comics filled the second drawer. *Dandy*, *Hotspur*, *Beano*. They all looked as if they'd been read many times.

In the bottom drawer she found a folder, almost an inch thick, containing carbon copies of letters. Glancing around, she noticed a manual typewriter on the table. These were copies of letters that Jim had written on that machine. How in the world did he manage to find new ribbons for it, she wondered, in these days of computer printers?

She didn't hear Laura come in from playing with the goats. She was lost in the strange world of Jim Frazer. The letters started with the earliest, and Rosemary found herself reading outrageous accusations about local people, dating back twenty years.

'What have you got there?' Laura asked. 'It looks a bit private to me.'

Rosemary forced herself to stop reading. 'Martin said we could look at anything we wanted,' she said defensively.

Laura was forced to agree. 'He did, yes,' she said, and added, 'Besides, once a person's dead, nothing's private any longer.'

Rosemary frowned. 'Isn't that going a bit too far?'

'I'm afraid not. Think about it. People have to go through their papers, looking for a will or insurance policies or forgotten savings accounts. They're bound to find letters and diaries and so forth, in the process. Besides,' she added darkly, 'when it's a suspicious death, there's a *duty* to examine everything.'

'Maybe so – but not *your* duty.'

Laura looked around. 'Gosh, it's a sort of time warp, isn't it. Look at these wonderful things! Airfix models! Oh, I used to love them. I made all the cars in the series.'

'You were a boy as a child, then, were you? You never said.'

Laura guffawed. 'I thought I was, for a while. But I was never very keen on aeroplanes. Looks as if Jim favoured planes over everything else.'

'These letters,' Rosemary flourished the folder. 'They're dynamite. I've only glimpsed a few, but he says *awful* things about people. How in the world did he get away with it?'

'Squire's cousin,' said Laura. 'He'll have been protected,

tolerated. Even forgiven by most, I imagine – they must have realised he was a bit psycho.'

'But there are about fifty reasons here why he could have been murdered.' Rosemary stopped, her mouth open. It was the first time the word had been uttered in relation to Jim. Except that Constable Stuart had come close, standing on the riverbank with Rosemary on Monday morning. Had she been carrying that remark around with her ever since, harbouring a suspicion that nobody else appeared to share?

Laura was slow to react. She was tapping experimentally on the old typewriter, a look of nostalgia on her face. 'My mother had one of these,' she said. 'She used to love it.'

'I think we should go,' Rosemary said. 'We've got what we came for.'

'Have we? You mean you've seen enough. What about upstairs?'

'We can come back another day. I'm hungry.'

'OK.' Laura went to the door. 'I'll just say bye-bye to the goats. Poor things – they're awfully lonely.'

A moment or two later, Rosemary followed her.

Gwynne approached Jim's cottage from the opposite direction to the one Laura and Rosemary used. She drove up five minutes after they had departed, and got out of her car. Then she opened the hatch at the back and extracted a large cat basket. The goats, still recovering from Laura's enthusiastic pettings, took little notice of her, but the hens ran up to her, hoping for some corn.

Without warning, she reached over the chicken wire and grabbed one of them, deftly popping it into the basket. The remaining three stepped back nervously when she tried to repeat the procedure. It took her ten minutes to

corner and capture all of them, by which time the goats had
realised something interesting was happening, and were
straining over their fence to watch.

'Your turn tomorrow,' she told them. 'Unless you fancy
a two-mile walk.' They stared blankly at her and she
laughed. 'I thought not. Transport will be provided, in that
case. You won't know what's hit you,' she added. 'More
attention than you've ever had in your lives.'

There was no reason for Gwynne to go into the house
that afternoon. Everything she needed for the animals was
in a small shed off to one side. But for once she was in no
hurry, so she stayed close to the goats for a few more
minutes, savouring the sense that an era had ended. Now
that the inquest was over, Martin would be able to get on
with the paperwork required for arranging the funeral and
disposing of the cottage. Jim's possessions would have to
be sorted, too. Suzanne would no doubt have ideas about
that, and Gwynne suspected she would urge Martin to sell
the place, to realise some useful capital.

The cottage was part of Gwynne's earliest memories.
When she and the boys had played in these woods, an old
man named Grumpy Garth had lived here. He had kept
goats, too, as well as a huge Gloucester Old Spot sow, who
had dozens of babies more or less continuously. The
children had been nervous of old Betsy, provoking her into
chasing them and running off screaming. Looking back,
Gwynne suspected that the pig had fully understood the
game, and had been happy to pretend to a ferocity she
didn't really possess. In any event, the cottage symbolised
a world and a way of life that Gwynne remembered with
affection. When Martin had suggested exasperatedly that
Jim ought to make it his home, nearly twenty years ago,
Gwynne had not been surprised that Jim accepted. It was a

clever way of embarrassing his cousin, making an unnecessary show of poverty, when he actually had quite adequate means to live in a more normal fashion.

And there was another reason why Jim elected to stay so close to Abbotslea. With a sigh, Gwynne let the memories take over. The yearning looks he would give her, every time he saw her. The utterly loyal and undying devotion he maintained, over so many years. She had come to take it for granted, almost as if he'd been a dog. It had become part of the background of life in Lyvedon. And it had been incumbent upon her not to abuse his feelings. She liked to think she had been unfailingly pleasant and friendly towards him. She had spent Sunday afternoons with him, now and then, walking along the river or sitting in his disorderly living room eating biscuits that he made himself. She had always felt perfectly safe with him, even when as a confused teenager she had revealed some of her emotional entanglements with other men. Jim had always shown sympathy and support, when anyone else would have been consumed with jealousy. He seemed to have accepted his role in her life as friend, but never anything more. He might be eccentric, or perhaps something rather more serious than that, but she never regarded him as dangerous.

She ought to leave; there were several other things she could be doing, but somehow she felt reluctant. Her mind was full of the strain of the past few days, the suspicious looks people had been exchanging, the trouble arising from the gardening women who seemed intent on stirring up as much mud as they could. Rather like Jim, she though wryly. Then an idea struck her. Jim's letters! Hadn't he often said he'd kept copies of them all, a dossier on the many transgressions he'd observed amongst the people of Lyvedon? It had to be here in the cottage.

Hurriedly, she opened every drawer and cupboard in the house. She looked at the back of the wardrobe and on top of it, where there was a good inch of dust and fluff but no letters. She looked warily under the bed, and down the back of the sofa cushions.

They weren't there. She paused to think. Would he have gone to the trouble to hide them in the goat shed or under a flagstone outside? She thought not. Besides, she dimly remembered a day, three or fours years earlier, when he had pulled open a drawer of his desk and tapped a folder with a meaningful look. That folder was what she was searching for now. And it was nowhere to be found. Her eyes widened at the realisation that someone else had taken it. Someone else was reading all those twisted insinuations about herself and Katy and Rob and just about everyone she knew.

Laura bustled about preparing their supper as soon as they got back to the campsite. She lit the campfire and hummed cheerfully as she warmed some soup and cut slices from a granary loaf. 'Do you want a bottle of beer?' she asked Rosemary, who was in the tent. 'There are still quite a few left.'

Rosemary didn't reply, which Laura presumed to be a negative. Some minutes later, she called out again. 'It's ready! Come and get it.'

Still there was no response. Laura put her head through the tent opening. 'Are you asleep in there? Or what?'

Rosemary looked up from where she was sitting on her airbed, a wad of paper in her hand. 'Laura, this stuff is amazing,' she breathed. 'Wait until you hear some of it.'

'What is it?' asked Laura, knowing only too well.

'Jim's letters, of course,' said Rosemary, with an air of innocence. 'What do you think?'

'You stole them from the cottage? But…I mean…'

'Borrowed, not stole. Martin said it would be all right.'

'He did not and you know it.'

'Well, somebody ought to keep them safe. They're red hot.'

'You can read them to me later. The soup's ready,' said Laura firmly.

'All right,' said Rosemary, obligingly. 'It smells good. What flavour is it?'

'Tomato with basil.'

'Again,' said Rosemary carefully. 'Are we having anything else?'

'We're out of sausages and the bread's nearly finished, but we might manage a ham sandwich each. Tomorrow we'll have to go shopping for more supplies.'

'Right.'

When they'd finished, and Rosemary had caught up with her beer allocation, Laura began to think about the airbed and the night ahead. 'You've left the flap open,' she accused Rosemary. 'The mosquitoes will get in.'

'What mosquitoes?'

'The ones that bite me in the night. I suppose they breed in the river or something.'

'I'll go and shut it,' Rosemary offered. 'And I can fetch my remedy at the same time.'

Laura's eyebrows rose. 'You're still taking it?'

'Oh, yes. It's nearly all gone now. Haven't you noticed how much better it's made me?'

'How can it be all gone? You're only meant to have three drops two or three times a day.'

Rosemary looked over the river evasively. 'Well, I thought it wouldn't hurt to increase the dose a bit.'

Laura chuckled. 'If Katy's right, and it's really only plain water, you could probably take a bucketful with no ill effects.'

'Don't knock it,' Rosemary advised. 'I think it really does work.'

'She said something about the power of water,' Laura remembered. 'It didn't make much sense. But sitting here, watching the river, I can understand it better. When you think of the way the water has formed the landscape, carving its way through the soil and down to the rocks, bending around to make that promontory where the village is – it's a real force of nature, isn't it.'

'And it can kill people,' Rosemary pointed out.

'That too. Maybe she's onto something, after all. Didn't that Teed man say something about it remembering dramatic events?'

Rosemary shivered. 'He scared me at the time. It makes you wonder whether this place really is a time warp, where they still cling to ancient superstitions.'

'Sacred wells and so forth, you mean?'

'They'd be part of it – but it goes a lot deeper than that. Sitting here, it isn't hard to believe that the river has its own spirit, that it can actually retain some sort of trace. It doesn't sound as daft as all that.'

'Katy's a fascinating person, isn't she. I think I'll try to have another chat with her tomorrow when I go for my session with Chris.'

'I thought she was a bit sinister, to be honest. That voice of hers! It seems to penetrate, somehow.'

'We're getting whimsical,' said Laura, giving herself a shake. 'Not our usual style at all.'

'No, I know. It's something about this place, the ancient feel to it. As if nothing has really changed for hundreds of years. Maybe even thousands.'

They sat peaceably for another hour, watching the fading light flickering over the water, hearing occasional plops from fish jumping, somewhere to their right, and woodland birds singing their end-of-day arias. 'Lovely, isn't it,' Laura murmured, trying not to think of the night ahead.

'It's absolutely glorious,' Rosemary enthused. 'I'm so glad you made me do it. I have to admit I was horrified at the idea of camping, but you've converted me. This is the life, all right.'

Laura swallowed back the sigh that was threatening to erupt.

Martin had offered to take a turn reading to the boys, but Suzanne explained that they were two-thirds of the way through a book, and it wouldn't make any sense to him. 'Besides,' she said, 'I don't want to miss any of it.'

So he had kissed each boy, ruffling their hair and promising an outing the next day, and gone down to the kitchen where the debris of a family supper still awaited attention. He stacked it all in the dishwasher, worried that Suzanne would find fault with his system, and then opened a bottle of his wife's favourite wine. The evening was almost over, but they could sit outside for a while, enjoying the sudden warm spell after so much rain.

Unusually, Suzanne made no demur when he called her to his side. She took the wine and sank onto the comfortable lounger with a satisfied murmur. 'We should do this more often,' she said.

'Definitely,' he agreed, fighting the impulse to take her words as a reproach for his frequent absences.

'Will you really take the boys out tomorrow?' she asked after a brief silence.

'Not just me,' he objected. 'I want us all to go.'

'Where?'

'Oh, I don't know. The sea. Or the Castle. We can ask them what they'd like. Half-term's almost over and they haven't had much of a holiday, poor chaps. This business with Jim has cast a pretty grim cloud over us all.'

'But that's done with now,' she said, reaching out a hand to him. 'We can forget all about it. Why don't we go to Yarnwood and row over to the island? We haven't done that for years.'

'It's a long way.'

'We'll have to make an early start, then. The dogs can come, too.'

The island was small and uninhabited. Martin's father had been a close friend of the owner, who had accorded all the Frazers perpetual visiting rights, forty years previously. At Yarnwood, dinghies could be hired to get across the intervening strait, and once on the island it was as if the rest of the world no longer existed.

'They'll soon be too old to enjoy it,' Martin said sadly. 'I remember, when I got to fifteen or sixteen, how dull it began to seem.'

'But then you came to love it again, when you grew up.'

'True,' he said, thinking that his cousin Jim had remained in the pre-adolescent state of delight in the driftwood and shells and tangled undergrowth. Jim had never really grown up, and there were aspects of that condition that Martin rather envied.

'We leave at seven,' said Suzanne decisively. 'The garden people can cope without you, I assume?'

'Oh yes. I'll leave them a note, pinned to the garden door.'

* * *

Rosemary had her torch trained on the copies of Jim's letters until well after darkness fell. She repeatedly read sections out to Laura, who could hear her very clearly from the adjacent section of the tent.

'Listen to this! *"Does anybody know who the father of young Fern Evans really is? Is the story she puts about really true? Her mother is not exactly a vestal virgin, as everybody knows. Lucky for her, then, that the child so closely resembles the mother."*'

'That's nasty,' said Laura. 'I had the impression that Gwynne was fond of Jim, too. That must have been awfully wounding.'

'She probably never knew he'd written it. There's no way that would get printed in the paper. And it's dated fifteen years ago.'

'Surely Teed wouldn't print any of it,' said Laura.

'Well, that's not quite true. Jim does show genuine concern for the village, every now and then. He wanted a street light put up outside the meeting house, for example. And he was passionate about that little postbox at the end of the drive.'

'Boring,' said Laura. 'Read me some more gossip.'

Rosemary flicked through some more pages, before stopping. 'Hello! There's a top copy here as well. Must be one he decided not to send. It isn't dated, either.'

'What does it say?'

'*"Even Martin Frazer can break the law when it suits him. By tearing down the cherished little chapel in the walled garden, he has become a vandal, worse than any on an urban estate. No planning permission has been sought or obtained. The Lord of the Manor has chosen to ride roughshod over both law and sensitive feeling in his cavalier behaviour."* I do like his prose style, don't you?'

'It's a howl of pain,' said Laura sadly. 'So even his cousin was not ultimately immune from his attentions.'

'Except that Jim never sent this letter. He must have had second thoughts.'

'Not necessarily. Maybe that's just a first draft you've got there, and he polished it up a bit and then sent a better copy.'

'It's possible,' Rosemary agreed doubtfully and riffled through another few letters, before reading the next one out.

'Heavens – this is a good one! *"Wouldn't we like to know just what the medicines that Katy Stevens makes have in them? She works at the hospital. She could help herself to all those drugs. She has half the village banging on her door for the stuff. Are they addicted? Is she finding ways of controlling them, or fleecing them of their cash?"*'

'What an inventive mind!' said Laura.

'And there's another one, a few months later. *"Can we be certain that Mr and Mrs Stevens satisfied all the international legal requirements when they brought that little Chinese girl home with them? Or was she abducted?"*'

'Oh, Lord,' said Laura.

'There's a dreadful spite to it,' mused Rosemary. 'He always goes for the weak spot, playing on people's natural fears and sensitivities. He makes accusations that could just be true. Gwynne did have a child when she was in her teens. Katy does have access to all sorts of powerful drugs. If anybody actually listened to him, he could have done a lot of damage.'

'We never did find a photo of him,' Laura remembered.

'No. And until we do, we still can't be certain it wasn't him I saw go into the river.'

'We'll keep trying,' said Laura. 'We could go and ask at the newspaper office.'

'Good idea,' Rosemary agreed.

'Well, that's enough for tonight. It's time to go to sleep.' Laura wriggled further down her sleeping bag, and listened intently for any sounds of a mosquito. Nothing. After the excitement of the inquest, the energetic work of the afternoon and the beer, she thought it just possible she might manage a proper sleep for once.

'Night, night, then,' said Rosemary, switching off her torch.

Chapter Thirteen

Friday morning began greyly, and was much cooler than previous days. Rosemary awoke to find her nose and fingers uncomfortably chilled. When she had struggled free of her sleeping bag, she hurriedly pulled on her jacket before venturing outside for water. She had insisted on continuing this task despite the dreadful experience of Monday morning. Laura was always slow to get going in the morning, and Rosemary needed her tea badly enough to brave the river and its memories.

From the house she could hear voices, and then the sound of a car engine. Looking at her watch, she saw that it was only seven-fifteen. What were they doing going off so early, she wondered? Martin hadn't said anything about another court case in some distant town.

An hour later, she learned the answer. Arriving at the garden door with Laura, Rosemary quickly found the note pinned to it. *Gone off for the day, with boys, dogs and picnic. Not due home until after dark. Hope you can manage without us. Have fun!*

Martin & Suzanne

'Well, good for them,' said Laura, meaning it. 'Pity about the weather, though.' There were dark clouds overhead and a wind was blowing up.

Rosemary shivered. 'We can't do much in the garden if

it rains hard,' she said. 'We'll just ruin the ground.'

'We can't do much of *anything* if it rains,' Laura said. 'Where would we go?'

'We'll have to huddle in the barn or somewhere until it stops.'

'Along with the prisoners, I suppose?'

Rosemary smiled uncertainly. 'Maybe not,' she said. 'That barn isn't very big.'

Mr Coutts had evidently shared their worries. When he arrived, jumping down from the driving seat of the minibus, he hurried to reassure them. 'I've been listening to the weather forecast,' he announced. 'It won't be very much. All over by eleven, they say.'

As if in mockery, the skies opened almost before he'd finished speaking. The prisoners stayed where they were in the bus, and Laura and Rosemary, without even thinking, scrambled in with them. 'Oh, dear,' said Waldo. 'This isn't very nice, is it?'

'Poor Martin,' groaned Laura. 'What a day to choose for a picnic.'

Ten minutes later, Rosemary had grown restless. 'This is a waste of time,' she announced. 'I'm going into the village. I've got a little errand to do. Laura, you'd better stay here and get the men organised if the rain stops.'

Katy and Chris Stevens set off at ten on their mission to retrieve their children. Katy's parents lived almost two hours away, and the plan was for them all to have lunch together before returning home. 'We must be back by four,' Chris insisted. 'I've got work to do. That garden woman's coming. The King's last mistress.'

Katy giggled. 'Which King are we talking about?'

Chris shook his head. 'Can't remember,' he admitted. 'A

French one, I think. There's no encouragement from the editor to aim for historical accuracy.'

'What time did she say she'd come?'

'Half five, six, something like that.'

Katy gave him a mock slap on his chest. 'The worst possible time, in other words. Won't you ever learn? I'll be left getting the kids' supper, putting Bonnie to bed, and the rest of it.'

'It's still half-term,' he reminded her. 'Let them stay up. We can all eat together when the mistress has gone. I'll do a Welcome Home chilli – they all like that.'

'Look at this weather,' said Katy. 'It's bucketing down. My mother's going to be driven crazy by three kids cooped up inside all morning.'

'If you ask me, your mother needs to understand about taking the rough with the smooth. She gets almost a week of quality time with her beloved grandchildren – something she's been angling for ever since Bonnie was out of nappies – and throws a wobbly over a few tears at bedtime. I have to say she's gone down in my estimation.'

'Well, don't say anything like that to her. She might never have them again if you do.'

The reunion between parents and children was more muted than expected. Grandpa had belatedly remembered the existence of a clockwork train set stored in boxes in the attic, and had devoted most of Thursday to laying it out in the spare bedroom and along the landing. All three children had been instantly captivated, shrieking with laughter when the locomotive left the rails, and building fanciful scenery to border the tracks. A hurried trip to town early on Friday had been made to purchase plasticine and glue, so that Bonnie could fashion a nation of Blobbies to interact with the railway. The arrival of Chris and Katy produced horrified protests that they couldn't possibly go home yet. Not for *days*, insisted Freddie.

But things eventually followed the ordained plan. The train set was packed away and promises made for a return visit in the summer holidays. Granny produced a mountain of golden chips and chicken legs, which quickly disappeared. Somehow or other, everybody was happy and smiling as the Volvo full of the Stevens family headed back to Lyvedon only half an hour later than planned.

George Hamilton Teed was in the office, as was his habit on Fridays. He began early and finished late, scanning websites for unusual local events and answering his mail. Local people knew he could always be found there and would phone or visit with items of news. The rain made little difference to him; if anything, it was rather welcome. It made him feel cosy and complacent, sitting indoors and watching the sodden passers-by in the street outside.

He had only been there for five minutes when he had a visitor. With some excitement he recognised the woman who had made a fool of herself at the inquest. She, in fact, had been on his list of people to try to speak to that day, in the faint hope of some kind of follow up to his story about the inquest. Her face was sure to be on the front page of next week's *Observer* and he liked to think it was not an unflattering image.

She ran in, dripping from the downpour. 'Morning,' she said cheerily. 'Have you got a few minutes?'

He spread his hands in welcome. 'Certainly,' he smiled. 'What can I do for you?'

'Archives,' she said. 'I assume you keep them?'

He raised his eyebrows and indicated a row of filing cabinets. 'Of course.'

'Well, what I am specifically looking for is a picture of Jim Frazer,' she said.

His eyebrows shot up. 'May I ask why?'

'You were at the inquest,' she said. 'You heard me tell the Coroner that I saw the man who jumped in the river in Long Horton the next day.'

'Yes, and then you admitted you were probably mistaken.'

'So – the quickest way to resolve it is to find a picture of Jim and check that it really was him I saw on Monday. Simple.' She smiled at him.

'And if it isn't? Him, I mean.'

'Then something fishy has been going on.'

Teed snorted. 'Not very likely,' he said. 'We don't have violent deaths in Lyvedon.'

'I think that's what everybody says. So – do you have a photo of Jim?'

'Oh, well, I suppose you can see it. I don't think it'll help you much, though.' He began to rummage through the untidy papers on his desk. 'I asked Martin for it, earlier in the week. I scanned it and imported it into the article in this week's paper. You could have seen it yesterday if you'd bought a copy. Of course, the real story will be next week.' He went on talking as he flicked through the chaos. 'Goodness me, I really ought to do a bit of tidying. I can never understand how it gets like this so quickly. It's not even as if I was here every day.'

Rosemary turned her attention to the rest of his office, which seemed well equipped and surprisingly spacious. Outside, the rain cascaded onto the cobbles of the courtyard. The offices opposite looked deserted.

'Here it is!' He held up a black and white photograph, which had been enlarged to half-plate size. 'Martin asked me to keep it safe, so I put it in an envelope. No wonder I couldn't find it.'

Rosemary took it carefully by the edges and stared at the two faces. They were boys, aged about twelve, standing in a garden, either side of a piece of stonework. Teed watched her face, as she blinked and then stared for several more seconds. 'Martin and Jim – right?' she said. 'Which is which?'

'The one on the left is Martin. Can't you recognise him?'

'Not really,' she admitted. 'So this must be Jim.'

The boy's face had a patch of shadow across it, further impeding any attempt at recognition. It might have been the man she'd seen and it just as easily might not. 'Haven't you got anything more recent?' she asked.

'Sorry. Obviously it would have been useful for the paper, but Martin says there's nothing. Jim might have been a major part of the Lyvedon scene, but he never had his picture taken. According to Martin he was one of those people who hated the camera. I've been right through the files. Apparently he never even had a passport, or a driving licence.'

'He sounds like a total hermit,' said Rosemary irritably. 'And rather a nuisance.'

'A nuisance, yes. But not exactly a hermit.' Teed sucked his teeth thoughtfully. 'Jim Frazer had a good heart, you know. He felt passionately about Lyvedon and Abbotslea. He wanted it to be a good place. Good in the sense of virtuous. He saw himself as the conscience of the village, if you like.' He smiled ruefully. 'And you know – it worked. Everybody wanted to be in Jim's good books. They craved his good opinion. Isn't that strange?'

'But those letters!' Rosemary burst out. 'He says such

terrible things about everybody. And you must have read them all. They were sent to you. Even if a quarter of them are true – well!' She ran out of words. 'People must have been *terrified* of him.'

'Nervous, anyway,' Teed nodded, giving her a quizzical look. 'You've seen the letters then, have you? Jim made copies, I suppose.' He went to one of the filing cabinets and pulled open the bottom drawer. 'I thought I was the only person in possession of them.' He dragged out a bulging folder and flipped it open. 'They go back nearly twenty years,' he said.

'You kept all of them? Even the ones you didn't print in the paper?'

'Habit,' he said. 'I never throw anything away. I imagine the copies you've seen are only the more recent ones. I understood from Jim that he hadn't known about carbon paper until about ten years ago.' He crinkled his eyebrows at her like a schoolmaster questioning an errant pupil. 'Or have I got that wrong?'

Rosemary flushed and evaded his gaze. 'Martin gave me the key to Jim's cottage,' she said uncomfortably. 'He said I could look at anything I found.'

'And if I phone him and check that, he'll confirm it, will he?'

She bristled. 'Of course he will. Besides – you can't phone him because he's gone out for the day.'

He shrugged. 'Never mind. But you do have to understand the way things work here. It isn't really how it seems. We all understood that. In a way Jim was a kind of deranged chronicler, I suppose. He invented a great deal, but he also captured something that was real, just below the surface. I can't explain it, but at heart we were all very fond of poor old Jim.'

'So, do *you* believe he killed himself deliberately?'

Teed cocked his head. 'Not for me to say,' he smiled. 'I'm just here to report the facts.'

'And Martin,' Rosemary said.

'What about him?'

'It sounds as if Jim was a big embarrassment to him, hanging around and annoying Suzanne. That cottage – it's a disgrace. It's as if Jim was deliberately trying to highlight the differences between himself and his cousin.'

Hamilton Teed narrowed his eyes and extended an aggressive forefinger, just short of prodding her in the chest. 'Now listen to me,' he said. 'This village owes everything to Martin Frazer. He works tirelessly to keep things the way they are, fending off developers and new roads and waste incinerators. It's only thanks to Martin that the local school is still there, and the ambulance station. He's a one-man campaigner for Lyvedon and the whole community loves him. If they could hear you making the slightest accusation against him, they'd probably lynch you. So be careful what you say. As for Jim – well, I've already done my best to explain how it was with him. Now – leave well alone, and get back to your gardening.'

'Well, thanks anyway,' said Rosemary, very subdued by this outburst.

She looked out at the driving rain, and Teed felt a moment's concern. But then he noticed she was wearing good waterproof boots and had an efficient-looking mackintosh. She'd be all right.

'It's set in for the day,' he observed, peering up at the sky. 'You can always tell.'

'Oh, I don't think so,' she disagreed. 'Mr Coutts says it'll be gone by eleven.'

'Then Mr Coutts is wrong,' said George Hamilton Teed.

Something in his voice made Rosemary pause. 'Do you know him?'

'Went to school with him, as a matter of fact. That's if we mean Cyril Coutts, presently working as a prison officer at Bleakmoor.'

'That's him. So he's another one who grew up around here, is he?'

'Lyvedon gets under a person's skin,' he told her. 'Even the ones who leave generally come back again after a few years. Like Miss Evans, for example.'

Rosemary could delay no longer. 'Well – here goes,' she said, and launched herself into the downpour.

When his visitor was out of sight, Teed quickly flipped through his rotary phone directory, until he found the Fs. 'Mobile – what's his mobile number?' he muttered. 'Ah!' He keyed the digits, and waited. If Martin was on the road, he wouldn't reply, but the thing was obviously switched on, at least.

A voice answered. 'Martin? Sorry to trouble you, it's GH here. I thought I should just check with you – that Boxer woman has just been here. It's plain that she's been reading the carbon copies of Jim's letters, and I thought it might be wise to shred the top copies. Then you can deal with the carbons yourself.'

Martin answered succinctly.

'Right. I'll get straight onto it,' Teed replied. 'Is it raining where you are?… Oh, dear. You poor things. Maybe you can find a coffee shop or something.'

The answer caused him to laugh sympathetically, before he put the phone down.

Shredding was always a pleasing activity. He found it soothing and oddly cleansing. The results were bagged up and given to a local farm for animal bedding. By twos and threes, all Jim Frazer's letters disappeared. 'Good riddance!' murmured George Hamilton Teed.

Next he turned his attention back to the mess on his desk. He had picked up a handful of mail from the doormat when he'd first arrived and still hadn't had a chance to open it.

It was with shocked disbelief that he recognised one of Jim's long white envelopes, and the lettering from the antiquated typewriter. How could that be, he asked himself, feeling icy ripples run through his veins. Was it possible that the Boxer woman was right after all, and Martin had wrongly identified the body of his cousin?

Shakily he opened the letter. As always it was dated, and laid out in the strict style taught in all good primary schools in days gone by. The date, he worked out with the help of his calendar, was a full week ago. If Jim had posted it in the little box on Friday evening, it would not have been collected until Tuesday. And since it only carried a second class stamp, it probably wouldn't have been delivered until yesterday, Thursday. So there was nothing sinister about it after all. Teed breathed a deep steadying breath and began to read.

After some deep thought he was still unsure as to what he ought to do. Other tasks had occupied him, and he had gone out for a quick takeaway lunch of a pork pie and soft drink. He was waiting, he realised, for Martin Frazer to get home. It was not something he wanted to talk about on a crackly mobile with children and dogs causing havoc. He needed to see his friend in person.

Finally, he called the Abbotslea number. 'Martin,' he said, in a sombre voice, 'there's something you should know. I've just had another letter from your cousin Jim, posted before he died. It concerns an affair that could affect the whole village, and I think you ought to come over as soon as you can and see it.'

The weather proved Mr Teed right and Mr Coutts wrong. By twelve, there was no sign at all of it relenting. Laura and Rosemary sent the prisoners away, having arranged for them to come back next morning if it was dry.

They were not surprised to see the Frazer family returning in the early afternoon, having abandoned their plans. Suzanne jumped out first and ran into the house, followed by the dogs. Martin and the boys began to unload the car, stopping to talk to the very wet gardeners who approached them.

'Gosh, you poor things,' said Laura. 'What a swizz.'

'A swizz,' Timmy echoed delightedly. 'Yes, it was a swizz. We wanted to go to the island anyway, but Mum wouldn't let us. She's in a bad mood now.'

'Who can blame her?' said Laura.

'You look soaked,' Martin noticed with concern. 'I suppose there isn't really anywhere you can get some shelter. I never thought of that.'

'Well, we could have gone into your garage,' said Laura. 'But we decided there were a few things we could get on with, and we won't melt.'

'You must come into the house and get dry. You'll want to change your clothes and all that. Gosh, what a fiasco!'

Toby and Timmy were making no effort to keep themselves dry, seeming to relish the deluge. 'Even the dogs have got more sense than you two,' said their father. 'Get along into the house.'

The boys were in no hurry to obey, but eventually everybody was gathered in the hall, dripping onto the marble floor. Suzanne appeared from the kitchen, looking as if she'd had enough for one day.

'We sent the prisoners home,' Laura told Martin. 'I hope that's OK?'

Martin nodded absently. 'We had such plans,' he mourned, and explained about the island. 'But the only way to get there is in an open dinghy, and it was absolutely pouring.'

'We'd have filled up with water and capsized,' shouted Timmy, still much too exuberant for the situation.

'Shut up, Tim,' said Suzanne. 'I can't imagine what you're so happy about.'

'He likes water,' said Martin. 'He's some sort of throwback to our fishy ancestors.'

Laura and Rosemary laughed at this, but Suzanne didn't.

Feeling very much in the way, Laura suggested they go to the tent and test its water-repellent qualities. 'The man did say it was showerproof,' she said. 'And if it isn't, we'll have to salvage the things inside and get them somewhere dry.'

Rosemary followed her with alacrity. The atmosphere inside Abbotslea was fractious, thanks to the disappointing change of plan. 'If it stops, of course we'll get straight back to work,' Laura assured Martin.

They gazed optimistically at the sky for a few seconds, once they'd left the house. 'It could be a little bit lighter over there,' said Rosemary. 'Don't you think?'

Laura pursed her lips. 'A *very* little bit,' she conceded.

The tent was remarkably dry inside, greatly to their relief. 'The trick is not to touch the sides or top,' said Laura. 'That lets the water in.'

'Really?' Rosemary was sceptical. 'Is that what you learned in the Brownies?'

Laura nodded.

'Maybe they've improved the material they use since then,' said Rosemary, poking one corner of the tent with a gentle finger. 'Look – nothing happens.'

They settled down to wait for the rain to stop. Rosemary went back to the folder containing the copies of Jim's letters, and Laura picked up her paperback novel. Once or twice Rosemary would read out part of a letter, but on the whole she judged most of them to be disappointingly dull. 'I think I've seen the best of them,' she said, putting them aside, with only a handful still unread.

Laura recognised the signs, and set her book aside. 'You haven't told me what happened at the newspaper office this morning,' she invited. 'I assume nothing very exciting?'

Rosemary shrugged and recounted how Teed had produced the old picture. 'He said Jim was one of those people who can't abide having their photo taken. He talked quite a lot about him, actually. Said everybody felt quite fond of him, in spite of the things he said about them. Then, when I cast aspersions on Martin, he got really annoyed with me. Gave me a lecture about how Martin's the protector of the whole village.'

'Exactly what aspersions did you cast?'

'I don't think it was anything specific. But you can't even *hint* at his being less than perfect around here.'

'Don't they realise how out of step they are?' Laura wondered. 'It's positively feudal, the way they go on.'

'I know. But it works well enough. And they don't have to put up with it if they don't like it.'

'We haven't asked Martin and Suzanne yet if they've got a photo of Jim,' Laura reminded her. 'They're the obvious people to have one.'

Rosemary shuddered. 'If I ask them, they'll say I'm accusing Martin of foul play or something and get angry again.'

Laura gave this some thought. 'They shouldn't really be angry if they want us to get at the truth. If Martin's got nothing to hide, he ought to be on the same side as us. I think we should ask him.'

'Feel free,' said Rosemary. 'After all, it's me he's angry with, not you.'

Laura almost forgot her appointment with Chris Stevens for late that afternoon. 'I wonder if he'd mind if I was early?' she said. 'It would be better than slopping about here doing nothing.'

'He'll probably be delighted,' Rosemary said.

Laura changed into a smart top and inserted a pair of dangly ear-rings for the occasion. 'Fancy me being on the cover of a book!' she crowed.

'People are going to stop you in the street,' Rosemary teased. 'What did you say the book was called?'

'I can't remember. Something romantic and dashing. He seems very artistic, don't you think?'

'Oh, yes,' affirmed Rosemary.

Laura was suddenly nervous. 'He said I had the ideal face and figure. You don't think – I mean—' She shuddered, half alarmed, half excited.

'Who knows?' teased Rosemary.

'Well, I'd better go. Are you sure I look all right?' Laura asked, for the third time.

'You look the perfect artist's model,' Rosemary assured her.

Laura suddenly started to declaim:

'While Titian was mixing rose madder
His model reclined on a ladder.
Her position to Titian
Suggested coition,
So he ran up the ladder and 'ad 'er.

'That must be why I'm feeling wimbly about it. All those associations with posing for an artist.'

'Laura, for heaven's sake. It's a book cover, not a centrefold. And he's a happily married man with a gaggle of small children. They'll probably be watching the whole procedure. Go, will you.'

Laura braced herself. 'Right. Yes – I'm off. Will you be OK?'

Rosemary listened to the rain pattering on the top of the tent. 'I'll be fine, but you're going to get wet. You'll take the wagon, of course?'

'If it hasn't been washed away. But how are we going to get the campfire going?'

'We're not,' said Rosemary. 'Obviously. Listen – when you're finished, come back for me and we'll go to that pub for a meal. The Lamb, isn't it? After all, we've done a full week here now. We owe ourselves a bit of a treat.'

'Good idea,' said Laura. 'See you later.'

Chapter Fourteen

Chris Stevens had a substantial sandwich in his hand when he answered the door to Laura. 'Sorry I'm a bit early,' she said.

'No problem,' he mumbled. 'I'm just having a bite to eat.' He waved the sandwich in unnecessary explanation.

'Don't mind me,' said Laura.

'You found us all right, then?'

'Can't really miss you. It's a lovely house.'

She had parked the Land Rover as close to the house as she could get, beside a rather muddy family car. The Stevens residence was not as old or as impressive as Abbotslea, but still a handsome edifice. 'Georgian?' she asked Chris.

'That's right. Like a lot of people around here, I inherited it. My family actually built it in 1804.'

'Heavens! And do you have a resentful cousin out there somewhere as well? Or a disinherited younger brother?'

Chris laughed. 'Actually, I *am* the younger brother. There are three ahead of me, but none of them wanted to stay in Lyvedon all their lives. We managed to reach an amicable compromise, at least for the time being.'

He led her through an untidy hallway, from which the loud voices of the children could be clearly heard, and down a corridor into a large light rectangular room. It was fitted out with a small platform in the middle, surrounded by lights and cameras mounted on tripods. Half the room seemed to have been transported from a travelling theatre, with coloured drapes, strange costumes, and a host of ever stranger objects. Laura could see a wicked-looking cudgel, as well as a scythe, a splendid old bicycle complete with basket fixed to the handlebars and a tigerskin. 'Oh, my!' she breathed. 'Aladdin's cave!'

'Tools of the trade,' he said. 'I pick them up at car boot sales mainly, or eBay. The bike was a mistake, though. I still haven't had an opportunity to use it and it takes up far too much space.'

Laura tried to imagine a novel for which the cover might suitably include a 1950s cycle. Something by Barbara Pym, perhaps.

'So, which props am I going to need?' she asked excitedly.

'I thought this,' he said, yanking at a length of crimson velvet. 'And this,' he added, rummaging in a pile that seemed to consist of dead animals. He produced a very bouffant wig with a lot of ringlets dangling from it. Laura winced. 'It looks a bit – um, *dusty*,' she objected.

Chris shook it, experimentally. 'No, it's OK,' he said. 'Try it on. There's a mirror down there, look.'

She followed his pointing finger, and found the mirror alongside a large pinboard covered with book jackets. 'Oh – are these all yours?' she asked.

'Of course,' he said. 'They're only my most recent ones. Can you recognise anybody?'

Laura peered closer. 'There's Gywnne,' she said, noticing a familiar face surrounded by wreaths of spring flowers. *'Floral Frolics,'* she read. 'Sounds a bit saucy.'

'Probably is,' he agreed.

Another cover caught her eye, near the bottom of the display. The book was entitled *Oktober* and showed a man's face in extreme close-up, eyes wide with alarm, hair standing on end. She found it oddly disturbing and looked away, finding something more appealing to comment on.

'Are these your children?' She pointed to an illustration of three youngsters piled in an awkward pyramid, all grinning maniacally. The lettering read *Julian's Jungle Gym*.

'I'm afraid so. That book never got published, for some politically incorrect reason. Mind you, it did have a few dodgy elements that I noticed when I flicked through it. I'm quite relieved my children haven't been associated with it. But it's a fine picture, even so.'

'Very fine,' Laura agreed. She was still looking at the faces of Chris's three children. 'Your little one – she's oriental, I see.'

'That's right. Didn't we tell you? We adopted her in China, two and a half years ago. She's the light of all our lives. An absolute darling. You must meet her when we've finished.'

'So you often use local people as models,' she said, with another look at the covers. 'What about Jim Frazer?'

Chris snorted. 'I'm afraid he's one person I would never have used. Katy would have had good reason to veto such an idea if I'd ever been daft enough to raise it.'

Mindful of the letters Rosemary had read to her, concerning Katy and her access to hospital drugs, as well as accusations about Bonnie, Laura thought she could understand.

She looked around, taking in more of the actual building they were in. 'Was this a stable or something?' The walls were of unplastered brick, with the timbers showing between them. 'It makes a brilliant studio.'

'Well guessed,' he approved. 'It was originally separate from the house, but we had them connected up. It all works pretty well.'

Laura turned her attention to the wig, which was an uncomfortably tight fit. The upper part, which was supposed to stand up in a sort of pompadour effect, kept flopping sideways. 'Wait a mo,' said Chris, and started rooting through a box of rattly items. He produced a pair of knitting needles. 'Let's see if these work.'

Five minutes later she was on the platform, draped in velvet, with a backdrop suggesting wild moorland and rough weather. Chris pointed the camera at her and told her to look surprised.

'Eyebrows raised, mouth half open,' he ordered. Laura did her best to comply. 'No, no, you trollop,' he snapped, 'that's rubbish.'

Her instant reaction was of outrage at being addressed so rudely. Before she knew it, the flash bulbs were popping, shocking her into an even more startled expression.

'Great!' Chris enthused. 'Much better.' He took a few more shots, moving a little to one side. Then he lowered the camera and took a few more.

It was over in no time, and he helped her to get back to normal. Still bemused by the flashes and the speed of it all, Laura let herself be unwrapped and dewigged. 'Now we'd better do the paperwork,' he said.

He went to a large oak kneehole desk in the far corner of the studio and took a hand-written ledger out of a desk drawer. In it he carefully noted name, book title and how much his sitter had been paid. Laura watched the screensaver on the computer sitting on the desk. It seemed to be composed of several book jacket illustrations. As they floated quickly across the screen, Laura glimpsed again the *Oktober* cover, with the face that now looked uncomfortably familiar.

'Who is that man?' she asked Chris.

He gave the cover a brief glance. 'Can't remember,' he said, with a forced carelessness that Laura found strange.

But before she think any more of it, Chris spoke. 'Will a cheque be all right?'

She blinked. 'I didn't realise you were going to *pay* me,' she gasped.

'Oh yes. And I'm afraid you have to sign a disclaimer, giving me permission to use your likeness in any way I see fit.' He held out a printed page, which Laura skimmed quickly before signing it.

'I don't suppose you'll use it for anything too dreadful,' she laughed.

'Trust me,' he beamed at her, before writing a cheque for a sum considerably larger than she could ever have expected.

Then he said, 'I'll have to finish up in here now. Can you give me a minute? Go and get yourself a drink, why don't you? You might find Katy out there somewhere. Try the second door on the left.'

She followed Chris's instructions and found herself in a large well-equipped kitchen. There was no sign of Katy or the children. Not liking to make free with the kettle, she opted for fruit juice, if she could find some in the fridge.

There was something about the room that was making her uneasy. Trying to work out what it was, she thought again of the letter about drugs that Rosemary had read out to her the previous evening. Could there be any truth in it? If, as she and Rosemary were increasingly coming to suspect, Jim had been deliberately pushed into the river at some point over the weekend, were Chris and Katy immune from suspicion? The image of the great cudgel in Chris's studio floated before her eyes. Jim could have been bashed on the head first – the cause of death had, after all, been a head injury rather than drowning.

Katy had a responsible, well-paid job. If she were to be dismissed for theft of drugs, she would never work in a hospital again. Even if Jim's accusations were groundless, the taint might remain in people's minds, if they got to hear about it.

Laura resumed her search for some juice. She located the fridge and opened it. Inside, on two of the four shelves, was a mass of small plastic pots all containing clear liquid. It was a bizarre sight, and she could only stare at them until a voice came from only a few inches behind her.

'My remedies,' said Katy calmly.

'Oh! Yes, of course.' Laura had forgotten the remedies. 'Rosemary felt much better after taking the one you gave her.'

'I'm glad.'

'You really do make them yourself then? Where do you get the ingredients?' Perhaps this did, after all, connect with the hospital job. Perhaps Jim had had a point?

Katy smiled. 'I thought I'd already explained, the other day. The "ingredients" are minute. One drop would be more than enough for a thousand of these little pots. Ten thousand, even. It's diluted almost infinitely, you see.'

Laura frowned. 'I don't think I realised that.'

'The theory is, essentially, that the water *remembers* the active substance, without ever having to be physically mixed with it. The energy simply passes from pot to pot, in a process we still don't fully understand.'

Laura held up a hand. 'Katy,' she said firmly. 'You've got

a proper scientific medical qualification. You're a trained anaesthetist. It's not possible that you believe all this stuff.'

Katy's smile stiffened slightly. 'You said yourself that your friend was helped by the remedy I gave her.'

'She did seem better,' said Laura carefully. 'But perhaps she would have got better anyway. I think this is just a placebo.'

'You undervalue the power of suggestion,' said Katy.

'You don't believe it could make a person kill himself, do you?' Laura asked.

Katy hesitated. 'I doubt it,' she said. 'Unless the person was weak and vulnerable – and really needed to die.'

The words hung in the air, making Laura's heart pound. She wanted to argue and protest, but Katy's steady gaze quelled her. At last she managed to stammer a reply. 'I can't believe that,' she said.

Katy's deep brown eyes followed Laura's, their expression full of complexity. 'It doesn't really matter to me what you believe,' she said. 'I only judge by results.'

Laura struggled to muster her thoughts. 'I didn't mean to criticise,' she blurted. 'I'm genuinely interested. I get the feeling there's much more you could explain to me.'

Katy leaned towards her. 'It's all quite simple. You just have to think about what I've told you. The water remembers. Water retains a memory, like a kind of energy or imagining. Don't try to understand it, just let it be true.' Her voice was slow and rhythmic.

Laura felt the words bloom inside her head, resonating with power. With an effort she focused on normal things – the kitchen, her own foot, children's voices in a room close by. She thought about Rosemary and the events at Abbotslea. 'So – does the river remember that Jim drowned in it?' she asked. 'Would it know if he had not intended to kill himself?'

Katy's eyes narrowed. 'Don't mock,' she said. 'Whatever you think, this is not a subject for ridicule.'

'I'm sorry,' said Laura, glad to find the spell had been broken. Resisting Katy Stevens was not comfortable.

The Lamb was quiet when Rosemary and Laura arrived, but it began to fill up over the next quarter of an hour. The rain had finally stopped, but everywhere felt damp and chilly, with summer in sudden retreat. There was even a log fire burning in the bar, which felt rather excessive for the end of May.

After a day of inactivity, they were surprised at how hungry they felt – until they remembered they'd had virtually nothing for lunch. Having ordered substantial meals from Rob, the amiable landlord, they sat at a table some distance from the fire. Laura began to describe her visit to the Stevens, when Fern Evans appeared with the cutlery and condiments for their dinner.

'Oh, hello!' said Laura. 'I'd forgotten you worked here.'

Rosemary met the girl's eye. 'Am I forgiven?' she asked. 'You were awfully cross with me yesterday, after the inquest.'

Fern flushed. 'Well, I was worried for Martin, that's all. He doesn't deserve all that's going on just now.'

'You're obviously fond of him,' Laura said.

'He and my mum go back forever. He's always been a good friend to us. I often tell her she should have grabbed him before Suzanne did.'

'He told us your mum was the first girl he kissed,' said Rosemary.

'Yeah – he tells everybody that. I think she was ten at

the time. She used to play with him and Jim in the school holidays, right through their teens.' A sudden scowl darkened her face. 'That was before Jim turned into such a headcase.'

Laura and Rosemary waited, saying nothing.

'She really tried with him, you know. But he threw everything back in her face. She always made excuses for him, until I could have screamed. But before all that, they seem to have been just a happy bunch of kids.'

'And then she had you,' said Laura, wishing she had the courage to simply ask Fern outright for the whole story. All they'd learned so far was an ambiguous collection of hints and muddled facts.

Fern giggled. 'She did. She doesn't talk much about that time, but it doesn't sound as if I came as too big a shock.'

'She certainly comes over as a coper.'

'She's that all right. She wouldn't marry my father, anyway. Wanted to hang on to her independence. I don't blame her – she was only twenty. Who wants to be married at twenty?'

'Good question,' said Rosemary. 'So long as you don't miss having a dad around.'

Fern gave them a look of surprised superiority. 'Of course not,' she said. 'I mean – I still see him almost every week.'

Across the room someone waved for Fern's attention. 'Oops – better stop chatting,' she said, and moved quickly away.

Laura and Rosemary put their heads close together. 'So – who *is* her father?' Rosemary asked. 'Am I missing something?'

'It must be Martin, I suppose. But if that's right, wouldn't Jim have known? So why did he write that letter?'

'It was written when Fern was only three. Maybe it was a secret to begin with. Or something.' Rosemary shook her head in confusion.

'I don't suppose it matters, anyway,' sighed Laura.

'It might. Maybe Martin has managed to keep it from Suzanne, and was scared Jim would tell her.'

'That isn't very likely, given what good friends Suzanne and Gwynne are.'

'Besides – how on earth could it stay a secret?' Rosemary wondered. 'How could they keep it from everybody in the village?'

'Quite easily, I imagine,' said Laura. 'Isn't village life full of secrets like that?'

'So – maybe Martin *thinks* he's the father, but really he isn't. Jim finds out, and tells Martin. Then he threatens to tell the whole village, which might be very embarrassing. Especially for Fern.'

'You know what you're doing?' Laura suddenly realised.

'What?'

'You're searching for reasons why Martin might want to arrange for his cousin's death.'

Rosemary shook her head. 'No, I'm not. What a thing to say.'

Well it sounds as if you still think he's guilty of something.'

Rosemary glanced around the room. Nobody seemed to be able to hear their conversation. 'I can't help it,' she said. 'There are so many pointers. The chapel, for one. And Jim's simmering resentment. And his being such a nuisance to Suzanne all the time. Now Fern as well. It adds up to quite a case for the prosecution.'

'Except,' said Laura, 'we still can't be sure that Jim didn't simply drown himself, after all.'

Rosemary clutched her head. 'If only we could find a proper picture of him,' she wailed. 'That would clinch it, once and for all.'

'Sshh,' said Laura. Fern was approaching with two plates of food. 'Mixed grill and lasagne and chips,' she announced.

Laura took the grill eagerly. 'That looks fabulous,' she said.

Fern looked around the bar, as if expecting to see someone.

'Somebody missing?' asked Laura.

'Mr Teed. He's always here on a Friday at this time.'

'I saw him today,' said Rosemary. 'I think I annoyed him rather.'

'Oh?'

'More of the same, I'm afraid. He leapt to Martin's defence, the same as everyone does around here.'

'Because Lyvedon depends on Martin,' Fern said, her voice rising emphatically. 'Without him we'd be over-run with all the usual rubbish – supermarkets and new housing and all the rest of it.'

'So Mr Teed explained to me this morning,' said Rosemary.

Fern glanced around again, seeming to want reassurance that nobody was listening. 'Actually,' she began. 'I did want to talk to somebody about Jim, and the way he died. And there's really nobody…' she tailed off, looking uncertain.

'Go on,' Laura invited her.

Fern bent low over the table. 'It sounds awful, I know, but I know there was something between my mum and Jim, years ago, and now, since he died, she's been behaving strangely. Avoiding me, for a start. And every time anybody mentions Jim's name, she goes sort of – peculiar.

Her face seems to sag, and her eyes go all big.' She lowered her voice even further. 'What if he had some sort of hold over her? And she got to the point where she couldn't bear it, and—'

'And what?' Rosemary asked the girl directly. 'You don't think your mother arranged his death somehow?'

Fern went even paler. 'I've been trying my best *not* to think it,' she pleaded. 'I always thought she'd told me everything about her life here, since she was little. But that's just it, you see.' Her voice grew stronger and more urgent. 'They're all so *connected*. There's so much history.'

Laura put a hand on the girl's arm. 'Yes, there is,' she said. 'But I don't think you need worry too much about your mum. She really doesn't look like a criminal to me.'

Fern shook free impatiently, and glanced towards the kitchen, where she knew there was work waiting for her. 'You don't understand,' she went on. 'Jim would never have killed himself. Not while Mum was still here. He loved her, that's the thing. Adored her. He lit up when he saw her. And she felt nothing for him.'

'So…' Rosemary looked up at the girl. 'That sounds like rather a common motive for suicide to me.'

'No.' Fern shook her head violently. 'He didn't just love her. He wanted to *protect* her as well. He was convinced she needed him.'

Rosemary frowned her puzzlement. 'So why did he tell that story about the Lyvedon Trust? He must have known how angry it would make her.'

'Attention,' said Fern simply. 'He would do anything to gain her attention.'

Laura noticed Rob, the barman, waving crossly in Fern's direction. 'You're needed,' she said. 'Better go.'

The girl stood up straight, and nodded at her boss.

'Coming,' she said. Then she addressed Laura once more. 'It sounds muddled, I know,' she said. 'But I know for certain that Jim did not drown himself deliberately. I saw him last Friday evening, and he told me then that he had plans for Bank Holiday Monday. He had something he wanted to give Mum, and I was to be sure she was by the old bridge in the woods after Suzanne's lunch. Besides,' she flung over her shoulder, careless of who might hear her, 'there's no way a body could get all the way from Abbotslea to Westover in the river, in a single day.'

In the office of the *Lyvedon Observer*, George Hamilton Teed was boiling a kettle for a mug of tea. He had effectively finished for the day, and was already turning his thoughts to the lasagne he planned to make for himself that evening. Living alone, he found that life slipped into routines, whether you wanted it to or not. He would read his weekly magazines, do the crossword in the *Spectator* and watch the television news. All that after an hour or so at The Lamb, of course. Just time to quaff a reviving pint of Best after a hard day's work.

He heard the outer door of the office open and close, while he was still in his little kitchen area. Stepping sideways, he peered out to see who was visiting. 'Oh, it's you,' he said with a smile of welcome. 'What good timing. I'll make you some tea, shall I?'

The caller nodded. 'Thanks.'

The two mugs sat companionably on the worktop, waiting for the tea that would never be poured. As he switched off the kettle, and reached for a second teabag, George Hamilton Teed felt a strange swoosh of air close to his ear. Then something happened to his head. It didn't hurt, but there was a huge sound that obliterated the whole world. A sound of disintegration and terrible fatal damage. He never felt himself hit the ground, or saw his visitor walk calmly out of the office, pushing the murder weapon into a clear plastic bag, and then dropping it into another larger holdall.

Chapter Fifteen

The walk along the river bank, just as darkness was falling, felt like the end of a long and frustrating day. Laura had recounted every detail of her visit to the Stevens household, trying to give a balanced report of Katy's theories about water. 'That voice of hers,' she said. 'It's got such strength behind it. I'm sure she could make anybody do anything she liked. She even said as much.'

'She's a kind of hypnotist, do you think?'

'I'm not sure I'd quite say that...' Laura stopped and sniffed. 'Funny smell,' she remarked.

Rosemary took no notice. 'What if Katy managed to suggest to Jim that he kill himself? Would that count as murder, do you think? Undue influence, power of suggestion, is there anything about that in the law?'

'Not that I can recall. For a start, you'd never be able to prove it.'

Rosemary's nose twitched. 'Hey! That's burning!' she shouted.

They were less than a minute away from their campsite at a walking pace. Running they seemed to get there instantly. 'My God!' gasped Laura. 'The tent!'

A golden glow was emanating from inside the nylon sheeting. Rosemary dived instinctively towards it, with Laura behind her. The tent's door flap was closed, and as

Rosemary fumbled with it, the glow inside turned to a larger creature, making a roar as it climbed voraciously up the rear wall of Rosemary's sleeping area.

'Back!' urged Laura. 'It's got too much of a hold.'

'No,' Rosemary resisted her. 'Water. We have to get some water.' She grabbed the big plastic box that had contained their food and drink. Emptying the last few items onto the ground, she ran down to the river to fill it.

Laura went to help her, more from a need to be doing something than from any hope that they could douse the fire. The box when full of water was very awkward to carry. They scuttled sideways, each holding an end, and slopped nearly half the contents.

'Throw it over the top,' said Laura. 'We might save something that way.'

The water hissed as it met the flames, and dark smoke billowed from the growing hole at the back of the tent. For a moment it seemed hopeful, but then the fire monster leaped sideways and attacked Laura's sleeping area.

'Somebody's poured petrol over everything,' Laura said, in horror. 'I can smell it.' She pulled Rosemary back. 'We can't do anything more. It could turn into a real fireball.'

Her forebodings were not entirely realised, but the destruction was comprehensive, just the same.

'My *things*,' moaned Laura. 'My best dressing gown and three pairs of earrings.'

'My cord trousers and work boots,' chimed in Rosemary. 'And where are we going to *sleep*?'

'This is deliberate arson,' Laura said solemnly. 'Somebody did this on purpose.'

'But why on earth?' Rosemary clapped a hand over her

mouth. 'I know why,' she exclaimed. 'It's those copies of Jim's letter. Somebody wanted them destroyed – badly enough to burn everything we possess.'

Martin, Suzanne, boys and dogs were all assembled, staring helplessly at the small pile of smoking debris. 'Your boots might still be all right,' Martin said at last. 'I doubt if it had time to really work up much heat. You'll probably find your earrings as well,' he told Laura.

'But,' Laura looked abjectly at Suzanne. 'Where will we sleep?'

'The Lamb,' said Rosemary. 'They do accommodation. We'll stay there.'

Suzanne cleared her throat, as if there was smoke in it. 'Well,' she said. 'You *could* have our guest room, except—'

'No, no. We wouldn't dream of it,' said Laura emphatically. 'That's the last thing you need, two more people to cater for.'

'The Lamb is very comfortable, I understand,' said Martin, looking awkward. 'And it would save my poor long-suffering wife a pile of laundry if you stayed there.'

Even in the midst of such a crisis, Laura winced at this piece of insensitivity. Suzanne seemed to feel the same. She gave Martin a look that women had been giving their husbands for centuries. Helpless frustration threaded with suppressed fury came close to describing it.

'Then that's decided,' said Rosemary, who had evidently missed the momentary interchange. 'After all, we've only got another three or four days' work here, anyway. Another trip to Long Horton market on Tuesday, and a full day on Wednesday putting everything in, and then we'll just leave it to settle down for a few weeks.'

'What about the sundial?' asked Suzanne. 'I'm

beginning to think that's never going to be moved.' She lifted her chin at Martin as if to remind him that without her he'd be entirely useless.

'Tomorrow,' said Martin. 'We'll do it tomorrow.'

The Lamb was almost deserted when they arrived back in the bar, carrying their few remaining possessions. Suzanne had lent them some nightwear, and they had found their spongebags intact, having been tidily placed with the cooking pan and packets of food in a stout plastic box. The box had gone soft and misshapen, but the contents were undamaged.

Fern had gone home and the landlord was stacking the few glasses that had been used that evening into a dishwasher. When he heard them come in, he popped his head around the door of the kitchen. 'Oh, hello,' he said in surprise. 'Did you forget something?'

Laura explained why they'd returned. He suddenly became much more businesslike. 'Was it arson, do you think? Because if so, I'll have to file a report. I'm with the Specials, you see – if you know what that means.'

Laura considered him for a moment. 'I would never have guessed,' she said with excessive honesty. 'I used to be in the force myself. I like to think I can always spot a fellow officer.'

He grinned. 'I try to keep my two roles separate as much as possible,' he explained. Then he grew serious again. 'Could your tent have caught fire accidentally?'

'Absolutely not,' said Laura. 'I could smell petrol, quite distinctly.'

'And you didn't call the cops? You really should have done.'

Rosemary snorted. 'It was only a tent,' she said. 'And nobody was hurt.'

'But *why* would anybody do such a thing?' Rob demanded.

Laura was already regretting telling him about it. She was tired and cross and befuddled by the events of the evening. 'Can we talk about it in the morning?' she begged.

Rob looked dubious. 'You ought to log it with the police, if only for the insurance claim.'

'What insurance claim?' Laura said glumly.

Rob showed them to their room, and offered them a nightcap on the house. Gratefully they accepted, and then settled down for the night. Laura rolled experimentally from one side of the bed to the other. She stretched her arms and legs, and let her head sink into the spongy pillows. 'Bliss,' she murmured softly to herself. 'A real bed. It's an ill wind, as they say.' And she was asleep within seconds.

The prisoners arrived early on Saturday, eager to make up for the lost time the previous day. The sun was shining warmly, as if its shocking dereliction of duty on Friday had never happened. Steam rose gently from the damp ground. The water that had gathered in the new trenches in the garden rapidly disappeared. Laura and Rosemary presented themselves at eight-thirty, only to find Mr Coutts and his gang were ahead of them. 'They want to knock off early, if that's all right,' said the warder. 'There's a ping-pong tournament this evening, and two of them are involved.'

Nobody enquired as to which two, but Laura privately thought Rupert Waldo might lack the necessary killer instinct for competitive sport.

'First job on the list is the sundial,' said Rosemary. 'It's a big thing, and we have to move it from one of Martin's sheds to the middle of the garden.'

Martin himself turned up a few minutes later, followed by Jess and Cabbage. 'They'll have to keep out of the way,' said Laura. 'We might drop it on one of their paws.'

Martin nodded. 'They were bothering Suzanne, so I let them come with me. She's got a headache, poor love. She's still sorry about yesterday's wrecked plans. I've told her to stay in bed for a bit.'

Somehow the idea of the inexhaustible Suzanne spending a couple of extra hours in bed struck Laura as improbable. But even the most active people had off days, she supposed.

Moving the sundial turned out to be not unlike an SAS training exercise, where brawn, brains and sheer determination were all brought into play. Rosemary began by trying to issue instructions from a safe distance, only to find that they all ignored her. Huxton Rymer was evidently experienced in shifting large objects, and came in useful at the point when they had to manoeuvre it through the garden door with millimetres to spare. George Marsden Plummer was the brawn, lifting one end with relative ease. Laura insisted on taking a corner with Martin. 'We'd have done better to construct some sort of transport for it,' said Rosemary. 'What about trundling it on logs?'

'Up those steps?' scoffed Laura. 'I don't think so.' There was a short flight of three shallow steps to negotiate, which nobody was looking forward to.

It took them an hour, but they managed it, with a triumphant cheer when it finally sank into place. 'I hereby swear that it will never be moved again,' said Martin, hand on heart. 'It must have a core of solid lead, under that brickwork.'

'Quite likely,' said Rosemary. 'These things were really made to last.'

'Are we sure it's positioned properly, though?' Laura worried. 'I mean – what's the point of a sundial if the sun's shadow doesn't fall in the right place?'

Martin cut through the alarmed groans from the prisoners with a reassuring hand. 'It can be adjusted independently, look.' He showed them how the actual dial was attached with a few easily removed screws. 'I suggest we do it at exactly midday, assuming the sun's still shining then.'

'It will be,' said Mr Coutts, undeterred by his poor showing as a weather forecaster the previous day. 'A lovely day to be working outdoors, getting so much healthy exercise.' He was swiping his hands together as if he'd been working as hard as anybody. In reality, he had kept clear of actual physical involve-ment, joining Rosemary in verbal encouragement. 'Bad back, you see,' he'd defended himself. 'Besides, I'm not here as part of the workforce.'

Aware of mutinous glances, he went to the minibus and fetched a bag containing a large flask of coffee and some biscuits. 'Time for elevenses,' he announced. 'Then it's back to some serious digging.'

Martin had gone back to the house, but before he went, Laura observed a curious exchange between him and George Marsden Plummer. Thinking they were unobserved, at the further end of the garden, Martin discreetly handed George a roll of banknotes. Laura glimpsed the distinctive brown of a ten pound note before it disappeared rapidly into the prisoner's pocket. She was convinced there had been more than one in the bundle. What was Martin paying for so furtively, she wondered. Then she remembered George's reputation as an arsonist.

Martin left the workers alone, having done his duty by the sundial. The digging was focused on the upper end of the garden, where the chapel had been, and where most of the mysterious holes had been dug. Ten minutes into the work, Rupert Waldo let out a cry. 'Hey! I've found something,' he called.

Laura, Rosemary and the other prisoners all converged on the spot. Mr Coutts remained at his post by the door, but craned his neck to see what was happening. Rupert carefully dug around four sides of an object roughly a foot square. 'It's an unexploded bomb!' said Huxton Rymer in alarm. 'Watch out!'

'It's nothing of the sort,' said Rupert. 'But it is made of metal.'

'Treasure trove,' said George Marsden Plummer. 'Put there by an Elizabethan aristocrat. No – probably a bit later than that, during the Civil War. I bet they were all Royalists around here.'

Finally, Rupert extracted a tin box, with vestiges of coloured decoration still visible. 'A biscuit tin,' said Laura.

They opened it gingerly, elbowing each other to see what was inside. Laura was first to reach in and finger the contents. 'A toy robot. And a comic,' she said, lifting the *Beano*. 'And a Dinky car. And a page with writing on.' She looked up. 'It's a time capsule! Remember when we all did them, as children?'

George uttered a sound halfway between a chuckle and a groan. 'Oh, my word – yes. But I dug mine up again six months later because I wanted the aeroplane I'd buried.'

'Somebody must have been searching for it,' Rosemary said. 'That's what all those funny holes are. He'd have found it if he'd carried on just a bit longer, too. See how close he got!'

Laura read from the page in her hand. '*Friendship Pact. We the undersigned do solemnly declare this lifelong pact of*

*loyalty and fidelity and may he who breaks it or betrays the
other suffer dark days, disgrace and a horrible death. Signed
in their hearts blood this 13th October.*

Martin Frazer. James Anthony Frazer.'

She looked up, her face suddenly sad. 'Oh dear,' she
said.

'I suppose Jim made all the holes, then,' realised
Rosemary. 'He must have been looking for this, for some
reason.'

Laura nodded. 'He must have wanted to confront
Martin with it – to remind him of how close they once
were. Do you think?'

'Which means he thought Martin had broken or
betrayed the pact,' said Rosemary slowly.

Rosemary had been pursuing her own private thoughts
through most of the morning. As the men took charge of
the garden work, she lapsed into a reverie about the death of
Jim Frazer. The loss of the copies of the letters before she
had finished reading them struck her as a decisive piece of
proof that there was foul play afoot, with someone
desperately needing Jim's letters to be destroyed. There were
now only the original letters available to point suspicion at
those who had wanted Jim silenced. And she could not trust
George Hamilton Teed not to shred them at any moment.
She was going to have to stop him, she concluded.

'Laura, how do you fancy a little stroll down to the
village?' she suggested.

Laura lowered the handles of the wheelbarrow she was
pushing, and scanned the garden. 'Now?' she queried.

'They can get on without us for a bit. It's all quite
straightforward. And it *is* Saturday. We deserve a bit of a
break at the weekend.'

'All right then.' Laura pulled off her gardening gloves and looked down at herself. 'Do we have to change?'

'No, of course not. We can buy something for lunch while we're there and bring it back with us. And I thought I might see if Mr Teed's in his office.'

'I wouldn't think he works on a Saturday.'

'He might,' said Rosemary.

They walked through Lyvedon to the more modern end of the village, where there was a small food shop and a wonderful old-fashioned store selling everything from mousetraps and notepads to dishcloths and candles. It also had a table outside stacked with second-hand books. They separated, Rosemary to buy their lunch and Laura to browse through the books. 'I need something to read in the evenings,' she said. 'My other book got burnt.'

When Rosemary emerged with a bag of bread and sliced ham, Laura beckoned her excitedly. 'See this?' she said, waving a book in Rosemary's face. 'Does it remind you of anyone?'

Rosemary took the book and stared at the cover. '*Oktober*,' she read. 'Never heard of it.' Then she looked again. 'My God!' she breathed. 'It's him.' The face on the cover had been exagge-rated, the eyes wide with fear, and the person's hands held up on either side of the head, fingers splayed. But the features were clear enough. The crisp jawline and the strongly etched mouth were etched on Rosemary's memory. 'It's the man I saw fall into the river,' she said, one hand to her chest. 'And in the market.'

Laura took the book from her, and waved it in the air. 'I saw this picture at Chris Stevens' house. I thought then it was familiar. It's only just come to me who it is.' She opened the book at the second page. 'It was published only three years ago. Now all we need to do is get hold of Chris's ledger and see who this is.'

'Ledger?'

'Didn't I tell you? He writes every job down in a big book – name, date, fee, everything. We can just go and ask him right away.'

Rosemary shook her head slowly. 'No,' she said. 'What if he's involved somehow? We don't want to tell *anybody* about this until we've got more of the facts. They all stick together so tightly around here, it would be common knowledge by bedtime that we're still not satisfied that Jim committed suicide.'

'So what do we do?'

Rosemary shrugged. 'Search me.'

'We have to get a name for this man. It definitely isn't Jim Frazer, because Chris said he'd never used him as a model.' She looked at her friend. 'We're almost there,' she said solemnly. 'This is very close to proof that Jim was murdered.'

'Except we still don't know who that man is.'

'No,' agreed Laura.

'Well, somebody will have to go back to Chris's house and check in that ledger of his,' said Rosemary, fixing Laura with an appraising look.

'Somebody?' Laura pretended to look behind her for a likely person. 'Who?'

'Who do you think?'

Laura took a step back. 'You mean I have to sneak in without them seeing me and search through the ledger.'

'Exactly. You could go now.'

Laura shook her head. 'No, I couldn't. I'll go tomorrow morning. I need time to prepare a cover story for if I'm caught.'

* * *

Gwynne Evans saw the two women outside Harry's Hardware as she drove past on her way to Long Horton, but thought little of it. She had a long list of tasks for the day, including consulting with Martin about Jim's funeral and finding something to wear for the occasion, for Fern as well as herself.

Soon, she thought hopefully, things would be back to normal. The Elizabethan garden would be completed, Timmy and Toby would go back to school, and the first shock of Jim's death would fade. Her irritation with Hamilton Teed over the piece in the paper was already assuaged by his letter of explanation, and she intended to visit or phone him at some point to let him know he was forgiven. While she was in Long Horton, she would have to pop in to the Lyvedon Trust charity shop, which was run by a formidable woman named Marigold, and let her know that no suspicion about mishandling of funds lay at her door. Marigold had been the first to see the article, screaming at Gwynne down the phone that they would have to sue the paper for every penny it possessed.

And threaded through all these thoughts was the worry about Fern. Her daughter had been unusually quiet since Jim's inquest, snapping when spoken to and avoiding being in the house with her mother whenever she could. It was inevitable, Gwynne knew, that the girl would be shocked at a sudden death so close to home. Inevitable, too, that it would make her think about the whole Lyvedon community and her own place in it. Fern's parentage had never been an issue between them. Although her father was still so close by, with younger children to which he devoted almost all his attention, Fern had never seemed to feel hard done by. She was relaxed with the situation, probably because it had never occurred to her that other people might find it unusual, or suggest that she could have a legitimate grievance. Now that everybody was discussing Jim and the unfairness of his life compared to his brother's, Gwynne was afraid that Fern might start to feel some of the same resentment.

But there wasn't much she could do about it. Some things, she had accepted long ago, simply couldn't be changed.

Rosemary left Laura to walk back to Abbotslea with the bag of shopping while she took a quick detour into the office of the *Lyvedon Observer*. 'Won't be long,' she said. 'I just want to let him know that there are no longer any copies of Jim's letters. And I suppose there's no harm in telling him about the fire. He might be able to make a little story out of it.'

'He won't be there,' Laura said. 'I bet you.'

Rosemary shrugged. 'Well, I might as well try.'

The door to the office opened at her push, and she walked in, calling 'Mr Teed?' softly. There was no sign of him. Idly she glanced at his desk, which was quite a lot tidier than it had been the day before. In the middle, as if waiting for some sort of action, was a long white envelope. The address was typed, with the same slightly uneven lettering as the copies of Jim's letters. Rosemary knew the look of it all too well. Picking it up, she realised that it was empty, and there was no sign of its contents.

On the floor beside the desk sat an office shredding machine, with its red light winking. Rosemary went to it and peeped into the bin beneath the grooved top. It seemed to be full of strips of white paper with black lettering. Furtively, she reached in and took a few of them. There was no mistaking the old-fashioned typewriting.

'Jim's letters!' she breathed. 'He's gone and destroyed them.'

'Mr Teed?' she called again. Something made her move towards the small kitchen and toilet area behind the main room. 'Hello?' she said. 'Are you there?'

The day was mild, so the sound of a large fly buzzing about did not surprise her. Glancing into the kitchen, at first all she saw was two china mugs sitting side by side on the worktop. There was a great stillness, except for the fly.

Then she took a step forward, and her foot nudged something.

It was some seconds before she identified just what it was. Out of context, a man's leg, stiff with rigor mortis, lying on a kitchen floor, was not easily understood. The mental picture of a whole body, lying face down, hands outspread, seemed to take an age to come into proper focus.

'Mr Teed?' she whispered. 'Hello, Mr Teed?'

It was foolish, she knew. He couldn't hear her. He was never going to hear anything again. The pity of it overwhelmed her. Who, she asked herself furiously, would do such a thing to a man so inoffensive?

Jerkily, she backed out of the little room and into the office. What were you supposed to do, she wondered confusedly? He was beyond help, but somebody had to come and remove him. Somebody had to keep the flies away and make him decent and dignified.

And somebody had to catch and punish the wicked person who had done this deed.

Chapter Sixteen

Laura ate her bread and ham in the garden with the prisoners, having grown tired of waiting for Rosemary after fifteen minutes. She must have found Teed and got chatting to him, she supposed. The conversation in the garden drifted aimlessly until Laura had the idea that some of the stone from the demolished chapel could come in useful as a surround for the sundial.

'Where did you say the stone was, exactly?' she asked George.

He did his best to explain. 'But we weren't allowed to go there ourselves,' he added. 'It can't be too hard to find, even if Martin did try to hide it.'

'Hide it?' she repeated. 'You make it sound like a guilty secret.'

Rupert Waldo just smiled and shrugged. 'Not for us to comment,' he said.

Laura tried to remember what Jim Frazer's undelivered letter had said about the chapel. 'Why didn't Martin just apply for permission to demolish it?' she asked, not expecting an answer.

'Because they'd never let him, that's why,' said George, with an air of finally sharing a worrying secret. 'Something like that has all kinds of preservation orders and so forth slapped on it, if anybody threatens to demolish it. No – I regret to say our Mr Frazer did it on the sly, hoping everybody would just forget about it.'

Waldo's eyes widened. 'You mean you think Martin's broken the law?'

'Must have done,' nodded George. 'Can't see it being any other way. Be a hefty fine if they catch him, and a loss of face amongst his serfs.'

'Serfs!' scoffed Laura. 'That's a bit much, isn't it.'

'Open your eyes, love. What would *you* call it? That Miss Evans, for a start. Consults him about every little thing that happens. We heard her one day last week. *Do you think we might let Mrs Hooper open up her fireplace again? Harold Minton's keen to build a new wall at the bottom of his garden.* It all gets put up for His Majesty's permission. And as I know for a fact, he's only a junior barrister. What's it to do with him?'

Laura rubbed her nose. 'I see what you mean,' she said. 'But they all think it's a good thing that he watches over them and keeps the place the way they like it.'

'Well my word for that is Feudal with a capital F.'

'Which must have been annoying for his cousin Jim,' suggested Rupert. 'Couldn't take it any longer, I suppose. Poor bloke, watching his cousin get all the power and glory while he lives like a vagrant.'

'It was not like that *at all*,' came a very angry voice from the other side of the garden wall. Laura realised they kept forgetting the way sound could easily cross the apparently solid brick barrier. Martin pushed his way in past Mr Coutts at his usual post, his face rigid with fury.

'Jim *chose* to live that way. He was ill, don't you understand? He couldn't take a proper place in the community. He never held down a job, or even passed his driving test. It started when he was seventeen and was a terrible family tragedy. All this ignorant gossip is completely wrong, and I'm very disappointed in you, Laura, for encouraging it.'

Laura's jaw dropped in outrage. She spluttered inarticulately. Before she could utter a word in her own defence, Martin had swept out again.

'Well, get *him*,' muttered Rupert.

Laura took a deep breath. 'And how are we going to show him the time capsule after that?' she wondered.

Rosemary had to answer a lot of questions when Constable Stuart and a more senior officer arrived at the premises of the *Observer*. When she had last seen Mr Teed alive, why she was there, who she had seen. Then the police doctor put in an appearance and from his muttered comments Rosemary man-aged to gather that the man had been dead since the previous day. 'Probably sometime yesterday afternoon,' she heard.

She agreed that she could be found either at Abbotslea or The Lamb at any time over the coming few days, and was permitted to leave. Constable Stuart gave her a critical scrutiny. 'Will you be all right?' he asked.

'I think so,' Rosemary said limply. 'I do feel rather wobbly. Not surprising, I suppose, after last week.'

The Inspector accompanying Stuart looked up from his examination of the contents of Mr Teed's office. 'Last week?' he repeated.

'Well, it was *this* week, strictly speaking, I suppose. It seems much longer ago than that. You must know about it. On Monday I witnessed a man fall into the river, and on Tuesday a body was found, downstream. Constable Stuart was there – he can tell you about it.' She had been slow to acknowledge to herself that the unambiguous murder of

Mr Teed had confirmed many of her suspicions about the death of Jim Frazer. *More* than confirmed most of them. She wanted to explain it all to the police, but could not find the words or the energy.

'Oh, yes. James Frazer,' said the Inspector, somewhat carelessly. 'Suicide.'

'You might find that needs re-examining,' said Rosemary weakly. 'But for now I'm going back to my garden, if that's all right.'

She walked steadily along the High Street and up the quiet stretch of road to Abbotslea. Poor Mr Teed, she thought. What secret had he been keeping that made somebody kill him? And was it a secret that she, Rosemary, also knew from her reading of Jim's letters? If so, she suddenly realised, *she* might be next on the killer's list.

Glancing around nervously, she quickened her pace. There was a long avenue of thick rhododendrons before she came in sight of the house. Anybody might be lurking there, ready to jump out at her. By the time she got to the garden her heart was racing and she was quite out of breath.

The prisoners were highly excited at the news. A babble of speculation arose, as they compared the Lyvedon events with numerous anecdotes they had gleaned from fellow inmates, and avid reading of thrillers from the prison library. Laura left them to it, and went to the far end of the garden with Rosemary.

'Are you all right?' she asked, with real concern. Her friend was pale and shaking slightly.

'It was pretty awful,' she admitted. 'That poor man. I can't think that he ever did anybody any harm. But I pulled myself together quite well, at first. Then my imagination started up and I thought I might be the next victim. I mean

– it's got to have something to do with Jim, and the things he knew about everybody, don't you think?'

'Because Teed's got the letters on file,' nodded Laura. 'That makes sense.'

'Except he's shredded them all,' said Rosemary, going on to explain her findings in the newspaper office.

'Oh dear,' said Laura. 'So there's no hard evidence now existing as to what Jim wrote about people.'

'More important than that,' Rosemary remembered, 'there was another letter from Jim.'

'From where?' demanded Laura. 'Beyond the grave?'

'No, no. From that little postbox at the end of the drive. Fern saw him posting something last Friday, remember? They only empty it twice a week. I saw the envelope on his desk, but the letter wasn't there. It must have said something incriminating. I think he phoned the person to warn them about it, and that signed his own death warrant.'

'Yes, but *who*?'

Rosemary glanced around. Martin Frazer was standing in the doorway of the garden, his fury of an hour ago all forgotten, to be replaced with shocked confusion. 'I'll tell you later,' Rosemary whispered.

Martin was obviously dismissing the prisoners for the day. They gathered up their few bits and pieces and headed for the minibus. Then, without even looking at Laura or Rosemary, Martin walked away.

'Do you get the feeling that things are coming to a head?' Laura said. 'I can smell it in the air.'

Rosemary shivered. 'I don't know,' she said. 'All I can think of just now is that I'm very glad we don't have to spend the night in that tent. Not with a double murderer on the prowl.'

Laura rolled her eyes. 'Not half as glad as I am,' she confessed. 'I hate to admit it, but I never *ever* want to sleep in a tent again as long as I live.'

'Laura!' Rosemary stared at her in amazement. 'I thought you liked it.'

'Well, I didn't,' said Laura, 'and that's the honest truth.'

They spent a few minutes assessing the progress on the garden. Four symmetrical new beds had been created, meeting at the sundial in the middle. Since its repositioning, the effect had been transformed into that of a unified whole, the eye drawn to the ornate stone artefact, and then out to the corners, taking in the colourful displays in the beds. Although these still needed considerable embellishment, the basic design was complete. No obvious colour scheme had been imposed, but Rosemary had selected a predominance of pinks and reds, avoiding blue entirely. 'I could be wrong,' she said, 'but I just don't see blue as an Elizabethan colour.'

'Lavender?' Laura queried. 'Wasn't that a big favourite?'

'I'll find one that's as purple as possible,' Rosemary decided. 'It'll pick up the reds, then. It's magic how that happens, if you get the right colours in conjunction.'

The plants were a long way from their final glory, still recovering from being moved. There were many empty gaps and not yet any of the small hedges that would eventually mark the edges of the beds. 'It's going to be gorgeous,' said Laura. 'A triumph.'

'Just give it time,' agreed Rosemary, feeling, as always, much better after a soothing spell in a garden.

They left the garden, and started walking towards the Land Rover with no clear object in mind. Toby and Timmy were sitting beside the river halfway down the drive, throwing sticks into the water.

'I wonder if you ought to try going to the Stevenses now,' said Rosemary.

'Definitely not.'

'Why?'

'Well – for all we know, they're related to Mr Teed or something. And the police might be there.'

Rosemary shook her head. 'But everything's even more urgent now. We know there's definitely been one murder, and that makes it a lot more likely that Jim was murdered as well. The obvious suspect is the mystery man I saw on Monday morning, and again in the market on Tuesday. We *must* find out who he is.'

'Yes, we will,' Laura assured her. 'But not until tomorrow.'

Rosemary twisted her hands together impatiently. 'It's hard to see why the mystery man would murder Mr Teed, though. I mean – what would be the reason?'

'Only that Teed had somehow discovered what he'd done, I suppose.'

Then Rosemary had a thought. 'Listen,' she said, glancing around furtively, 'I need to tell you something else.'

But the chance had disappeared. Suzanne was coming towards them, looking as if she had something to say. They waited for her to reach them, their expressions politely receptive.

'I just wanted to ask if you were comfortable at The Lamb,' she said. 'I feel very bad not having you here – but I'm sure you understand.'

'Of course we do,' said Laura. 'Rob's been wonderful. The food's good, too.'

'We're sorry we've disrupted you so much as it is,' said Rosemary. 'It's turned out to be rather bad timing, hasn't it?'

Suzanne looked as if she was unsure what was meant. A puzzled frown creased her brow. 'Timing?' she repeated.

'You know – with Jim and poor Mr Teed and everything. Inquests and funerals and so forth going on, and the boys here.' She tailed off weakly, with Suzanne looking at her intently, as if expecting something more significant.

'I see,' she said, after a moment. 'No, that's all right.' And she walked back to the house.

'She seems in rather a daze,' said Laura, when Suzanne was safely out of earshot.

'She's been like that for a while now. Poor thing – she has got a lot to cope with.'

Laura fiddled with the small stud in her ear. 'I'm wondering about Martin,' she said. 'He's been really losing it today. He shouted at me earlier on, and you saw what a state he was in just now.'

'So?'

'So now we have much stronger reasons for thinking Jim was really murdered, and your list of questions about Martin suddenly seems a lot less fanciful. For a start, there's the whole thing about Fern. If Martin's her father, and the village people don't know, then he could have killed Jim to stop him spilling the beans.'

'On that basis, it might have been Gwynne, for the same reason.' Rosemary wondered at her own perverse desire to argue. The discovery of Teed's body had put a new perspective onto the whole situation, and she found herself hoping that Martin Frazer could, after all, be trusted. She grasped anxiously at alternative candidates. 'And I'm still not completely sure about Katy Stevens and her bizarre remedies,' she went on. 'It all sounds so airy-fairy for a medical professional. As if it might be a cover for something more sinister.'

'And what about that little girl they've adopted?' Laura suggested. 'Bending the rules, abducting her from China, that sort of thing.'

Rosemary nodded. 'When it comes to it, just about anybody in Lyvedon might have done it,' she sighed. 'Even Martin.'

Laura gave her a look. '*Especially* Martin, I'm sorry to say.'

The police called at Abbotslea quite late on Saturday afternoon. 'Just routine, Mr Frazer,' said Constable Stuart, who had been detailed to do the door-to-door work. 'Won't keep you more than a few minutes.'

Martin ushered him into the living room, where Suzanne was watching television with the boys. 'Switch it off, Tim,' said Martin. 'Just for a bit.'

The constable rather embarrassedly went through his checklist of questions. 'When did you last see Mr George Hamilton Teed? Where were you yesterday afternoon? Have you noticed any unusual activity in the area over the past day or two? Do you know of anybody with any reason to wish harm to Mr Teed?'

The family answered as a group, explaining about their aborted day out, and their return at approximately two o'clock. 'I went out to the village shop to get some milk and a few other things,' said Suzanne. 'Probably about half past three. Mrs Hodges can verify that if necessary.'

'And I went off at five-thirty to the same shop to buy an emergency box of dog biscuits,' said Martin with a short laugh. 'Suzanne forgot them, you see.'

They could not think of any reason why Mr Teed should have been deliberately killed. It was a ghastly thing to happen, especially so soon after losing Jim. Timmy looked intently at Constable Stuart, as he was closing his notebook. 'Is there a serial killer on the loose?' he asked anxiously.

'Serial killer? What makes you say that?' the policeman wondered. 'There's only been one killing that I know of.'

Timmy looked at the floor, rubbing his finger hard under his nose as everybody stared at him. 'Oh, right. I know that,' he muttered. 'Only some people might think Jim was – sort of – you know – murdered as well.'

Suzanne reached out and pulled the boy to her. 'Who says that, darling?' she asked him.

Timmy merely shook his head.

'Well, it isn't true, not at all. Miss Boxer saw him throw himself in the river, you know she did. And probably it was some stranger who killed Mr Teed, thinking he had a lot of money hidden away. Something like that. A robbery that went wrong.' She looked pleadingly at Constable Stuart. 'Isn't that right, officer?' she said.

'Can't say just yet, ma'am,' he answered stolidly. 'But there's no need for you to worry, young sir. No need at all. We'll have the person who did it locked up in no time. Just you see.'

'I hope so,' said Timmy fervently. 'I liked Mr Teed. He took us fishing, you know.'

Mindful of many more visits to be made, the policeman took scant notice of this last observation. 'Did he?' he said carelessly. 'That was kind of him.'

'OK boys,' said Martin, decisively. 'Sorry, Donald – you know what they're like,' he said to Constable Stuart. 'Is that it for now?'

The constable nodded and ruffled Toby's hair. 'You've been very helpful,' he said. 'Both of you.' He looked at Martin. 'What can I say?' he sighed. 'Whoever would have thought such a thing could happen in Lyvedon?'

'Who indeed?' Martin said. 'I don't suppose we've seen the last of you, have we?'

Donald Stuart smiled wryly. 'I shouldn't think you have,' he agreed.

Chapter Seventeen

Saturday evening at The Lamb was gloomy by any standards. The dining area was sparsely occupied and the food seemed to have been prepared with unaccustomed carelessness. When they were kept waiting fifteen minutes for their coffee, Laura got her new book out of her bag and began to read it.

'Manners,' said Rosemary.

Laura winked at her and held up the book for her friend to see. 'I'm hoping to get somebody to identify the model,' she said.

Her hopes were quickly realised. Fern Evans eventually brought their coffee, with a sullen expression and several heavy sighs. 'It's nearly knocking off time,' Rosemary told her encouragingly. 'Must have been a hard day for you, losing your friend like that.'

Fern gave her a grateful look. 'I'm being very selfish,' she said. 'It must have been far worse for you, finding him like that.'

Rosemary nodded. 'Horrible,' she admitted.

Idly, Fern looked at Laura's paperback. 'Oh, that's one of Chris's covers,' she said. 'I've seen it in his studio.'

'Is it?' Laura feigned ignorance. 'Who's the model – do you know?'

Fern tilted her head to see it better. 'He's a local chap. I forget his name. He does odd jobs for Martin and various other people.'

'Bingo!' Rosemary mouthed silently as Fern went back to the kitchen.

Chris Stevens answered the knock on the door, at ten o'clock on Sunday morning. A bull-necked young man stood there, a piece of paper in his hand. 'Mornin' mate,' he said. 'Am I right for Mr Stevens?'

Chris nodded blearily.

'Got a box for you. Special delivery.'

'On a Sunday?'

'Twenty-four seven these days, mate.' The man grinned. 'To be honest, I got all behind with myself yesterday and they've said if I don't get everything up to date by the end of today I'll be looking for another job. Can't have that, now can we?'

'Go and get it then. Where's Ken, anyway? He's the usual chap.'

'Falariki,' came the laconic reply.

The box was almost too big for the man to manage, but Chris made no move to help him. Perpetually on the alert for a suitable model for one of his commissions, a phrase had come into his head as he watched the muscular arms and shoulders heaving the parcel out of the van. *Thrud the Barbarian.*

'It'll be the African stone head I bought on eBay,' he remembered. 'Carry it through to the hall, will you? And – could you come in for a bit? I've got a little job for you. It'll only take half an hour.'

'Job?' The man registered Chris's appraising looks at his muscles with apprehension. 'You're not – I mean, I don't—'

'Don't worry,' Chris laughed. 'My wife and kids are here to protect you. Now, how do you fancy being on the front cover of a nice new paperback?'

'Sign this first,' said the man. 'Signature there, printed name there.' He produced a pen and Chris quickly obliged. 'So what's this about a book, then? Don't have much truck with books, me.'

Chris smiled. 'You'd like this one,' he said. 'Now just follow me. There's good money in it, of course.'

The man rubbed his cheek for a few seconds and then went into the house as invited.

Laura felt like a burglar as she lurked in the bushes at the side of the house, despite it being broad daylight. She had seen the delivery man go into the house and decided it would be easier to make a quick dash into the studio while Chris was occupied with his parcel, find the page of the ledger, and dash out again. If she was seen, she would brazen it out by saying she had come to see the results of her session with Chris on Friday.

The door was on the latch, and she let herself in as silently as a ghost. It was almost magically easy after that – at least for the first few minutes. She could hear the delivery man and Chris in the kitchen, talking softly, presumably to avoid disturbing Katy upstairs. Tiptoeing down the corridor, Laura was in the studio in moments. The ledger was in the same desk drawer as before, and she whisked it out, thumbing rapidly back through the pages.

There it was! 'Oktober, 24th March. Odd-job man. £50. Modelling fee.'

Laura groaned in frustration. Did the dratted man not have a name?

But before she could do anything more, she heard

Chris's voice approaching. 'It'll only take half an hour or so,' he breezed. 'Just step in here and we'll get cracking.'

Without conscious thought, Laura dropped to her knees and crawled into the cramped space under the desk. She huddled there, scarcely breathing, while the cover illustration for *Thrud the Barbarian* was carefully created.

'Aarghh!' came a deep male snarl. 'Ggrrrr!'

'Better, but give it more *menace*,' came Chris's voice. 'It's kill or be killed. Imagine it's your boss on the floor in front of you.'

That seemed to work. As Laura listened, it all sounded very authentic. At one point she risked a wary peek from her hiding place, to witness a very well-muscled young man, wearing only a ragged piece of animal hide and daubed with something that looked like mud, thrust viciously at his imagined employer with a sharpened stick. His face was contorted with loathing. 'AAARGGGHHHH!!' he roared, and Chris's flash went off several times in rapid succession.

It seemed to last for hours, until Laura thought she would never be able to stand up straight again. Thrud seemed to be tiring, too. 'Can't we stop now?' he whined. 'I'm meant to be back at the depot by eleven.'

'Just a couple more,' Chris promised, before the sound of a telephone cut him short. 'Drat! I'll have to answer that,' he said. 'Don't go away.'

Laura could see the bare feet approaching, from under the desk. Bored, the model was examining the strange objects that Chris had collected. She heard him ring the bell on the bicycle, before he came closer, perhaps to admire himself in the mirror. Crouching even lower, Laura knew what was going to happen.

Sure enough, seconds later, the feet were standing

directly in front of her. Slowly she raised her head and met his eye. 'Hello,' he said, pushing out his chest. 'I'm a Barbarian. What are you?'

Laura gulped, and said, 'A Hobbit in a Hole,' and laid a warning finger across her lips.

Then Chris came back, and his model stepped away from the desk and Laura. 'Can I go now?' he asked.

'Actually,' said Chris slowly, 'I was just thinking. There's another commission that came in yesterday. *Shadows and Secrets*. I thought we might have you in silhouette, back hunched, wearing some sort of hat. It seems a shame to waste you, now you're here. You're not in any real rush, are you – and it would mean twice as much money.'

'Whatever,' said the man, and Laura's heart sank. The words that now repeated through her head, over and over were *Odd-Job Man*.

Fern served a traditional roast Sunday lunch to Laura and Rosemary at The Lamb, but did not linger to chat to them. She was already regretting some of the things she had said to them on Friday evening. With the death of poor Mr Teed, everything suddenly seemed much more frightening, with many of the villagers giving each other doubtful looks. The theory that he might have interrupted an intruder was plainly the favourite, at least in the conversations Fern had heard, but she doubted whether anybody truly believed it. Why would somebody try to burgle a newspaper office in the middle of the day?

And yet nobody spoke openly about a connection between the death of Jim Frazer and the murder of George Hamilton Teed. Fern herself hesitated to dwell on the questions that were raised by any hint of such a connection. It made her think of past events involving her mother and others in her generation. It made her wonder whether the apparently relaxed and easygoing relationship Gwynne had with her – Fern's – father was actually as it seemed. Were there some dark undercurrents that she had been shielded from all her life? Had Jim Frazer been causing even more alarm than usual by his unrestrained remarks?

Specifically, Fern was afraid that her mother had something to hide. Gywnne had been behaving oddly in the past few days, dashing around the place in a whirlwind of activity that seemed to Fern to be almost hysterical at times. When Fern had tried to talk to her about Jim, Gwynne had brushed her aside, pretending she had to be somewhere on some errand for Martin.

The pub was doing a busy trade in lunches, as it generally did on a Sunday. Although the Stevens family weren't there, two tables were already full of children and their parents, out in the garden. Fern was kept well occupied taking food out to them and collecting up used glasses. It being the last day of half-term, many people seemed to have an end-of-the-holiday feeling, letting the children run wild and buying them extra treats. They were helped by the weather, which had excelled itself for the second day running, after the deluge of Friday.

The landlord seemed tired and not entirely focused on the job. Little wonder, Fern thought, with another sudden death on his patch. Until now, being a special policeman had not caused him any great conflicts of interest, and he had maintained both jobs with a relaxed manner. Now he seemed to share in the general sense of suspicion and bewilderment as to how such a thing could have happened.

Suddenly, there was a burst of noise from inside the bar. Raised voices, and the crash of breaking glass. Fern hurried in to see what was going on. A man she did not recognise was standing aggressively confronting Rob, his lower jaw stuck out as if daring the landlord to hit him.

'Say that again,' he invited. 'Just say that again.'

The larger of the two garden women – Laura Whatever-it-was – stood up, looking pale and uncomfortable. 'Mr Coutts,' she chided. 'Calm down. Really, you ought to know better. You and Rob are both professionals. You're behaving like children.'

'I won't have my prisoners slandered like that,' Mr Coutts growled. 'It's well out of order.'

Fern went over to the other woman and quietly asked her what was going on. Rosemary explained briefly. 'That's the man in charge of the prison workers, who've been helping us in the garden. We were talking about our tent burning down on Friday – you remember. Rob said he thought it must have been deliberate, and wasn't one of the prisoners serving time for arson. It looks as if Mr Coutts took it a bit personally.'

'So what did he do?'

'Nothing much. He just stood up too quickly and knocked a glass over. Rob told him to mind what he was doing, and Mr Coutts started shouting. I think Laura's got them under control now,' she finished.

She was right. The men had backed off and were looking more than slightly embarrassed. 'In any case,' said Laura reasonably, 'George Marsden Plummer couldn't possibly have burned the tent. When would he have had a chance?'

'I never meant to say he did,' defended Rob.

'It sure sounded like it,' Mr Coutts complained.

'Well, come and have another drink with us,' Laura invited him. 'I'll pay for it. What are you doing back here on a Sunday, anyway?'

'Didn't I tell you? My auntie Sarah lives just outside Lyvedon. I go over sometimes for tea and a chat. She's eighty-seven now, but a sprightly old bird. She likes to keep up with the gossip.'

'But you won't tell her you've been fighting with the landlord of The Lamb, I don't suppose,' teased Laura.

'No,' he snorted. 'She'd give me a right telling off if I did.' Then he seemed to relax. 'And how do you like having to stay here, instead of in your nice new tent?'

'Well, it's an ill wind, as they say,' Laura admitted. 'I wasn't sleeping terribly well in the tent.'

Rosemary rolled her eyes. 'Well I was enjoying it tremendously. So much fresh air and the lovely woodland sounds.' She sighed. 'Now there's just a central heating boiler chugging in my ear and more traffic than I'd ever have expected.'

'I think my camping days are over,' said Laura with a flicker of regret.

Mr Coutts nodded sympathetically. 'Never liked it myself,' he agreed. 'But I tell you what I *do* like.' His eyes twinkled. His listeners waited for the revelation. 'Being on a canal,' he finished. 'Gently rocking in a narrowboat, sleeping with the doors and windows wide open in the middle of summer. You get all the scenery you could wish for, and amazing water birds. Everything done at a walking pace. Fabulous!'

'What if it rains?' asked Laura.

'When it rains it's the most miserable activity in the world,' he said. 'That just makes the good bits all the better.'

'I like your philosophy,' said Rosemary.

Laura looked around at their fellow drinkers. 'Can't see anybody we know,' she remarked. 'Other than Fern.'

Mr Coutts pulled a face. 'They'll be scared,' he said. 'Wondering who did for the newspaper chap.'

'But wouldn't it be more normal for them all to be here, gossiping about it, and keeping an eye on each other?' Rosemary said.

'Give them a couple more days, and that's how it'll be. For now, they feel safer indoors.'

'You're probably right,' said Laura, trying to recall how it was from her time as a police officer. 'People are easily frightened.'

'Not just that,' smiled Mr Coutts, 'There's an international football match on this afternoon.'

Rosemary groaned. 'I sometimes wonder if there's ever a day where there *isn't* an international football match.'

At Abbotslea, Timmy and Toby were running out of games to play. Although neither would ever have admitted it, they were not especially sorry that half-term was almost over. The frustration over the abandoned visit to the island had seemed to grow instead of diminish. Initially, it had seemed quite funny, but their mother's black mood and the persistence of the rain had quelled their buoyant spirits by the end of Friday. They'd seen Gwynne walking along the riverbank, just after lunch and asked her to spend some time with them, showing them more of her old childhood haunts, but she'd brushed them off saying she was busy. Even the dogs seemed aimless and depressed.

'We'll have to do homework on the train,' Toby grumbled. 'Why do we always leave it to the last minute?'

'They should *make* us do it sooner,' Timmy said. 'That's what parents are for.'

'They did try,' said fair-minded Toby. 'But other things kept distracting them.'

'Like Jim,' said Timmy, his eyes growing rounder. Their reaction to the death of their cousin had evolved from genuine shock to a deliberately melodramatic game, where they frightened themselves by intoning his name and acted out his desperate struggles to escape from the rapids. As for the murder of Mr Teed, they preferred not to think about that. A real murder, less than half a mile away, was a bit too scary to make into a game – especially when the grown ups were being so useless about it. They stopped talking when the boys came into earshot, and kept being cross with them for no reason.

If they hadn't been going back to school, they might have embarked on a game of detectives, following likely suspects and making notes about overheard conversations, but already half their minds were on Hampton's new iPod and Higgins's stated intention of getting himself a tattoo without his mother finding out. 'The dogs know we're going back tonight,' Timmy observed. 'That's why they're so quiet.'

Rosemary and Laura had an assignment for the afternoon. 'We'll have to show Martin that time capsule,' said Laura. 'I feel bad that I haven't done it already.'

'OK,' said Rosemary. 'Where is it?'

'I put it in the Land Rover, for safe keeping. The trouble is, I have a feeling it would be better if Suzanne wasn't there. She's so down on Jim, she might say something nasty and upset Martin.'

'So we don't just march up to the front door with it, then?'

'Preferably not.'

Rosemary had a thought. 'Didn't he say he was going to spend this afternoon clearing out the cottage? He's away again for most of next week, so this is his last chance.'

'Good thinking. We'll take it to him there. And we should probably confess about you stealing those carbon copies and then losing them in the fire. We should have told the police about them, by rights,' she added guiltily.

Rosemary frowned. 'Don't you think the fire was *because* of them? Somebody deliberately wanting to destroy them?'

'So who knew you'd got them?'

'Mr Teed. He didn't say anything, but I think I gave it away when I was talking about Jim. Then he could have told somebody else, and that's who killed him.'

Laura looked at her. 'Is there something you haven't told me?'

Rosemary wriggled. 'Well, it seems so *awful*. I know you like Martin a lot, and he's been really nice to us.'

'But you're not so sure about him, especially since he got so angry about what you said at the inquest.'

'Laura, every time I try to think through what's been happening, the finger of suspicion points directly at Martin Frazer. I try not to let it, but it just *does*.' Rosemary sagged helplessly. 'It isn't my fault. I don't want him to be a killer. Think of those boys, and this place – the entire community depends on him. But even so—'

'Tell me,' Laura interrupted.

'It was the phone in Teed's office. Just before I called the police, I pressed the Redial button. I don't know why – it was an impulse.'

'And?'

'I got the answerphone at Abbotslea. It was Suzanne's voice.'

Laura gave this news her careful consideration. 'OK,' she said slowly. 'It might look a bit bad, I agree. But it isn't proof of anything.'

'No, I know. That's what I keep telling myself. But it feels like another piece of a jigsaw. And the picture on the jigsaw definitely has Martin's face on it.'

Laura got up from the large rock beside the river, in the Dingle where the tent had been. Something about the place had drawn them back, despite it no longer being their home. 'Let's fetch the biscuit tin, then, and walk over to the cottage,' she decided.

In the house, Suzanne was trying her best to concentrate on collecting up all the paraphernalia that the boys would need to take back to school. 'Honestly!' she complained. 'How can everything get so strewn about in one short week?' Nobody replied. Martin was at Jim's cottage for the afternoon and the boys were finishing off their favourite jam in the kitchen. Already Suzanne was thinking about her return to work the next day. Her hours were complicated, and she kept a large chart pinned up in the kitchen to remind herself and anybody else when she had to be in class. The marking and lesson plans and assessments all had to be fitted in with her duties at Abbotslea.

In many ways, she realised, she was looking forward to the return to normality, just as she suspected that Toby and Timmy were. It had been a very distressing week by any standards. Trust Martin, she thought ruefully, to introduce those two garden women into the mix. That had really been the final straw, and the effort required to remain polite and hospitable towards them had been another strain. When Martin had told her on Saturday that they were coming, her initial reaction had been to groan and take her head in her hands.

'Will we have to *feed* them?' she'd demanded. 'And have

them here in the house? Really, Martin, I think that's a bit much. Can't we just enjoy a quiet family week together, for a change?'

Then he'd reminded her that he absolutely had to be away on Tuesday and Wednesday anyway, so Laura and Rosemary might actually be company for her.

Typical, she had groaned silently to herself. He always thought he knew what she wanted, what was best for her, and always got it wrong. And she could never openly complain about it, because he had her interests at heart. He loved and admired her as much as any husband could; the community regarded them as the perfect couple. And she loved him. Even more than that, she loved Abbotslea. She felt as if she was made of the same material as the house, so connected were they. Martin praised her endless labours to maintain it, offering sympathy when the work became overwhelming, but never grasping the central fact that it was him, Martin himself, who made it all so much harder than it need be. He valued her as a home-maker, mother, social asset – but she seldom felt appreciated for her own self, a woman with passions and needs.

Martin's sudden return home from Gloverton at ten o'clock on Saturday morning had been a mixed blessing. Suzanne had been up for as many hours as he had, and already felt the day was practically over. While her husband had been leaving Gloverton at six-thirty, she had been busy in and around the house, preparing for the very different demands on her time that half-term would bring. From a somewhat solitary life, with husband and sons away most of the time, there would be an abrupt change of pace and atmosphere, to which she would have to instantly adjust. The boys had been due to arrive home by train at two that afternoon, and everything had to be just right for them.

And now, a week later, everything was thrown into reverse. Her family would abandon her again, the dogs would follow her about looking reproachful, and once more she'd have to devise her own entertainment.

'Toby!' she shouted. 'Come and sort out these trainers. You can't possibly need to take four different pairs with you.'

Chapter Eighteen

The cottage carried an air of even greater dereliction to Rosemary's eyes as they approached it. There was a big skip outside the front door, which hadn't been there before, already half full. 'Oh look!' she cried, pointing to a jumble of model aeroplanes. 'They're the ones that were hanging from the ceiling.'

'You'd think Toby or Timmy might like them,' said Laura. 'I wonder if they've been consulted.'

'Not their sort of thing, probably. And all these comics. Isn't there a demand for them from collectors?'

'It's always the way,' Laura nodded. 'When somebody dies, there's hardly ever a relative who has the time or the inclination to dispose of their things properly. It all ends up in the landfill, even when plenty of people out there would love to have them. Wasteful, I call it.'

'Oh well, I suppose you can't keep everything. But it does seem sad.'

'Very,' Laura agreed.

They pushed the door open and went inside, Laura holding the time capsule under one arm. They could hear scuffling noises in the living room.

'Hello?' called Rosemary. 'Are you there?'

Martin stepped into view, his hair tousled and a cobweb draped across his chest. 'Oh, hello,' he puffed. 'This is a right old job, I can tell you. He's got cupboards that I swear haven't been opened for twenty years. I just scared a spider as big as a tennis ball.'

'Ooh-er,' said Rosemary, glancing around nervously.

'And what am I meant to *do* with it all?' Martin wailed.

'We saw the skip outside,' said Laura.

'Oh, did you. It's wicked waste, I know. But I just don't have the time to find homes for everything.'

'You could put the comics on eBay,' suggested Laura.

Rosemary gave her a look. 'What do you know about eBay?' she demanded.

'Not much. Just that people buy and sell things on it. Or through it. Don't they?'

Martin laughed impatiently. 'You have to upload pictures of everything, and then log on at least once a day to see how things are going. It's incredibly time-consuming.'

'Oh,' said Laura. 'I see.'

'What'll happen to this cottage now?' asked Rosemary.

Martin stirred up his hair all over again. 'That's another thing,' he groaned. 'Suzanne thinks we should sell it. We could do with the cash, and it would be nice to have someone taking better care of it. But...' he pulled a face, 'it's part of the estate, goes back generations. It's always been ingrained into me that you never sell property. My grandfather would come back to haunt me.'

'So rent it out at a realistic price. That'll bring in some steady income,' suggested Laura.

'Right,' Martin nodded. 'Except that before I can do that, I'll have to spend a small fortune on renovating it. It's a dilemma.'

Suddenly there were steps on the stairs, and Gwynne appeared through the door at the bottom. 'Oh, it's you,' she said with a broad smile. 'I thought I heard voices.'

She seemed flushed, and was carrying a large armful of clothes. Martin looked at her, an identical smile lighting up his face. Looking from one to the other, Laura caught a sense that she and Rosemary had walked into something warm and intimate.

'How's it going?' he asked.

'I can make good use of these in the charity shop,' she said. 'And there's another pile to go, even bigger. Marigold's going to be thrilled. I must say Jim had some good clothes. Surprising, really.'

'Mostly my cast offs,' said Martin. 'I doubt if he wore many of them. We did rather dump them on him.'

'He liked having your things,' said Gwynne, her voice soft and slow.

Martin sighed. 'This is an awful job. I can't help feeling we're rushing it, somehow.'

Laura nodded. 'I know what you mean. But it has to be done, and there's really no sense in delaying it.'

'Which charity are you donating them to?' Rosemary asked Gwynne.

'Oh, it's our own shop – run by the Lyvedon Trust. It's in Long Horton, a few doors down the street from my office. You should drop in if you've got a minute. There's a huge range of stock, books, tapes, furniture, toys – as well as clothes of course.'

Gwynne's customary briskness was returning, as she trotted outside with her bundle. But something was in the air, if Laura was not mistaken. Something sweet and secret between Martin and Gwynne, and even if they hadn't been acting on it, she would swear it existed.

'What's this?' Martin said suddenly, indicating the biscuit tin that Laura had put on Jim's table. 'It looks familiar.'

Laura smacked herself lightly on the forehead. 'Gosh –

I forgot! This is why we came.' She opened the lid carefully and displayed the contents. 'We dug it up in the garden, close to where the chapel used to be. We think somebody must have been searching for it – that's what all those holes were.' She lowered her voice. 'And it can only have been Jim, I imagine.'

Martin made a sort of groan, as he carefully put his hand into the tin and lifted the items, one by one. 'My Dinky car!' he said. 'And Jim's robot.'

Gwynne had come back from loading her car and the three women watched solicitously as Martin obviously struggled with his emotions. 'It must have been nearly thirty years ago,' he breathed. 'And it seems like just last week.'

'It'll be thirty years this October,' said Gwynne. 'You and Jim were twelve and I was eight.'

'A long time,' said Rosemary. 'We read the friendship pact.'

Martin unfolded the sheet of paper, and blinked a few times before reading it. '"Dark days, disgrace and a horrible death". That has an awful resonance now.' He looked at Gwynne. 'As he saw it, I must have broken the pact a thousand times over. Did he wish a horrible death for me, I wonder? How he must have hated me. Was he searching for this, to confront me with it, do you think? To show me what a swine I was being?'

Gwynne reached out, and gripped his arm. 'No, of course he didn't hate you. He loved you. He never stopped loving you, despite everything that happened. *That's* why he was looking for the tin – to remind himself of what you two had between you as boys. Perhaps to remind you, as well.'

'And now it's too late,' groaned Martin. 'I had completely forgotten about this. All I saw in Jim was a reproachful presence and a nuisance.'

'That's what was so tragic.' Gwynne swiped a hand across her eyes. 'Poor Jim,' she muttered. 'And if anything, I was even more cruel to him than you ever were. He loved me as well, in his way. And I went out of my way to avoid him. I pretended not to see him looking at me with those great yearning eyes.'

'He didn't make it easy for either of us,' Martin said. 'And those letters, they poisoned the air around him, making everybody afraid of him.'

Gwynne's expression changed. 'I'd forgotten!' she said. 'Somebody took the carbon copies of the letters. I went through the whole house last week, looking for them, and they'd gone.'

Martin looked at Laura and then Rosemary. 'We know where they went,' he said. 'Don't we?'

'I borrowed them,' Rosemary confessed, trying not to look sheepish. 'And left them in our tent. It was deliberately burned down, with them in it.'

'My God!' Gwynne clapped her hand over her mouth. 'I had no idea.'

Something about the dramatic display aroused Laura's suspicions. 'You must have known we'd moved to The Lamb,' she said. 'Fern would have told you.'

'Yes, but I had no idea you were deliberately burnt out. That's dreadful.'

Martin had moved to the bottom of the stairs, saying nothing. Resisting the urge to pacify Gwynne with assurances that no harm had been done, Laura nudged Rosemary towards the door. 'Time we left you to get on,' she said. 'We only came to show Martin the time capsule.'

They were glad of the open air and blue sky outside. 'Phew!' said Laura. 'That was getting a bit heavy.'

* * *

Monday brought cloudy skies and a renewed vigour amongst the garden workers. The prisoners were only available for two more days, before their period of comparative freedom came to an end. 'We've got assessments for the rest of the week,' explained Huxton Rymer. 'Group work, and a lot of navel-gazing. We're all eligible for early release, so long as we can demonstrate we're no further risk to the community.'

Rupert Waldo gazed around the garden, and gave an exasperated sigh. 'I hate to leave it so unfinished,' he complained.

'Then we'd better get it finished by the end of tomorrow,' said Rosemary robustly.

'What?' squawked Rupert. 'Impossible.'

Rosemary explained that the hard work had all been achieved already. 'It looks so unfinished because we haven't put the hedges in,' she said. 'I'll zoom off to Long Horton again tomorrow, early, and fetch fifty little boxes, and it'll be transformed by teatime.'

'Boxes?'

'Box hedge plants,' she explained.

'We need your help with this knot garden,' George called to Rosemary. 'I can't see where the centre section fits.'

Rosemary trotted over to his side. 'No, you've got it wrong,' she told him. 'Have another look at the plan. There's a crossover just there, see.' She sketched the line of the eventual box hedging with a stick. 'If you think this is complicated, you should see some of the originals,' she teased him. 'Three different colours for the hedges, leaving convoluted beds which were filled with rosemary and sage and hyssop – all flowering in subtly different shades of purple and pink.'

'And smelling rather wonderful into the bargain,' George said. 'Must have been gorgeous.'

Rosemary had felt awkward towards George ever since the tent had burned down. Despite Mr Coutts's indignation, it was difficult to abandon all suspicious feelings concerning him. And Laura had reminded her that morning about the episode between Huxton Rymer and Jim, when the prisoners had been at Abbotslea demolishing the chapel. 'We mustn't forget that these are three very clever men,' Laura had pointed out. 'Between them, they might have hatched up a conspiracy to dispose of Jim.'

'They can't be as clever as all that,' said Rosemary.

'Why not?'

'Because they got caught. Obviously.'

Laura laughed. 'That's true,' she acknowledged.

Laura joined them now with a list of questions about pathways. The originals, made of bricks set in herringbone designs, were still in place, revealed by the diligent digging of the prisoners. 'Are we sowing low-growing herbs here and there on the actual paths?' Laura asked. 'Or would that be sacrilege?'

Rosemary tapped her teeth. 'Some thyme would work well – maybe dotted along the edges, rather than between actual bricks. And chamomile's nice.'

'If you're having thyme, then you've got to have rosemary as well,' joked George. 'Keep it fair.'

'Don't worry – there's already plenty of rosemary,' said Rosemary.

Without Toby and Timmy the place seemed disturbingly quiet. The dogs mooched about dejectedly, occasionally chasing Jim's hens, which had instantly made themselves at home. 'They can live in one of the sheds until we can decide what'll happen to them,' Martin had told Suzanne. 'During the day they can wander where they like.'

Suzanne had gritted her teeth. 'Hens and gardens are a bad mix, you know. They make dust baths where things have just been planted, and drop their – droppings – just where people walk.'

'It's only temporary,' said Martin. 'Somebody in the village is sure to give them a home. Be thankful I didn't bring the goats over here as well.'

'Oh, I am,' said Suzanne with veiled sarcasm. The goats had been adopted by Rob at The Lamb, who said they would be the foundation of a small children's zoo in one corner of the garden. 'Rabbits and lambs next,' he'd said.

'Why not hens?' Martin had asked.

'I just don't like them,' came the unassailable reply.

'At least Fern's happy,' Martin said now to his wife. 'She wanted Gwynne to take the whole lot, but this way she gets plenty of contact with the goats while she's working at the pub. She's always liked them.'

Martin had spent some time on the telephone that morning, arranging his cousin's funeral. The parish church had been booked for Wednesday afternoon, and Martin had to speak with the undertaker, the vicar and a number of other people. 'It's rather short notice, I know,' he said repeatedly. 'But there doesn't seem to be any reason to delay. It won't be a very big affair, in the circumstances.'

Suzanne had three sessions of Modern American Fiction that afternoon, with an unruly crowd of Year Eights and Year Nines, and was bracing herself accordingly. Martin had a complicated brief to study before disappearing again on Wednesday evening for another long case. They both had a feeling of choppy waters survived and the duller but much more predictable stretches of normal work ahead for the next seven or eight weeks.

'I need to phone Gwynne,' Suzanne said, 'and see how she got on this morning. I just hope she's managed to subdue 9GG for me. They can be murder.'

'Poor old Gwynne,' muttered Martin, who always thought it rather unfair that most of Gwynne's work was in the mornings when the schoolchildren were full of energy and mischief, whereas Suzanne mainly got them after lunch, when the worst problem was that some of them went to sleep if the weather was warm – especially those from homes where nobody went to bed before midnight.

Suzanne ignored his remark and went to make her phone call.

Whilst his wife was occupied, Martin went out to the garden, drawn to it by a sense that with the work almost completed he ought to be showing his appreciation. Laura met him at the door, as she emerged with a wheelbarrow full of discarded plant pots. She was walking very stiffly, he noticed.

'Hurt your back?' he asked solicitously.

She made a brave face. 'It's seized up on me,' she admitted. 'Nothing to worry about, really. Rosemary's making me go to the market with her tomorrow, so I'll have to be better by then.'

'I ought to tell you – Jim's funeral is at three o'clock on Wednesday, at the village church. It would be good if you and Rosemary could be there.'

'Oh!' Laura hesitated. 'Can we think about it? We might still be planting hedges then, and we definitely want to be away by the end of Wednesday.'

'It's up to you, of course,' he said. 'But we would be pleased to see you at the service.'

He moved off to speak to Rupert Waldo, who was preparing a wide border along the furthest wall. Laura watched him, wondering how Rosemary would react to their invitation to the funeral.

She would have been even more concerned if she could have heard Martin's conversation with Rosemary, five minutes later. 'There's obviously going to be an inquest on George Hamilton Teed,' he told her. 'And because it's clearly a violent death, it might take rather longer than Jim's did.'

Rosemary gave him a startled look. 'I have to give evidence again, I suppose. It won't be – you know who, will it?'

Martin grinned. 'I think we can safely assume not. His parting words last time were along the lines of *I never want to set foot in this godforsaken village again.*'

Rosemary giggled. 'How rude,' she said.

'The police seem to think his killer was a petty thief, looking for cash, who panicked when he was interrupted,' he told her, with the air of sharing privileged information.

'And you agree with them?' The disbelief in her voice was impossible to ignore. 'How many petty thieves are there in Lyvedon? I thought the place was unadulterated by modern scourges like that.'

He gave her a look full of reproach. 'It's hard to think of any other feasible explanation,' he said.

'Is it?' muttered Rosemary, to his departing back. 'Not from where I'm standing, it isn't.'

On Tuesday, they set out early for Long Horton, Rosemary suffering from an unsettling sense of déjà vu. A week ago she had seen the man who had claimed to be Jim Frazer, and suspected herself of near insanity. Since then, poor Mr Teed had been murdered and the whole business was still a confusing tangle. But one thing was now certain – the man she had seen near the fruit stall was the odd-job man, who had close connections with Abbotslea. Since the weekend that she and Laura had arrived, he had remained invisible – a fact that everyone seemed to think was out of character. The clear assumption had to be that he had killed Jim Frazer and then pretended to drown himself in front of a woman who did not know him or Jim.

And that might have been relatively straightforward if George Hamilton Teed had not been killed a few days later, after opening the last letter to be posted by Jim. Then she remembered the newspaperman regularly went fishing, sometimes in the Abbotslea woods. Had he seen something incriminating? Was his death quite unconnected with his phone call, after all?

She sighed. So many questions and so little hope of finding answers to them. In the passenger seat beside her, Laura was equally lost in thought. At the sound of Rosemary's sigh, she stirred herself and remarked on the pretty country lane they were traversing. 'Makes you wonder why people do such beastly things, when they've got such a marvellous place to live in,' she said.

'That's more or less what Martin seemed to be saying to me yesterday. It's nonsense, of course. People are people, wherever they live. Jealous, vengeful, greedy – all the usual reasons for killing somebody. It might even be worse in these tiny villages where they all know each other's business – or think they do.'

'Which leads us to wonder why the odd-job man would want to kill his employer's cousin, doesn't it?' said Laura.

'Because his employer paid him to, in all probability,' Rosemary replied. 'As simple as that.'

'Maybe,' said Laura.

Parking the Land Rover was every bit as difficult as it had been the week before. They finally found a space across the street from a row of pretty eighteenth century houses that had all been converted into shops or offices. One of them had 'The Lyvedon Trust' emblazoned across the front window. A memory was jogged and Rosemary peered through the glass, hoping to see some sign of life inside.

She was rewarded with a clear view of Gwynne Evans, busily collating various sheets of papers from piles on a large desk. Suddenly it seemed to Rosemary that there might be at least a few answers to be had, if she could engage Gwynne in friendly conversation for a few minutes.

But first she had to see Bernie about fifty little boxes.

The plants were waiting, and Laura's persistently stiff back meant she was unable to do much on her own. Rosemary found herself thinking it might have been better if Laura had stayed in the comfort of The Lamb for the morning, instead of taking up space in the Land Rover. But she didn't say anything until the task was accomplished. Then she excused herself. 'Give me ten minutes,' she said mysteriously. 'I'll meet you in front of the war memorial and we can go for a coffee.'

The bell over the door clanged loudly, and Gwynne turned quickly to see who had come in. 'Oh, hello,' she said, with little sign of welcome. Now she was inside, Rosemary had to acknowledge that there could be no good reason for her to be there, other than to bother Gwynne with intrusive questions or idle gossip.

'Sorry to interrupt,' she said. 'It just occurred to me to ask you – does your Trust get involved in giving permission to demolish listed buildings?'

Gwynne's mind worked with impressive speed. 'You're talking about Martin's Victorian chapel, aren't you?' she said crossly. 'You're seeking to make trouble for him, on the basis of some ignorant gossip from those convicts. Well, the answer is, no – the Trust has no power to give or withhold permission for anything. It acts as an advisory body in conjunction with the Council Planning Department.'

'Oh,' said Rosemary. 'I see.'

But Gwynne wasn't finished. 'You're determined to persecute Martin, aren't you? I can't imagine what you think you know, but I assure you you're completely wrong. Hasn't it struck you yet that everybody in Lyvedon *worships* him? And with good reason.'

Rosemary held up a hand. 'Yes, I know. Everybody's been telling us what a saint he is. And I agree – he's a very nice man. I'm sure he's greatly loved –' Gwynne's sudden blush did not escape her notice, and did nothing to allay Rosemary's suspicions, '– but surely he isn't above the law? If he demolished that chapel without permission, then—'

Gwynne cut her short. 'The chapel was in ruins anyway. It was an eyesore. It had no preservation order on it, and wasn't listed. He was completely within his rights to tear it down. Now, are you satisfied?'

'Absolutely,' nodded Rosemary. 'I'm sorry I annoyed you.' She turned to go. 'Oh – just one more little thing. Do you happen to know the name of Martin's odd-job man, by any chance?'

Gwynne's attention had returned to the stacks of leaflets in front of her. 'Eddie,' she said casually. 'Eddie Brooks.'

Rosemary left the office feeling small and rather silly. If it had been that easy, why hadn't they asked somebody days ago? *Eddie Brooks*, she repeated to herself. *Now let's see if I can find him.*

She made her way to the thronged market square, and her rendezvous with Laura. On the way she passed a man selling a wide range of tools, most of them very good quality. Making a sudden connection, she stopped and waited for him to finish serving a bearded man who wanted a set of chisels.

'Excuse me,' she said, 'but do you know a chap called Eddie Brooks?'

'Course I do,' said the stallholder. 'He was here ten minutes ago. Bought my best hammer, saying his old one's gone missing. But he doesn't like to be called Eddie, you know.'

'Oh?'

'No, he likes everybody to call him the "odd-job man". Makes quite a thing of it, he does.'

'You don't know where I might find him, I suppose?'

The man gazed rather vaguely across the crowded square. 'Could be anywhere, love,' he said.

'Well, thanks anyway.' She smiled and moved on, with a sense of closing in on her quarry. With a name, face and line of work, the man was as good as captured. If she couldn't physically arrest him herself, she could rally the police to her aid. She had no idea that her conversation with the stallholder had been overheard by the very subject of her questions. Nor that Eddie Brooks was carefully flitting amongst the festoons of towels and stacks of DVDs, shadowing her as she rejoined Laura. With a stony expression, he loitered in the street while Rosemary and Laura lingered over coffee, and then trailed them to the

Land Rover. His own vehicle was parked close by, and as soon as the two women drove off, he was quickly in pursuit, despite having a very good idea of exactly where they were headed.

Chapter Nineteen

Laura was still discussing stonework with the prisoners in the last hours before they left for good. 'The sundial needs something more to really give it impact,' she repeated, walking around the centrepiece of the garden and examining it from all sides. 'It looks naked like that. It would have had more embellishment.'

'I thought you were going to have a look at the stone from the old chapel,' asked George Marsden Plummer. 'There were some splendid twiddly bits from the windows.'

'Oh, I forgot,' she said. 'And I think I know where it is now. Rosemary and I saw a stack of something knobbly under a tarpaulin, across the river.'

'That's it,' he confirmed.

Laura didn't have time to say any more. She heard Rosemary calling for assistance, as she unloaded their purchases from the Land Rover. 'Come on,' said Rupert Waldo. 'Action stations! Let's get these hedges in.'

The next two hours were devoted to concentrated teamwork, getting the new hedges planted, with Rosemary everywhere at once, measuring, straightening and instructing. They completed three of the four corner beds by four o'clock. Everyone stepped back to examine the effect.

'Amazing!' exclaimed Rupert Waldo. 'Considering I for

one had hardly any idea of what I was doing, it's turned out wonderfully.'

'It looks magnificent,' boasted Laura. 'Such symmetry! Such clever use of colour!'

'And this is just the bare skeleton of what it will be like later in the summer,' said Rosemary. 'I hope Martin likes it.'

'Go and fetch him,' urged Laura. 'Right away.'

Rosemary needed no encouragement, and went quickly over to the house to look for Martin. It took her less than five minutes to find him and lead him back to the garden. Laura could hear her chattering nervously as they approached.

'Of course it isn't really finished yet – we need another two dozen or so of box plants and a lot more herbs and things yet. But the lower half is more or less done. It should give you a pretty good idea.'

Martin followed her through the door, and stopped in genuine astonishment. 'But – but…' he spluttered. 'How did you…? I mean, only this morning, it was…'

Rosemary giggled at his confusion. 'The hedges make all the difference, you see,' she explained. 'And now George has brushed the brick paths clean, you can see exactly how it used to look. Well,' she amended, '*almost* how it used to look. We have simplified the designs of the beds themselves. Their basic shape's the same, though.'

Martin couldn't take his eyes off the display. 'It's glorious!' he enthused. 'Absolutely marvellous.' Then his eye fell on the sundial, and a small frown crossed his face. 'Is it me, or does it seem just a bit – well, *naked*?'

'Don't worry,' said Laura confidently. 'We're working on that next. With luck, we'll have everything done by this time tomorrow.'

'You've worked miracles,' he told them.

The prisoners departed, glowing with pride at the results of their labours. Jim's hens were shooed away from the garden door, and many of the tools returned to the shed.

'It's great,' said Martin again.

The three of them stood together outside the garden for an indecisive moment, before Martin excused himself, saying he still had a lot of reading to do. He invited Laura and Rosemary to make themselves tea in the Abbotslea kitchen, but they declined. 'We haven't quite finished for the day,' said Rosemary, vaguely. 'But you get on. We'll see you tomorrow, I expect.'

Martin nodded. 'Of course. But I'll be very occupied with the funeral, of course. They're bringing the coffin here at midday, and we'll all proceed to the church at three.'

Rosemary visualised the procession, wondering how many of the local people would take part. 'Not the boys?' she queried.

Martin shook his head. 'We thought it would be better to let them carry on as normal, especially as they've only just gone back to school.'

Chris Stevens was on his own in the house. Katy was working a long shift at the hospital and the children were all at school. They were not due back for another hour or two, the boys staying late for their judo club and Bonnie going to tea with her friend Tessa. It was all written up on a sheet of paper that Katy had attached to the fridge door with a magnet. It covered the whole week, with her own working hours listed in detail and any clubs or social engagements the children might have. Chris was conspicuously absent. His time was fluid and unpredictable. He could act with a spontaneity the rest of the family could scarcely dream of. And he often did.

The covers for the five Thrud books were almost complete. Constable Stevens had a prominent role, and appeared in three of them. In one he was ravaging poor Fern, who shrank back timorously from his uncouth advances. The most recent one, featuring the delivery man, had Thrud himself in difficulties, with another barbarian to reckon with. Chris hoped he'd got that right – he could scarcely bear to read the actual stories, merely flicking through a few pages and relying heavily on the publisher's blurb.

Already he was working on a new commission entitled *Beguiling Blossoms*, which seemed to be a very soppy romance set on a small old-fashioned farm with a lot of apple trees. The request from the editor stressed the importance of blossom, preferably apple.

'Stupid woman,' Chris muttered to himself. 'Doesn't she know the blossom's finished by this time?'

Then he remembered that the farm above Abbotslea had an orchard containing some late varieties of apple, which just might still be in flower. They also had a winsome daughter of fifteen who would be ideal for the heroine of the story. He looked outside – it was a clear afternoon, with just the right sort of shadows. He could go straight away and get some outdoor shots. 'Make a nice change,' he said to himself, and lifted to phone to make sure young Fiona was going to be at home.

Laura and Rosemary walked briskly along the river bank, leaving their Dingle behind them and heading towards the old stone bridge. The afternoon light slanted through the trees, flickering on the river and turning the woodlands to a wonderland of fresh greens. 'Everything about this place is so *beautiful*,' sighed Rosemary. 'It's like all my childhood memories gathered together. Those boys can't have any idea how privileged they are. It seems a shame to send them off to boarding school when they could spend their lives running free in these woods.'

Laura made a doubtful sound. 'Seeing what happened to Cousin Jim when he spent his time roaming free, that might not strike them as such a good idea. You can't avoid civilisation altogether.'

'We still don't really know how Jim himself felt about it. We've been prejudiced against him from the start. And then when everybody insisted he'd killed himself, we regarded him as some desperately depressed misfit. We know he didn't commit suicide, so all that's completely wrong.'

'He still doesn't sound too cheerful an individual,' Laura said. 'The misfit part is right, surely?'

'Somebody called him "the conscience of the village" didn't they? Sounds positively medieval, like a scapegoat.'

'Rosemary, this whole place is medieval.'

'Except I don't believe the motives for the murders were. I think that's something entirely modern.'

'Oh?'

'Look, it's always sensible to take the most obvious explanation – don't you agree?'

'In theory, I suppose I do.'

'So this Eddie Brooks has to be the murderer. He killed Jim sometime on Saturday or Sunday, just before we arrived here, threw the body in the river, and then staged that elaborate pantomime purely for our benefit. But somehow George Hamilton Teed got suspicious, so he had to be killed as well. Then Eddie went into hiding, and nobody's seen him since.'

'Except for a few hundred people in Long Horton, last week and this.'

'Right,' Rosemary nodded. 'That's twelve miles away. He'd have assumed he was safe there. Besides,' the thought hit her without warning, 'why would it matter if anybody from Lyvedon *did* see him? He didn't have to go into hiding. The only people he had to hide from was you and me. As soon as we leave here, he can just get back to his normal life.'

'It could easily have worked,' Laura realised. 'His biggest mistake was killing Teed as well. That was very stupid.'

'He probably thought he had no choice.'

'Here we are, look,' Laura pointed across the river to the stack of material under the tarpaulin. 'This is going to be interesting.'

They walked over the bridge, pausing to watch the sparkling water running beneath them. 'This has to be five hundred years old,' Rosemary said, stroking the weathered stone. 'And still strong enough to take road traffic.' She looked at the ground. 'Those tyre marks look as if they were made by a lorry. Amazing, isn't it.'

'Bridges are amazing,' Laura agreed. 'I've always thought so.'

They approached the demolished chapel down a wide track which had obviously been well used in recent times. They found themselves in a clearing not unlike the Dingle they'd camped in, but on more level ground. Laura lifted a corner of the tarpaulin and peered underneath.

'Remember, we want something that would make a base for the sundial,' Rosemary said. 'I'm not sure, actually—' she stopped as Laura began to climb on top of the stacked stone. 'Hey! Watch out. It could all shift and you'll find yourself crushed by a ton of granite.'

'It's not granite,' panted Laura. 'I think it's sandstone, isn't it?'

'Whatever it is, it's heavy.'

Laura had rolled more tarpaulin back, and was sitting halfway up the pile, gazing at a complete window, with carved arches and stone mullions. 'No glass in it,' she noted.

'Suzanne said it was in ruins. The glass must have disappeared ages ago.'

'What a waste,' sighed Laura. Then she leaned forward. 'Hello – what's this?'

'What?' Rosemary started tentatively to climb up after her friend.

Laura reached through the gaps where window panes had once been, and extracted a canvas holdall. She pulled it free and looked inside. Slowly she withdrew her hand, bringing out a heavy object in a plastic bag. She held it aloft, against the sky, peering at it in puzzlement. 'It's a hammer,' she said. 'Somebody's hidden it in the bag and then chucked it up here. How weird.'

'Let's see.' Rosemary had stopped climbing and beckoned Laura down. 'Come and show me.'

'Oh my God!' Laura squealed, giving the object a closer look. 'It's covered in blood and hair.' She stared in horror. 'This must be what killed Mr Teed.'

'That's horrible,' said Rosemary faintly. 'Why didn't the killer wash it first or throw it in the river?'

'Who knows? But listen – we'll have to get it to the police right away.' Laura glanced nervously around the woods, which suddenly seemed to come from dark tales of wolves and witches. 'If he finds us here, we'll be in big trouble.'

'Why would he find us?' Rosemary demanded.

'Because this is a village, and people notice things. We've been talking quite loudly, and there's a road only just over there. Anybody might have heard us.'

'So let's go,' said Rosemary.

Laura still didn't move. 'Wait a minute,' she said. 'I don't like to leave it unguarded. Why don't you go and alert the police, and I'll stay here? Take the wagon, and go to The Lamb. Rob is a Special. He'll know what to do.'

Rosemary frowned worriedly. 'Will you be all right?'

'Of course I will. I'm just being extra cautious. It would be so embarrassing if we both went, and when we got back with the law, the hammer was gone.'

'Why don't we just take it with us and both go?'

'Because,' said Laura patiently, 'it has to be seen in *context*. Exactly as we found it.'

'Oh.' Rosemary looked unconvinced, but as always when matters of police procedure were under discussion, Laura exerted superior knowledge and Rosemary had little choice but to comply. 'I'll be as quick as I can, then.' She crossed the bridge and returned the way they'd come, looking very much like a jogger out for an afternoon session. Laura watched her disappear, on the far side of the river, and hoped she'd made the right decision.

Chris Stevens used the small back road to Fotherdale's Farm, which ran parallel to the river for a mile or so, before crossing the lovely old stone bridge and charging up the steep hill to the farm. He drove quickly, realising he had limited time before he was supposed to collect Bonnie from Tessa's, and then meet the boys from the bus. He was thinking about life, his family, the Frazers, Lyvedon, all in a complicated medley of images and feelings, when a squirrel ran out in front of his car.

There was no conscious thought involved. He simply yanked the steering wheel hard to the right, in an instinctive desire not to kill the creature. If it had been a main road with other traffic, he might have been more careful to weigh up the implications. On a tiny country lane, there seemed to be no need. And another primitive factor influenced him: this was the squirrel's home, out here in the woods. It did not deserve to be slaughtered by a machine that should never have been in this quiet sylvan spot in the first place.

He had not been aware of the deep ditch running alongside the road. It was filled with spring grass and other wild vegetation. The car's offside wheels sank almost gracefully into it, tipping the whole thing alarmingly and making it impossible for Chris to escape from the driver's door. Instead he struggled across to the passenger side and managed to jump clear.

'Now what?' he muttered. It was only a twenty minute walk back to the centre of the village – but his problems would not be over simply by walking home. The car had to be salvaged. It was blocking the road, for one thing. Ruefully he thought of Katy's angry scorn at his carelessness and the complications that would arise if it had to go for expensive repairs.

So it was like a miracle when Constable Donald Stuart arrived on the scene in his shiny police car. 'Hello!' he said, jumping out of the vehicle. 'Problems?'

'What are you doing here?' Chris demanded. 'Nobody uses this road.'

'The traffic's being diverted down here for the rest of the day,' the constable explained. 'The gas board have discovered a leak in one of their mains, just past Abbotslea, and they've closed the road. Everything has to come past here now, to get to Lyvedon.'

'Except they can't because I'm in the way,' Chris pointed out.

The policeman was already speaking into his phone, ordering a breakdown lorry urgently. He switched it off with a satisfied smirk. 'Ten minutes, they say. How's that for service?'

'Incredible,' sighed Chris. 'You're better than the cavalry.'

They both heard the throaty diesel engine of the Land Rover several seconds before it appeared in sight. 'Oh-oh,' said Chris.

Rosemary pulled to a halt with an expression of furious frustration on her face. 'What now?' she screeched from the open window. 'This is like a nightmare. I've already been sent back once.' Then she registered Constable Stuart. 'Oh, thank heaven,' she cried.

The policeman walked towards her, his face puzzled. 'Good afternoon, Miss Boxer,' he said politely.

'Listen!' she panted, as if she'd been running instead of driving. 'We've found the murder weapon. The one used to kill Mr Teed. It's in the woods, by the old bridge,' she waved vigorously in the direction she thought was correct. 'Laura's with it. And we know who did the murder. You've got to come right away.'

To his credit, the constable did her the honour of listening attentively. 'All right,' he said. 'I'll make a few calls, and get a team to come and look.' He eyed the ditched car. 'I think you can squeeze past if you're careful. Go to The Lamb and fetch Rob. Explain that you've seen me, and he's to be at the old bridge asap. Can you do that?'

Rosemary lifted her chin. 'Of course I can. That was what I was trying to do anyway, before all the roads became impassable.'

Rosemary slewed the Land Rover to a crooked halt in front of the The Lamb and rushed in through the front door. Across the road, a man in a white van jerked upright in surprise. He had almost given up hope that his quarry would return before the end of the day. Parked on the verge, in the shade of a large beech tree, he had been listening to his iPod and praying nobody who knew him would drive past. Fortunately, there had been scarcely any traffic for the past hour or so. Moving quickly and purposefully, he grabbed something from the passenger seat and climbed out of the vehicle.

Ringing the bell on the bar for attention, Rosemary danced from one foot to the other, wondering where she should start looking for Rob if he didn't appear in the next thirty seconds. She leaned over the bar, trying to see through the frosted window into the kitchen. Suddenly, before she knew what was happening, an arm encircled her neck from behind and her head was plunged into darkness. A coarse material was held tightly around her neck, and she was dragged rapidly backwards, stumbling and choking and terrified. It wasn't until she had been bundled into a vehicle of some kind that she managed to work out that a bag had been put over her head.

She would never have imagined how terrifying it was to be deprived of all senses except touch. The thick material muffled sound, and the only smell was the residue of the potatoes which had previously occupied the hessian sack. Blinking feverishly, she found she could just make out a brown blur that was what the inside of a sack looked like.

She was being dragged part backwards, part sideways, outside and onto what felt like the road. Then she was inside a vehicle of some sort, and the engine was starting up.

She tried to scream, but her captor had knotted the sack so tightly around her neck that she could snatch very little air without a dreadful sense of choking. She was going to die, she decided, with a violent surge of desperation. He was driving her to a quiet spot where he would kill her.

When Rob finally responded to the insistent clamour of the bell, there was nobody to be seen. He stood staring around in bewilderment. Then he went slowly out again, to where he had been digging early potatoes in his back garden.

Rosemary was jolted from side to side, knocking against hard objects that she couldn't see. At one point she thought she heard a woman's voice calling something, but it was over too quickly for her to be sure.

The whole drive was less than ten minutes, and then the van stopped, and the back doors opened. She was manhandled out of the van and along ground that felt soft and spongy. Then they were in some kind of building, with a hard floor, and the bag was roughly yanked from her head. She found herself face to face with the odd-job man, the man who had said he was Jim, in the walled garden; the man who had dropped into the river before Rosemary's horrified eyes.

'You!' she said. 'You killed Jim Frazer, and Mr Teed. I suppose you think you can kill me as well.'

'I never killed nobody,' he said fiercely. He slammed her down on an old wooden chair. Reaching for a coil of rope, he wound it around her whole body and the chair several times. 'Just you try to get out of that,' he said, surveying his handiwork. 'You'll stay in here until—'

'Until what?' she demanded.

'Until it's safe to let you out again,' he snarled. 'Until I've got right away from this damned place. Why didn't you just leave it, instead of snooping into things that never concerned you? Why couldn't you just see what you were meant to see and then shut up?'

She glared at him. 'Because no decent person would turn a blind eye to murder.'

'Look,' he snarled, his face only inches from hers. 'I killed nobody. I've told you.'

'So can you explain how it is that we found your hammer covered in blood hidden in the chapel stones?'

'What?' He seemed frozen by her words. 'What did you say?'

'You heard me,' she snapped.

'In the chapel stones?' He repeated the words as if they still made little sense. 'Right.' He spun round and slammed out of the shed, apparently forgetting Rosemary entirely.

'Wait!' she yelled. 'You can't leave me here!'

But it was too late. She heard his van start up, and then there was silence.

Laura had carefully put the hammer back where she'd found it, and climbed down the stack of stone to sit under a tree. Halfway down, she had encountered a stone griffin, in near perfect condition. Almost absently, she picked it up, and now sat facing it in the shade of the great oak. She hummed some snatches of 'Hey, Jude' to herself, feeling in some obscure way that it was appropriate for the occasion. How many minutes would it take Rosemary to summon help, she wondered. Thirty, at least. And so far she calculated it couldn't have been more than fifteen. With a sigh, she leaned back against the tree trunk and tried to prepare herself to be patient.

She tried not to think about the murder weapon only a few yards away, the determined blow it had dealt to a living skull, the damage to the brain inside, the wickedness of such an act. She was only partly successful, forcing her thoughts to a consideration of the motives for the killing. The odd-job man must have had a guilty secret that Jim Frazer had discovered. Perhaps he had been stealing things from Abbotslea and disposing of them in Long Horton or somewhere. Perhaps he had family locally, with a shady history that Jim was threatening to expose. From the brief meeting she had had with him, Laura doubted whether the mystery involved anything to do with a woman. Although, she thought slowly, the strange manner he had adopted in the walled garden must have been a pretence. He wasn't actually bad looking. Well muscled, too. Quite a suitable candidate for one of Chris Stevens' pictures of barbarians, come to that.

It was difficult to pursue these thoughts logically. Other images persistently intruded, of Gwynne and Martin and Constable Stuart and the prisoners – all with possible involvement in the mysterious events of the past week or so. But she did her best to follow up the idea that the odd-job man might have had a romantic entanglement of some sort.

In the shed, Rosemary tried to assess her options calmly. The door was closed but not locked – the man had rushed off too quickly to do more than slam it behind himself. The chair she was attached to felt old and rickety, and her legs were not secured at all. She could actually stand up in a crabbed sort of way and totter a few steps. But with her arms so tightly bound, this was of limited use. She couldn't balance on one foot and kick anything. The only thing she could think of was to smash the chair to pieces and wriggle free of it. She tried running backwards against the wall, but the tiny steps she was restricted to meant she couldn't summon enough force to do any damage. She sat down again, rocking from side to side, testing the fragility of the chair beneath her.

There seemed only one course of action left. It was risky, since failure would see her hurt and stranded helplessly. But the alternative was unthinkable. No way would she simply wait for rescue – which might never come.

She rocked experimentally backwards two or three times, before thrusting hard with her feet and sending herself and the chair crashing over, landing on her back. For a moment it seemed as if it hadn't worked, until she wriggled her bottom and discovered the seat of the chair to be much looser than before. With a convulsive jerk of her hips, she straightened her legs, and the chair disintegrated into several pieces. She rolled over and knelt up. Her arms were still bound, but the ends of the rope were coming untied with the collapse of the chair. A strenuous working of her shoulders and elbows successfully detached her from the broken chair back, and she was free.

Outside, she hardly paused to get her bearings. Irrationally she feared that the man was still close by, waiting to attack her again. Some instinct sent her scrambling up a slope, towards a row of beech trees that seemed to offer security.

Her back and neck were hurting quite severely by the

time she reached the trees. She knew she'd be covered with bruises next day, but at least nothing seemed to be broken. All she had to do now was get back to Laura, who was herself in great danger from the odd-job man as he went in search of his incriminating hammer.

An approaching engine interrupted Laura's thoughts. She stood up excitedly, ready to beckon over the police officers. But then she saw the vehicle, which in no way resembled a police car. It was a white van, with writing on the side and a single occupant. Instinctively, Laura crouched behind her tree until she could see who he was.

The moment his face became visible, her heart leaped in alarm. It was the man she had just been thinking about – Eddie, the odd-job man. The murderer! Fearfully, she shrank back into the bracken that grew densely all around. Where was Rosemary? What was she supposed to do, all on her own?

Constable Stuart left the breakdown truck to pull Chris Stevens' Volvo out of the ditch, and drove quickly back to Abbotslea, mentally rehearsing procedure for such a situation. Since there was no suggestion that anybody was in immediate danger, he did not have the right to go rooting about on Martin Frazer's property without permission. So permission must be sought before any further action could be taken.

Martin opened the door quickly and listened to the policeman's summary of events as he understood them. Stuart had any sense of urgency well under control, standing easily on the doorstep, making it all sound like a bit of routine investigation, complicated by a somewhat hysterical female person. 'So all I need from you is formal permission to search that area of the woods,' he concluded.

'No problem at all,' said Martin. 'In fact, I'll come with you. The quickest way is to drive to the Dingle and walk from there.'

Leaving the van's engine running, the man ran to the pile of stonework, and began searching. Watching him for a moment, Laura was struck by the fact that he was on completely the wrong side of the stack. He had begun shifting large blocks from the side closest to the river, whereas the hammer was high on the opposite side. Surely he'd remember that much, she thought.

But she had other things to worry about. She had to stop him from taking the hammer and disposing of it more effectively, thus removing the only piece of evidence that might bring about a conviction for the murder of Jim Frazer, if not George Hamilton Teed as well.

There were a few yards of open ground between herself and the van. The man's back was turned. Taking a deep breath and bending almost double, she charged across to it, and grabbed the ignition key through the open door. Turning off the engine, she removed the key and then paused. What was her plan, she asked herself? How was she to keep the man in sight until help arrived?

Rosemary could see a farmyard a short distance along a lane beyond the beech trees just outside the hut. There was a handsome old farmhouse on the brow of the hill and several barns and sheds all around it. She trotted as fast as she could along the lane, hoping to summon assistance.

A young man was driving a quad bike across the yard,

with a bale of hay on the back. As Rosemary watched, he drew to a halt and heaved the bale off, walking into a shed with it. Without thinking, she ran to the vehicle and jumped onto the driving seat. The engine was still running, and she rapidly revved it and performed a wide sweep of the yard before setting off back down the hill, to where she hoped the lane would come to the old bridge across the river. She ignored the astonished cries behind her, as the lad watched his pride and joy disappear from view.

Eddie had heard the engine stop just as he finally located the hammer. With it in his hand, he peered through the trees, and saw Laura holding his key aloft. As he watched, she bent her arm and hurled them as far as she could into the dense undergrowth. 'There!' she called. 'Now I've got you.'

Instantly he started to run towards her, and she realised her danger. She leaped into the van and slammed the door behind her. The window was down, and she frantically wound it up, and pushed down the button that locked the door. The man slapped up against the window, pressing his face to it, his expression a mixture of rage and despair. Shudderingly, Laura shrank away from him, knowing he could break in and assault her if he really tried. But she had to hold on as long as possible, to give Rosemary and the police time to arrive.

Suddenly the man was gone, and for a second she thought something had scared him away. Then she understood what he was doing, and managed to lurch across to lock the passenger door a microsecond before he reached it.

Where was the hammer? she wondered. The vital piece of evidence, with hair and blood still attached to it. The hammer, she was certain, that had hung on the board in the shed at Abbotslea. The hammer that the odd-job man was seeking to replace in Long Horton market. Everything made complete sense at last, the jigsaw pieces dropping into place like magic. Which was very little comfort now she was face to face with the murderer himself.

An odd face it was too, as he pressed it horribly against the passenger side window looking uncannily like Chris Stevens' picture of him on the jacket of *Oktober*. He was deliberately trying to frighten her, that was obvious. And she was not going to be easily frightened. *Noise*, she thought. *I need to make a noise.* And the means for doing it were right in front of her. She pressed the van's horn with all her strength. The blast that emerged must have been heard miles away – surely it must?

As they trotted into the woods, Constable Stuart asked about the chapel stone. 'Funny place to put it,' he remarked casually.

'Not really,' said Martin. 'Suzanne wanted it out of sight, but close enough for us to salvage odd bits if we needed to. Eventually I expect I'll sell it to a reclamation outfit. Most of it is useless to me, like the windows. They can go to some nutcase thinking of building a folly.'

'I see,' said Constable Stuart, with a nagging sense that there were still questions to be asked concerning the demolished chapel.

They were at the Dingle when they heard the hooting of a horn, loud and insistent. 'Good Lord – what's going on?' said Martin.

'We'd better run,' said the constable, breaking into a fast trot.

* * *

Laura hooted the horn for the twentieth time. The man kept his face pressed to the window, mouthing words that she couldn't hear. In one hand he still held the blood-stained hammer in its bag. Any minute now, she thought, he'll get the idea of smashing the windscreen with it. Then what? For heaven's sake, she screamed inwardly, somebody come!

Rosemary had been right in her geographical calculations. But before she could be certain, she heard loud hoots from the horn of a car or truck, somewhere in the woods on the other side of the river. It had to be something to do with Laura, and automatically she hooted back. Whether she was offering hope to a friend in distress or sounding the alarm to a criminal, she neither knew nor cared. She bounced across the bridge at a reckless speed, and slewed the quad bike to a halt in the clearing beside the stacked stone.

It was a scene of confrontation. Laura was sitting inside the white van, looking much the same colour as its paintwork. Martin Frazer was standing in an attitude almost of supplication, his hands held out towards the murderer. Constable Stuart was speaking urgently into a telephone, while at the same time keeping a wary eye on Eddie Brooks.

'Come on now,' he was saying. 'It's all over and done with, don't you see? Just come with me, and we'll get everything sorted.'

Rosemary walked steadily towards the van and her friend. The odd-job man saw her, and pulled a face that seemed full of helpless despair. 'You!' he said hoarsely.

'Yes, me,' she replied, looking at the face of the man she had watched drop into the river less than a week before.

And as if he read her thoughts he quickly jumped from the bank onto a large rock, and then leaped to another one, right in the middle of the rushing water.

'Eddie!' called Martin, his voice thick with alarm. 'No, Eddie!' He took a step towards the river, but the policeman held him back. 'Don't,' he said. 'You'll make it worse.'

But the worst was already unfolding. As the horrified watchers hesitated on the riverbank, the man let his gaze rest on Rosemary.

Once again, their eyes locked, before he leaned forward, stretched his arms out at his sides and threw himself into the river for a second time. 'No!' screamed Rosemary. His head bobbed up, several yards down river of where he had taken his plunge, and still it seemed to her that his eyes held hers.

She wanted him to survive. The thought of his drowning, somehow for a second time, filled her with an immense dismay. Because despite what he had done to her, his violence and obvious rage, she couldn't wish him ill.

Neither, it seemed, could Martin Frazer. 'Eddie!' he yelled, fruitlessly, poised on the very edge of the water. He struggled against the restraining hand of the policeman.

The rushing water swept the man out of sight, before anyone could move. The speed alone seemed to paralyse them. Then Rosemary moved weakly to Laura's side, her face still covered in brown streaks from the potato sack, her whole body bruised from her fight with the chair. Neither said a word.

Chapter Twenty

Chris Stevens had a scramble to get to the bus for his boys, without having time to collect Bonnie first. He also had to make a number of phonecalls to get the car fixed and the insurance claim registered. Not to mention trying to catch Katy and ask her to fetch Bonnie on her way home.

And throughout all this, he could only really think about what might be going on in the Abbotslea woods. He re-ran the jumbled story that Rosemary Boxer had gasped out and wondered what it could possibly mean. A hammer with blood on it, hidden in the stones of the demolished chapel. Stuart had sent her to The Lamb, to alert Rob in his role as Special Policeman. And then what? No traffic had tried to pass while the Volvo was being pulled free. Everything had gone quiet and mysterious – and Chris Stevens really did not like a mystery.

He couldn't go out again and leave the boys, but neither could he reconcile himself to staying quietly at home until Katy got back. What he needed was a babysitter, and the person who normally held that position was Fern.

But Fern did not answer her phone when he called her. 'Dratted girl,' he muttered. It was still too early for her evening shift at the pub – so where was she?

Increasingly restless and desperate for some explanation of what had been going on in the woods, he did something

Katy had often ordered him not to do, and went across the street to Mrs Sampson.

She answered the door with the inevitable cigarette in her hand and slightly unfocused look in her eyes. Her feet were bare. 'I hate to bother you,' Chris said. 'But I really need to go out, and Katy's not back yet. She won't be long. Would you be an angel and keep an eye on the boys for me?'

If she was surprised, she didn't show it. 'No problem, love,' she said. 'I'll be right over.' She threw the cigarette into a plant pot in her hall and began to cast around for a pair of shoes. Chris waited as patiently as he could, and then trotted back to his house ahead of her, to warn Jasper and Freddie. 'Be good now,' he shouted, as he left. Mrs Sampson cackled throatily after him, 'I'll do my best, pet.'

Without the car, he had to jog the best part of a mile across fields and over stiles. He had no clear idea of precisely where he was going, but he knew that something vital was pulling at him. People were in trouble, and he was needed. Funny, he thought, as he went, the way everybody thinks it's Katy who's the psychic one, with her remedies and yoga. Very few people were aware of Chris's spiritual side, hiding beneath his bluff manner and constant jokes. Almost nobody knew that it was he, rather than Katy, who had insisted on bringing Bonnie back from her grim existence in a Chinese orphanage. And not even Katy suspected the depth of his grief for poor Jim Frazer.

Fern Evans was also in the Abbotslea woods that afternoon. She could not have explained quite why, but a reluctance to face her mother and a growing suspicion about the two recent deaths conspired to send her to where she knew she would find peace and quiet. She had dimly

heard the engines of the odd-job man's van and the quad
bike borrowed by Rosemary, but it was all too distant to
worry her. Somewhere further up the river, she calculated,
and most likely to do with the farm on the hill. When the
hooting began, however, she was forced to take more
notice. Why would two different vehicles start up such a
racket? Something was obviously going on.

Slowly, she pulled herself into a sitting position, from
where she had been lying in a sunny spot on the riverbank.
She had been dozing on and off, and reading an old copy of
Catcher in the Rye in the wakeful moments. Even with all
the noise, she could not summon any real anxiety.
Whatever it was, it wouldn't be her problem. Let
somebody else sort it out.

But then everything changed. Right in front of her, an
arm was waving in the swirling water of the river. As she
squinted through the dappled light, she discerned a man,
clinging desperately to one of the big rocks and waving at
her. 'Help!' he called, in a weak little-boy voice.

Without even thinking, Fern jumped up and leaped feet
first into the river. The water was freezing, and the slippery
stones beneath her feet were impossible to grip with her
toes. 'I'm coming!' she shouted. The man had let go of his
rock and been tumbled some yards further down river.
'Hold on!' she urged him.

But as she tried to resist the current, and save herself
from being dashed against rocks herself, she saw that the
man had lost consciousness. His head was half submerged,
and she thought she heard a horrible *thwack* as it struck
stone.

'Help!!' she screamed, ten times louder than the man
had called. 'Somebody come!' Then she launched herself,
horizon-tally, realising that was the only way she could

keep pace with the drowning man.

She reached him as his waist caught around another boulder, jack-knifing him like a rag doll. She gripped the man's arm fiercely with one hand, and clung to the rock with the other. The water thrust and heaved and battered at them both like a wild animal intent on killing them.

'Help!' she cried again.

Suddenly, on the opposite bank, a familiar figure appeared. In an instant, he had thrown off his shoes and shirt and was hurling himself into the water. It was shallower that side, and the current slower. 'Hang on, Fern,' he called. 'I'm almost there.'

'Oh, Dad!' she sobbed.

Chris Stevens reached his daughter and the man she had saved in a single desperate lunge. 'It's all right, baby,' he crooned, as he lifted her onto his shoulder. 'Everything's all right now.'

Martin and Suzanne Frazer had eaten supper almost in silence, each aware that they were enjoying a brief lull before more began to happen. Constable Stuart would be along shortly, and without it having been discussed, it was inevitable that the garden women would put in an appearance as well. It was almost a relief when Martin answered the front doorbell and found all three of them standing on the doorstep.

The policeman looked as if this was the most important day of his life. He was brimming with satisfaction at having apprehended a double murderer. But lurking beneath his sense of achievement, more complicated feelings could be detected. He glanced from face to face, first Martin, then Suzanne, then Laura, clearly wrestling with unanswered questions.

'Eddie's going to be all right,' he told them. 'We've got him wrapped up warm.'

They were all sitting round the big pine table. Martin opened a bottle of wine, but Constable Stuart refused to partake. 'I'm still on duty,' he pointed out. 'I'll have coffee, if that's all right.' Suzanne went to make it.

Laura had been carrying the hammer, still in its plastic bag. She put it on a kitchen worktop, drawing Stuart's attention to it. 'You rushed off without your main piece of evidence,' she reproached him. 'There's not much of a case without that.'

'Isn't there?' He frowned at her, trying to organise his thoughts.

'Not unless he confesses.'

Stuart took a mouthful of coffee. 'At least he *can* confess, thanks to young Fern and Chris Stevens. They were heroic.'

Martin had been sitting very still, staring at the floor, for some minutes. 'Eddie Brooks,' he kept saying, as if the man's name alone would make the story come clear for him. 'Eddie Brooks killed my cousin.'

'The thing is,' said the police constable, 'I can't for the life of me understand *why*.' He looked around for help. 'What was the motive?'

Laura gave Rosemary a meaningful look. 'We think we might be able to help you there,' she said. 'We've been very much involved from the start, and obviously we've thought it through.' She turned to Martin. 'I'm really sorry to say this, but we think Martin was behind it. We think he used the odd-job man's hammer to murder his cousin and Mr Teed, and then threatened to incriminate him with it. So Eddie was forced to cooperate with the cover up.'

She was not prepared for the chaos that her words

caused. Martin and Suzanne both jumped to their feet. Constable Stuart slapped both hands flat on the table, apparently trying to restore order. The dogs, which had been curled peacefully in their baskets, got up and began to bark. Martin shouted 'No!' several times and Suzanne went to pacify the animals.

'Lucky the boys aren't here,' said Laura, but only Rosemary heard her.

As rapidly as it had flared, the disturbance subsided again. Martin sat down and fixed Laura with a furious glare. 'Explain,' he said tightly. 'Just why do you think I would kill my own cousin?'

Laura gulped, and shifted her chair slightly closer to Rosemary's. 'Well...' she began. 'We think Jim knew secrets about you that you didn't want spread about.'

'OK.' Martin's stare did not waver. 'What secrets, exactly?'

Laura glanced worriedly at Suzanne, who was still at the other end of the room, clattering plates and murmuring to the dogs.

'I have no secrets from my wife, if that's what you're thinking,' Martin informed her.

'We realised quite early that Fern's your daughter,' Laura continued doggedly. 'And—'

Constable Stuart made a loud grunting sound, before he managed to say, 'Fern Evans isn't Martin's daughter. What are you talking about? Weren't you there when we pulled Fern and her dad out of the river?'

Rosemary took over. 'What? Fern and her dad? *Chris* is her father?'

'That's right,' said Martin. 'It's no secret. She babysits her little brothers and sister. Chris pays Gwynne maintenance for her. Everybody in Lyvedon knows that.'

'But – what about Katy?' Rosemary spluttered.

'What about her?' Martin sighed and began to elaborate. 'Chris and Gwynne lived together for a few months, when she was nineteen and he was twenty-four. They'd always known each other. It was all quite casual, in a way. I was at university, so I missed most of it, but they broke up just after Fern was born. Gwynne was quite happy to be a single mother – it suited her in several ways. She stayed in Lyvedon for another four or five years and then went off and got herself qualified as a teacher. Then she and Fern came back again, at the same time as Chris married Katy. Gwynne had had another boyfriend in the meantime, but that fizzled out before she came home.'

Constable Stuart took up the story. 'And in case you didn't realise, Fern jumped into the river this afternoon when she saw Brooks in difficulties. But the current was too strong for her, and we could well be looking at two more corpses at the weir, if it hadn't been for Chris. He says he had some sort of premonition that she needed him, and he went running up to the river, just in time to rescue them both.'

Martin had gone silent again. Now he said, 'So have I managed to clear my name?'

'What about the old chapel?' Rosemary asked, meekly. 'Jim wrote a letter saying you demolished it illegally, and hid the stone.'

Martin snorted. 'Jim was daft about that chapel. He begged me to spare it, and I was sorry to go against his wishes. But I got it down before it could have a preservation order slapped on it. Technically, I haven't broken any laws. Besides,' he said scornfully, 'that would hardly be a credible motive for murder, would it? At worst I'd have had my knuckles rapped by Jardine.'

'Ouch!' said Rosemary.

'He's right,' said Laura. 'I was never very convinced by the chapel argument.'

Suzanne was still clattering in the kitchen, filling the dishwasher and setting it going. Although she hadn't contributed to the discussion, she had obviously heard every word. Rosemary looked towards her. 'Suzanne – you must be very cross with us for thinking so badly of Martin.'

'Not really. There was a sort of logic to it, I suppose.' She came back to the table and sat down again.

'Which doesn't leave us any further forward,' Constable Stuart pointed out. 'Except that I am quite sure it had nothing to do with Martin.'

Rosemary squeezed her head tightly, and started to speak. 'There's a lot that doesn't add up, though. For one thing, Eddie genuinely didn't know the hammer was hidden in the stack of stone. When I told him, he went dashing off like a mad thing.'

'That's right,' Laura confirmed. 'When he got there, he had no idea which side of the stack to look.'

'But he behaved so suspiciously,' objected the policeman. 'Pretending to be Jim drowning himself, keeping out of sight for a week. What was all that about?'

'And what about George Hamilton Teed?' demanded Martin. 'The poor man was bashed on the head from behind.'

Laura could not resist asking, 'How do you know that?'

Martin sighed. 'Because I'm the local Coroner. And even if I don't preside at his inquest, I get to see the reports.'

Stuart had taken out his notebook and had a pencil poised above it. 'I need to write some of this down,' he said, and started writing. 'Brooks not aware of exact location of hammer.'

'So what about the burning tent?' remembered Rosemary. 'Somebody was desperate to destroy the copies of Jim's letters.' She narrowed her eyes at Martin. 'And I saw you passing some cash to George Marsden Plummer in the garden. He's an arsonist – was I wrong to make a connection?'

Martin laughed harshly. 'Totally wrong, yes. Those poor blokes get paid about fivepence a day. I was slipping him some extra for helping in the garden, that's all. Besides, how would he possibly have had an opportunity to go up to the Dingle that evening? It doesn't make sense.'

'No,' Rosemary agreed. 'So somebody else did it.'

'OK,' said Stuart. 'I think that's enough for now. We'll take some formal statements from all of you tomorrow—' The sudden ringing of the phone only a few feet from where he was sitting cut him short. Nobody moved to answer it, and after five or six rings, the automatic message cut in. Suzanne's recorded voice gave the usual invitation, but whoever was calling decided not to bother to speak to the machine.

Laura, meanwhile, was gazing at the telephone with very round eyes. 'Just a minute,' she said. 'Do you mind if I try something?' Laura got up and pressed a button. A voice rang out, loud in the sudden hush of the room. *Martin, there's something you should know. I've just had another letter from your cousin Jim, posted before he died. It concerns an affair that could affect the whole village, and I think you ought to come over as soon as you can and see it.*

It was gruesome, hearing the voice of a man who had died shortly after leaving the message. There was every reason to think these were the last words he had ever uttered, and everyone sat quietly for a moment.

'I have never heard that before,' said Martin. 'Suzanne always checks the messages as soon as she gets home. Then she wipes them.'

Suzanne said nothing, but got up and went back to the kitchen area. She picked up a tea towel and began twisting it.

'Why didn't you wipe it?' Martin asked her.

She shrugged. 'I forgot,' she said. 'I just forgot about it.'

Constable Stuart scratched his head. 'I don't think this is significant. We found the letter, out in the street. The killer must have picked it up and then just thrown it away. It was about the war memorial – Jim wanted it refurbished. He said it was in a disgraceful state of neglect.'

'But he uses the word "affair",' said Laura thoughtfully. 'Anybody hearing that message would think he was talking about a love affair – wouldn't they?'

Martin bristled. 'I can assure you that I am not having an affair.'

'Not you,' said Laura, her voice heavy with meaning.

Everyone turned to look at Suzanne as the implication became obvious.

'Suzanne?' pleaded Martin, getting up from his chair, his face ashen.

His wife said nothing, still twisting the tea towel and staring out of the window.

'I was worried about Jim bothering her,' said Martin brokenly. 'I asked Eddie to look after her when I was away.'

'He did that – and a bit more,' said Laura.

'But he didn't kill anybody,' said Rosemary. 'Did he, Suzanne? He merely betrayed your husband's trust.'

She turned on them suddenly, her eyes flickering from face to face before settling on Martin's. 'I don't have a husband,' she snarled. 'I'm married to a house and a history, and have to play the part of a silent saint who keeps it all together. Everybody says "Good old Suzanne, isn't she a rock". Well it was too much. The odd hour I had with Eddie was the only freedom I ever got.'

'Suzanne,' moaned Martin. 'Don't say any more.'

'Jim saw you, didn't he?' said Laura. 'And threatened to tell Martin. And in spite of what you might say now, you didn't want to lose your place as mistress of Abbotslea. If you were as sick of it as you claim to be, you would never have killed Jim to prevent him from telling Martin.'

Suzanne gave a harsh laugh. 'You don't understand me. Nobody does. Jim didn't just threaten to tell Martin – he went on and on about how I had the best husband in the world, how I didn't deserve him, I was a slut and a liar, and a dozen other things. I had to make him stop.' She lifted her chin. 'So I did.'

'With a hammer you conveniently had in your hand,' said Rosemary dryly.

Laura pressed the point. 'You must have set out with the deliberate intention of killing him,' she said.

'Oh, what does it matter?' Suzanne shouted. 'I'll go to prison in any case. And believe me, I won't mind it a bit. I'll be glad of the rest.'

Martin had become a frozen statue, staring at his wife as if he had never seen her before. 'When?' he croaked. 'When did it happen?'

'Early on Saturday.' She laughed harshly. 'You almost caught me, arriving back so soon from Gloverton. The boys were still in bed, and I went out at first light, to Jim's cottage. I took the hammer.'

Constable Stuart groaned. 'Premeditated,' he said miserably.

'I'm afraid so. We were by the river. When I hit him, he just dropped like a stone, and I rolled him into the water.'

'But wasn't he suspicious?' asked Martin. 'Why did he think you were visiting him so early?'

'He knew why. He understood exactly what I was trying to do – to explain to him why it would be a seriously bad idea to tell you about me and Eddie.'

'You threatened him?'

'Tried to,' she nodded. 'It didn't work.'

'Was Eddie there?' Laura asked. 'Did he see what you did?'

'Did he *help* you?' asked Donald Stuart with a sudden flicker of hope.

'Of course not,' Suzanne snarled. 'I came back here and phoned him, once I'd worked out the plan. It didn't take me long. It's amazing what desperation can achieve.'

'You knew we were coming,' Rosemary said slowly. 'And you persuaded Eddie to pretend to us he was Jim. Then he had to stage that fake suicide for our benefit.'

'Right. Well done.'

'Did you know we were planning to use a tent?'

Suzanne laughed again. 'I could hardly believe my luck!' she cried. 'I told Martin when he phoned that there was no way I could have you in the house for a week or more, with half-term and everything, but he never said anything about camping. It was as if fate was working on my side, when you went off to the Dingle so cheerfully. Until you saw Eddie in Long Horton, of course,' she added, savagely. 'That wrecked everything.'

'It was a rotten thing to do,' Rosemary said quietly. 'Making me think I'd witnessed someone's death.'

Suzanne shrugged. 'You got over it soon enough.'

'Eddie was defying your instructions, then, when he

went to the market on Tuesday?' Laura asked. 'He must have been told to stay right out of sight until we'd gone. What would have happened then? Would you have just carried on where you left off, if it had all gone according to plan?'

'Probably,' Suzanne admitted. 'He's quite something, you know.'

Martin moaned softly, and Constable Stuart held up his hand. 'I think that's enough,' he said. 'We get the idea.'

But Laura wasn't quite finished. 'And you killed Mr Teed because you thought he'd found out about you and Eddie?'

Suzanne nodded.

'With the hammer,' said Stuart.

'Yes.'

Laura suddenly looked at the place where she had left the weapon. 'Where is it?' she cried. 'It's our only piece of evidence.'

Suzanne's gaze flickered to the dishwasher. 'I think you'll find it isn't so useful now,' she said. 'Not that it matters, of course. I wasn't expecting to make a confession in front of you all when I put it in there.'

Martin went to the machine. Wrenching it open in mid-cycle, he reached in and extracted a shiny claw hammer, dripping with hot water and cleaning solution.

Rosemary emitted a horrified giggle, which was cut short by a sudden loud knock on the door. Constable Stuart went to open it. A muttered exchange took place with the two officers on the doorstep, and then he returned to the kitchen.

'We have Eddie Brooks outside,' he said. 'Mrs Frazer, I must ask you to come with us, now.'

Suzanne made no resistance, as she was escorted to one

of the waiting cars. Martin, Laura and Rosemary followed numbly. They all heard her words as she joined Eddie Brooks on the back seat.

'You weren't worth it,' she told him, and looked back at the house with an expression of the bitterest regret.

Martin groaned and tears began to slide quietly down his face.

Chapter Twenty-One

Six weeks later, Laura and Rosemary paid a return visit to Abbotslea. It was the first day of the school summer holiday, and Toby met them at the door. Laura noticed with a pang how much older he seemed. He smiled fleetingly and ushered them in. There was no sign of the dogs.

'Where's Jess? And Cabbage?' she asked.

'They live with Gwynne and Fern now,' he said. 'There wasn't anybody here to look after them, you see.'

Then Timmy appeared from the kitchen. 'They can come back here in the holidays,' he said. 'It won't be so different.'

But Laura could see only too clearly that life was in fact decidedly different already and would continue to be so. She turned to Rosemary and said with forced cheerfulness, 'Well, at least we've got good weather for our visit.'

Martin came running down the stairs, looking harassed. 'Hello,' he greeted them. 'I didn't hear the doorbell.'

After coffee, which they drank outside, he led them to the walled garden. 'I come here a lot,' he said. 'It's wonderfully soothing.'

The boys had not accompanied them, so Rosemary asked the first of a series of questions. 'Still awaiting trial, I suppose?'

Martin nodded. 'There's another two months or more

yet. She's going to plead guilty. It might not be too long a sentence.'

'Do the boys see her?'

'Oh, yes,' he replied. 'Although I'm not sure it's wise. They find it terribly upsetting, especially Toby. Timmy always looks on the bright side of everything.'

'That's good, isn't it?'

'Probably, but it's also very irritating.'

He pushed open the door, and stood back for them to enter the garden. They both blinked, and their jaws dropped. 'It's magic!' breathed Laura. 'How could it grow so much in such a short time?'

'All that fertiliser, for a start,' said Rosemary. 'And the protection of the walls. But I must admit it's come on much better than I expected.'

'It's magnificent, though I say so myself,' Laura crowed, starting towards the sundial in the centre of the garden. 'Look at the colours! And the paths – they're much more beautiful than I remembered.' Beneath her feet, the decorative brickwork was clean of all weeds and seemed to glow with colour.

Rosemary gave Martin a look. 'What have you done to them?'

'Nothing,' he assured her. 'Just a good brushing was all they needed.'

But the symmetrical beds with their flourishing box hedges were the main attraction. The foliage of the many different herbs formed a harmony with the bright colours of the flowering annuals interspersed between them. A riot of scents added to the impression that a small piece of fairyland had been offered for their enjoyment.

'It is good,' said Rosemary. 'Don't you think?'

'It's fabulous,' said Martin. 'And I'm more grateful to you than I can say.'

Then they heard voices beyond the wall. 'Visitors?' asked Laura.

'Just a few,' he said. 'It's a little garden-warming party, in your honour.'

Four people came slowly through the door. Gwynne, Fern, Chris and Katy stood in wondering amazement, exclaiming in delight.

'Haven't they seen it until now?' asked Laura.

Martin shook his head. 'I've been keeping it all to myself. It isn't saying too much when I tell you it preserved my sanity, these past weeks. I have you to thank for that.'

Rosemary pulled a dubious face. 'You also have us to thank for the exposure of Suzanne's crime,' she reminded him. 'We weren't sure how you might feel about that.'

Martin put a hand on her arm. 'I'm a barrister,' he said. 'A man of law. How do you expect me to feel?'

Laura nodded. 'You would have found out eventually, don't you think? Could she have kept it to herself, for the rest of your lives?'

'We'll never know, will we?' he said.

The little party seemed to have a therapeutic effect on everybody there. Chris Stevens approached Laura, his eyes twinkling as usual. 'You never did see this,' he said, producing a book's dust jacket from his pocket. It showed a sturdy woman, with a great deal of hair piled on top of her head, eyes and mouth perfect circles of shock. The lettering read *The King's Last Mistress*. Laura almost choked. 'That's not me, is it?' she squawked.

'Computer enhanced,' he nodded. 'It's one of my best.'

Laura pushed it back at him. 'Don't let Rosemary see it,' she begged.

Laughing, Chris returned it to his pocket. 'Funny,' he said. 'A lot of my models react like that.'

Fern seemed to be in a world of her own, drifting down to the far end of the garden, leaning to sniff the plants as she went. Rosemary decided to follow her.

'How are you?' she asked. 'Not long now until you're off to university.'

Fern gave a vague smile. 'I'm all right,' she said. 'More or less.' She was watching her mother, Rosemary realised, who had gone directly to Martin's side as soon as she entered the garden.

'You thought Martin was my father,' she said. 'He told us, a few days ago.'

'Stupid of us,' Rosemary admitted, in embarrassment.

'Not at all. He should have been. If my mum hadn't been so anti-marriage, so independent and proud, that's how it would have been. They were childhood sweethearts. She fought against her own destiny, and see what trouble it caused.'

'Heavens!' said Rosemary faintly. 'That's putting it rather strong, isn't it?'

'Maybe.' Fern looked at Chris. 'He hasn't been so bad. It just seems wrong – he and Mum never really loved each other.'

'He saved your life,' Rosemary said.

'That's true. And I can't deny I'm like him in a lot of ways. I've decided to study photography,' she burst out. 'He thinks I've got a talent for it.' She produced a camera from a shoulder bag. 'And I'm starting with a series on this garden,' she announced.

* * *

After a simple lunch with their friends, Gywnne and Martin walked down to the Dingle, carrying a package with them. When Katy called after them, Martin turned back for a moment. 'Something we have to do,' he said. 'We won't be long.' Chris gave his wife's back a little pat, as if to tell her to mind her own business.

'Well, what now?' Martin said, as he knelt on the riverbank, holding the urn full of his cousin's ashes. 'Do we say something?'

Gwynne brushed a finger beneath her eyes. 'Just "goodbye", I suppose.'

'Fond memories,' Martin added.

'Oh yes. And the water will always remember, won't it? Don't you think?'

'Yes.' He slowly tipped the urn over the water, which was flowing gently between the rocks. 'God speed, old friend,' he muttered. 'May all be forgiven.'